LONG MILES HOME

An Inspector Marshall Mystery

Emma Melville

Copyright © EMMA MELVILLE 2020
This book is sold subject to the condition that it shall not, by way of trade or otherwise, be lent, resold, hired out, or otherwise circulated without the publisher's prior consent in any form of binding or cover other than that in which it is published and without a similar condition including this condition being imposed on the subsequent publisher.
The moral right of EMMA MELVILLE has been asserted.
ISBN-13: 978-1-8380344-2-9

This is a work of fiction. Names, characters, businesses, organizations, places, events and incidents either are the product of the author's imagination or are used fictitiously. Any resemblance to actual persons, living or dead, events, or locales is entirely coincidental.

*A song once said that, given the choice, you should dance.
This book is for all those who have chosen not to sit it out.
Life is for living; whatever it throws at you.*

CONTENTS

ACKNOWLEDGEMENTS I
PROLOGUE 1

PART 1: THE FOOL 2
CHAPTER 1 2
CHAPTER 2 11
CHAPTER 3 17
CHAPTER 4 25
CHAPTER 5 31
CHAPTER 6 37
CHAPTER 7 44
CHAPTER 8 47

PART 2: THE WHITE STAG 56
CHAPTER 1 57
CHAPTER 2 67
CHAPTER 3 77
CHAPTER 4 84
CHAPTER 5 93
CHAPTER 6 102
CHAPTER 7 116
CHAPTER 8 121
CHAPTER 9 125
CHAPTER 10 137

PART 3: THE HUNTER 145
CHAPTER 1 145
CHAPTER 2 153
CHAPTER 3 163
CHAPTER 4 172
CHAPTER 5 180
CHAPTER 6 189

CHAPTER 7	195
CHAPTER 8	205
CHAPTER 9	214
CHAPTER 10	228
CHAPTER 11	239
CHAPTER 12	247
CHAPTER 13	260
PART 4: THE SMITH	269
CHAPTER 1	269
CHAPTER 2	282
EPILOGUE	290
ABOUT THE AUTHOR	293

ACKNOWLEDGEMENTS

Thank you to Paul for another fantastic cover. Thanks to Toby – it is most helpful to have a son who is a doctor and can correct all the medical information once he has finished laughing at my paltry attempts. Thanks to Dad, Mum, Hazel, Faye, Jack and Alan for the editing and grammar pass, geographical points and chronology notes on both this and *Journeyman*. Thanks to David for being the 'non-folky' adviser. And always, and forever, to Jon.

PROLOGUE

The car hurtled along the country lane, careering drunkenly from side to side. Its lack of grip on the icy road was exacerbated by its driver's inebriated condition.

The hedgerows lining the road glittered with frost in the cold dark of a Solstice night.

The knight appeared suddenly round a bend, the headlamps picking out the pure white of his surcoat and the sword strapped to his side.

He hit the bonnet with a resounding thud and the clang of metal upon metal.

Head over heels he spun, crashing into the road behind the rapidly disappearing car.

The blood which seeped from his fatal wounds was almost exactly the same scarlet as the cross on his chest.

PART 1: THE FOOL

CHAPTER 1

Jenny came back to the library slowly, the book closing gently as she finished the last page. She sat there for a while letting the high sun and blue skies of her imagination fade away to be replaced by the muted lighting above.

She glanced at her watch – it was after five. She hadn't realised it was so late; she was going to have to run to make it home for tea.

Sighing, she got up and swung her rucksack onto her shoulder, reluctant to return to the claustrophobic needs of her mother. Heading for the huge wooden doors of the entrance between the intricately carved shelves, she noticed that she was the last person here today. There wasn't even anyone on the desk as she passed.

Jenny smiled to herself. She liked David – the librarian here – but he wasn't very conscientious about manning his desk. Sometimes she spent half an hour searching amongst the shelves to find him so she could tell him she was leaving and wasn't around to help out. It wasn't an official arrangement, but he paid her a few pounds a week for her help. She thought it probably came out of his own pocket. It was just as well she didn't need anything today; she hadn't got the time to wait for him.

She put her hands to the massive wooden doors and pushed.

Nothing happened.

Jenny rattled the door thinking it may have stuck and then again, a bit louder, hoping she could attract David's attention. She'd never known the door to be shut; the library was always open to her needs.

When he didn't appear, she slung her rucksack off her back and searched through for her phone.

"Mum, hi, it's me. I," she paused considering how to avoid upsetting her mum; something that was all too easy. "I got to reading and I didn't realise the time. I might be a bit late for tea." No point telling her mum she'd got herself locked in just yet: time enough for that when she got home maybe. It might take a few minutes to find David to let her out, but surely not too long. This way she could stop her mother going overboard about her being locked in with a strange man. She was bound to imagine the worst – she always did these days – but Jenny knew David was all right. She couldn't have said how: just that he shared the same 'comfortable' feel as the armchair in her favourite corner. He fitted here – a part of the library.

"You don't think, do you?" Her mum's voice screeched from the earpiece. "I spend time cooking and all you care about is that bloody library."

Jenny sighed, stifling the desire to simply ring off. "Mum, I…"

"You better get going then or it'll burn." Her mum rang off abruptly.

Cursing under her breath, Jenny left her rucksack on the counter and set off for the librarian's office at the back.

*

It was empty.

Jenny paused and then, curious, pushed open the door and went in.

"David?" she said, though there was obviously no-one there.

She looked round enquiringly; it always felt like stepping back in time coming through to the office. There was no sign here of the technology which adorned the front desk. There was a large fireplace to one side and two high-backed armchairs stood in front of its cheery blaze. In the alcove to the far side she always felt sure she could see a bed spread with a patchwork counterpane, though only if she didn't look too hard. The whole room seemed cluttered yet welcoming, with books in need of repair heaped on a large wooden table at its centre. Scattered about at random were artefacts that looked as if they belonged in a museum, not a library; a gleaming silver sword hung above the mantelpiece, a goblet hidden amongst the books on the table, a set of framed golden coins hanging near to the door.

"David?" she said again, her voice less sure.

"He's in the garden," a voice said behind her, "there is trouble brewing."

Jenny whirled in surprise. She could have sworn she was alone.

A man dressed in black stood in the entrance to the office. He was tall and slim with long, dark hair which fell loose to his shoulders. His features were beautiful and clean shaven but the eyes were what held Jenny. They were a hawk's eyes, golden and fierce, the pupils dark slits.

"Who?... Where?" She gasped and stumbled backwards. There was a definite air of danger about the man and something more, an animalistic attraction which caught Jenny's breath and sent her heart racing. This was the sort of man her mother would warn her against; maybe she should have been more honest in her phone call.

"The garden," he said again, his tone insistent. He nodded towards the far wall.

She looked round quickly, wary of taking her eyes from him. What she had always taken for a large mirror on the office wall was now obviously a doorway. Through it she could see trees and flowers stretching into some unimaginable distance. She forgot her fears of the strange man and stepped closer to the garden entrance, fascinated.

"But," she frowned, her brain working furiously, "there's the car park behind there. That's not possible."

"And are you, so newly awake, to tell me what is and is not possible?" the man said and there was gentle amusement in the refined voice.

Jenny glanced back to him, "Who are you? How did you get in? The door's locked."

"I came from the garden," he said. "Some of us do."

Jenny looked again at the doorway. "But that can't be there. I don't get it." She took a deep breath. "All I want is to get out and go home." Though one rebellious part of her felt that losing herself in the pleasant place she could see was preferable to the argument and tears she would face at home. No sign there of the winter cold.

Another, deeper, part responded to the power in those golden eyes.

"David is in the garden," the man said again. "It is but a step to find him."

Jenny sighed. "Okay," she muttered, "it's a garden. I must be wrong about which side of the building we're on then." Not believing that for a moment, she stepped towards the doorway.

"Wait," the stranger said. "You may need this. Things are happening which could require action." He held out the sword he'd removed from the wall.

"What?" His glance caught and held hers as he stepped closer. She could feel herself drowning.

"Take the sword." Almost a command.

She reached out hesitantly, her fingers brushing his as she did so.

The slight touch set chills running down her spine. If her mum would have concerns about David, she would go into absolute fits over this one.

*

Inspector John Marshall scrawled his signature at the bottom of the final piece of paper and sat back in his chair. It had involved a couple of weeks of late nights, but he could tell Marian that the drug case was solved and the London thug who'd thought Fenwick an easy target was behind bars in time for Christmas.

His second Christmas in Fenwick and hopefully quieter than the last one. At least there had been no return of the travellers this winter.

In fact, after the frantic pace of policing the capital, Fenwick had given him a peaceful year. He'd managed holidays, weekends off and evenings out all without being summoned to distressing crime scenes. He'd even watched Sophie in her nativity play and got to Kate's school sports day; things he'd often despaired of ever seeing.

Sergeant Mark Sherbourne stuck his head round the door of Marshall's cubbyhole off the main office, "Done?"

Marshall tapped the sheaf of documents in front of him. "Send them to CPS, Mark, and then go take the rest of the day. We've done enough overtime recently. Tell Helen."

"She's taking a call."

"Tell them we're out," Marshall said.

Helen Lovell joined Mark in the doorway, "Library for you, John. It's David."

"David? Really?"

Marshall had made a point of dropping in to the Smith Foundation Library every couple of weeks to share a coffee and a chat with its strange librarian but David had never before contacted him at work.

Despite their rapport, Marshall had gained the distinct impression that David was too used to hiding and keeping secrets and not trusting the police unless he absolutely had to.

"Yes," Helen said, "Really."

Marshall made his way past the two of them into the main CID office and picked up the phone. He noticed, in doing so, that Ben Martin was seated at Helen's desk again. The uniformed constable had been Helen's partner before she joined CID and Marshall gained the impression Constable Martin was angling for a move to join her through the friendship.

Marshall thought Ben wasn't really innovative enough to cope with the variety of cases CID encountered or imaginative enough to handle their strange relationship with the library. The man was a good, solid copper and useful when a steady hand or shoulder was required but probably not CID material.

It was rumoured that Ben Martin had once been young, imaginative and ambitious before cancer took his wife and left him with a young daughter. As someone who'd moved out of London to avoid the risks that could threaten his family life, Marshall fully understood how such cares could curb a career though he hoped he retained more flair than Ben Martin seemed to.

Marshall nodded to the other man and picked up the receiver. "David, Hi, what can I do for you?"

"I don't know," the librarian sounded tired and more worried than Marshall had ever heard him.

"Is something wrong?"

"Again, I don't know. I'm sorry, John, I can't explain it but I just know something is different… possibly wrong."

"In what way?"

"What I feel from the library is wrong, like there's something missing or in the wrong place."

"What can I do?"

David sighed, "Probably nothing. My head tells me it isn't your problem."

"But?"

"I've been following my head all year; not involving you too much in the arcane, trying to let you be a policeman," David paused and sighed again, "It's lonely, John, I can't even share properly with Jenny." Jenny was David's young semi-assistant who helped out on Saturdays and evenings when she wasn't at college.

"So?" Marshall wasn't sure what David was driving at.

"So, I'm beginning to think I may have been mistaken in not involving you more. There's something wrong, like a storm brewing, and I feel you are going to be part of it. You coped well last Christmas so I'm ignoring my head and going with gut instinct. If I need you, if something bad happens, will you come? As someone who, at least partly, understands."

"Of course," Marshall said, silently hoping that he could get an evening off first.

"Thank you, err," David hesitated, "hopefully I... we... will recognise it when it happens."

"Thanks," Marshall said drily to the humming receiver as David cut the call.

"What did he want?" Mark asked.

"To be honest, I haven't the faintest. He thinks something is wrong but has no idea what."

"Useful," Mark said.

"Quite, but not something I'm going to worry about now. Home on time tonight, I think. You?"

"Um, well," Mark actually blushed slightly, "it's morris."

"Who?"

"Not who, morris dancing. I did a bit at University and then we saw some at our local over the summer and Lily suggested I should take it up again. I've been going along when I can. Tonight, I think we are practising the mummer's play."

"The what?"

"It's a play about St George which groups used to perform outside at this time of year, take it round the pubs. The Fenwick Morris Men do it at a couple of pubs on the closest weekend to the winter solstice. They lost their St George a couple of years ago, killed in a hit and run, so they asked me to take on a role."

"Where can I see it?" Marshall grinned at his Sergeant, "Sounds like a good evening out."

Mark grovelled around in his bag and pulled out a couple of wrinkled flyers. "Here, this should tell you. I was supposed to be putting one on the noticeboard but never got round to it."

"Was afraid we might all take the piss, more like," Helen Lovell said from across the room.

Mark balled up the second flyer and threw it at her.

"I think I vaguely remember the hit and run," she said catching the ball neatly, "two Christmases ago, before you got here. Ben and I did a bit of help on the interviews, didn't we?"

Ben shrugged, "Can't really remember," he muttered.

"No, it was a bit busy with the Christmas Present Thief."

"The what?" Marshall asked.

"Some idiot went around breaking into places and stealing stashes of presents parents had hid. We spent time tracking him down and then *The Advertiser* ran a campaign for replacing stolen presents and the entire station was swamped in bloody toys." Helen was still single and not, as far as Marshall could tell, fond of children.

The phone rang again, interrupting the conversation. Marshall rolled his eyes but picked it up. "Inspector Marshall, CID."

"Sergeant Wilson here, incident room. Is Ben there?"

"Yes, why?"

"We've had a call about a missing girl and the rest of the shift are out. I thought I saw Ben come in earlier with a shoplifter and hoped he'd still be around doing the paperwork."

Marshall thought it more likely that Ben was avoiding doing the paperwork and, with only an hour to go until the end of his shift, probably avoiding Sergeant Wilson too. "I'll pass you over," he said, ignoring Ben's grimace.

"I've done my share of overtime this week," he said handing Ben the phone, "and you've an hour left so will have time to find a missing person at speed."

"Great, thanks," Ben said drily, though Marshall knew he was a caring man and would make every effort to help.

"Go on, home, you two," Marshall said ushering Helen and Mark out of the office but then he hesitated – missing girls was too much of a memory from his first Christmas here.

"Library?" Ben said into the phone, "all right, I'll go and see the mother, give me an address." He scribbled something on a notebook in front of him.

"Library?" Marshall went back into the room properly as Ben but the phone down. "What was that all about?"

"Some woman's daughter gone missing. Last heard from at the library saying she was on her way home. Not made it and should have."

Marshall hesitated but the call came too soon after David's cryptic message to leave him totally happy. "Tell you what, I'll come with you," he told Ben, "see if we can clear it up quicker. Two heads better than one and all that."

CHAPTER 2

Annie checked the clock for the third time in as many minutes. Tea had been ready for nearly an hour now and Jenny still wasn't home.

It wasn't like Jenny to be so late. Annie knew, in her heart, that her daughter worried too much about her. Since Mike's death, Jenny had never stayed out late, never left Annie alone until she started going to the library. Perhaps she was selfish, clinging to her daughter but she felt unable to face this house without Jenny's cheer. She resented the time her daughter spent studying, though part of her was honest enough to admit that perhaps they both needed the time apart.

Annie picked up the phone again and rang her daughter's mobile. As before, it rang on and on without answer, even the voicemail was off. She replaced the receiver slowly, more convinced than ever that she had been right to call 999.

*

Marshall drove out to the Manor Estate, a suburban sprawl on the edge of Fenwick. Rows of sixties semis lined the streets, much more uniform than the new estates that were being built up towards West Cross. Conversation with Ben had been slightly stilted; he got the impression the constable was none too happy about a senior officer coming to oversee him when he was reaching the end of a shift and might be tempted to rush things.

"I'm supposed to be going to collect Lucy," Ben eventually admitted. "Need to bring her home from Uni and the traffic is going to be dreadful if I'm late going."

Marshall nodded, "Lucy? Your daughter?"

"Yes, had this weekend arranged all term. I'm supposed to be joining her at the end of term Christmas Ball tonight and then packing her up and bringing her home for the holidays."

Marshall's face must have registered his thoughts about a student taking her dad along to end of term balls because Ben continued.

"Not really my scene but it isn't really Lucy's either. I give her an excuse not to stop around late and get drunk. We, well we look after each other a lot after, well, you know, after Sarah."

"Yes, of course," Marshall couldn't really imagine how he would feel if he lost Marian though he hoped he would not inflict this seemingly claustrophobic and needy relationship on his own daughters if the worst ever happened.

They parked at the kerb outside 16 Didsbury Avenue; a neat, fairly nondescript semi amongst the sea of similar places.

Ben rang the doorbell in the small porch whilst Marshall had a glance round the front garden – neatly trimmed lawns, a couple of heathers and ground cover plants, nothing too time consuming in the way of maintenance.

"Mrs Williams? I'm Constable Martin." Ben's introduction drew Marshall back to the door. "This is Inspector Marshall, we're here about your daughter."

"Call me Annie, please." The woman who had opened the door was in her late forties; her blond hair cut in a shoulder-length bob which she wore tucked back behind her ears. Her red rimmed eyes spoiled an otherwise attractive face.

"Come in, please," she practically dragged them inside. "Have you found her?"

"Hang on, madam. We're here to collect some details. We don't know what we're dealing with yet." Marshall allowed Ben to do the talking; it was his call after all.

Broken eyes squeezed out another tear and then she nodded. "Yes, sorry, I... it's just I'm so worried."

"Shall we start at the beginning?" Ben got his notepad out, Marshall steered Annie Williams towards the lounge, and worried why the name 'Williams' was familiar.

"It's Jenny, she's missing."

Marshall sighed; they knew that much. Why did people have to repeat the obvious? "Full name?"

"Jenny, Jennifer Williams." Annie rushed on. "She said she'd be home for tea and she isn't and there's no answer on her phone and..."

"Slowly, Mrs Williams, please," Ben interrupted. "Let's sit down shall we?"

Marshall ushered her into the small living room to the right of the hall, noting as he did the family portraits on the mantelpiece – mother and daughter with a father who was noteworthy by his current absence.

"When did you last speak to your daughter?" Ben said once they were seated. Annie perched on the edge of her chair.

"Just after five."

Marshall checked his watch; it was seven fifteen.

"I'm not sure it's..." he began.

"She phoned from the library and said she was on her way," Annie ploughed on. "She..."

"The library?" Marshall frowned, the same slight jolt as before, and Jenny Williams he was now fairly sure from the photos was David's young helper. "Which library, Mrs Williams?"

"The Smith Foundation. She goes there a lot to research and things. Too much really. Why?"

"Would you hold on a moment, please," he told her and stepped out into the small hall to use his phone.

David didn't answer.

Was this the problem that he had been worried about? Marshall frowned, wishing he had rather more information to go on than David's vague concerns.

He returned slowly to the living room in time to hear Ben explain; "We had an odd report earlier from the library, Mrs Williams, suggesting something might be wrong." Marshall sighed; that was not the way to go about calming the woman.

"What?" As expected, Annie's voice rose, "What's happened to her. What do they know?"

"I have very little information at present," Ben prevaricated. No information would be nearer the truth, Marshall thought, and the constable would have been better served keeping it to himself. David had been fairly incoherent, meaning Marshall had little information and Ben was repeating the total lack of it third hand.

"Does she have friends at the library?" Marshall asked wishing he knew more about the young girl he occasionally nodded to on the desk as he passed.

"I don't know. I don't really know what she does there."

Marshall nodded slowly, his experience filling in the blanks about this pair. He thought he'd try something. "I think it might be an idea if we went over there," he said. "We may get more information. We can retrace her route home in case she's on her way. If you could wait for your husband..." he left it hanging.

"Died two years ago," she said crisply, cutting him off.

Marshall nodded, unsurprised. No wonder the daughter needed to escape. He could feel the same suffocating need here as he'd got from Ben when he talked about Lucy.

That meant there was the chance Jenny wasn't missing but running. Well, the Foundation Library was as good a place to start as any. He could ask David about things if nothing else.

"I'm coming too. She's my daughter."

"I think you should remain here, Mrs Williams, in case your daughter phones."

"I'll bring my mobile. Come on." She headed for the front door. "She needs me. Anything could have happened to her."

Ben and Marshall hurried after her, Marshall doing his best to dissuade her. Ben was less vociferous though Marshall guessed the constable probably better understood what was driving the woman.

"Mrs Williams, I really can't..."

"Should we walk or go in the car? If the problem is at the library then we need to get there as quickly as possible."

"We don't know that there is any problem, your daughter..."

She suddenly turned on him, her face crumpling. "I can't lose her as well, I just can't."

Marshall hesitated, moved by the tears.

"I'll walk with Mrs Williams, if you like, Sir," Ben said, his desire to get off to his own daughter obviously pushed to one side by this need in a victim, "check Jenny's usual route home and see if we can find her on the way. We'll meet you at the library."

Marshall paused briefly but decided Ben's insight into lost partners might make him a better companion on the walk. "All right, I'll see you there."

He watched the two of them head off, Annie leading, her heels clicking on the icy pavement.

*

The library was deserted, the door firmly locked.

Annie stared hard at it, as if her desperation were sufficient to let her peer within.

"Jenny must be in there," she said irrationally, "we haven't passed her."

"I've tried knocking," Marshall said. While waiting for them, he had also tried phoning David's mobile but the librarian resolutely wasn't answering. "There isn't any response." It was now half an hour past the end of the constable's shift and Marshall could see the irritation warring with the compassion in Ben's face.

"Let's try again," Ben said.

The two of them knocked hard on the unyielding wood, the sound echoing hollowly back to them from within the library.

No-one came.

"I'll try ringing," Marshall said. "Hang on." This time he rang the main desk rather than David's mobile. They could clearly hear the phone on the front desk ringing out unanswered from just behind the closed door.

"I'll try Jenny, again," Annie said looking to Ben who nodded encouragement.

She dialled her daughter and waited. In the quiet of the library porch, the three of them clearly heard a second phone ringing from the other side of the door.

CHAPTER 3

"Here." The dark stranger stopped beside a flowing trunk that sprang up beside the path. "Touch it."

Jenny placed the hand not holding the sword tentatively beside his on the smooth wood.

"Close your eyes," Hawkeye – as she had begun to think of him – said softly. "Just feel."

She glanced at him, prepared to argue that this wasn't finding David or a way home but he smiled and that made her heart jump again. She felt she could walk these paths with him forever.

"Just try," he said. "Humour me."

Feeling a little silly, she closed her eyes and pressed her hand gently against the trunk.

She stood beneath burning skies, the heat beat at her from a bright sun in an azure sky. The coliseum towered on the horizon and Jenny gasped in wonder. Legionaries in crimson cloaks strode in file towards her across the baked earth and she stepped back hurriedly.

She was once more in the garden. Her step back had separated her hand from the trunk. She looked round in surprise. "What?"

Hawkeye smiled and pulled her on to another tree. With greater trust this time, she stretched her fingers to the trunk.

She stood on a rampart amongst archers in mail, the tang of blood lay heavy in the air. A pale winter's sun hung low above her and a chill wind caressed her cheek. A shrill whistle brought her head up and she ducked as a flight of arrows flew over her head.

She opened her eyes slowly.

"How?" She shook her head. "What is this place?"

"This is the spirit," Hawkeye said. "Here is knowledge and conscience."

"Spirit?" Jenny groped towards understanding. "Of the books?"

"Of knowledge and history, fiction and fact, present and past, and sometimes of shadows still to come."

"And David?" She looked round half expecting the librarian to appear.

"Librarian, gardener and guardian," Hawkeye said, his face serious. "I fear for him."

"Why?"

"We change," he said softly. "The garden moves on. There are areas abandoned and forgotten which grow dangerous and other places where plants grow and twist so fast that they choke all life. Spirits walk who should never have been born as well as those who should have died long since."

"But it's beautiful," Jenny said, trying to drink in the sights around her.

"It can be deadly." Hawkeye lightly touched the sword she carried — a reminder. "This is no ornament."

Jenny looked at the weapon and then back up into the golden eyes that watched her. "So where is David?"

"I wish I knew," he said, looking away; an evasion. "Somewhere here. Deeper in, closer to the heart."

"Lead on," she said, caught by the magic in the air. All thoughts of home were buried under a desire to experience more. She didn't even think to ask why the librarian might be out here today rather than behind his desk though it did explain all the times she hadn't been able to find him.

*

They crossed the lawns and passed the manicured trees and entered a twisting path in what seemed to be a maze. Jenny was lost – in all senses of the word she knew. Her mind was drowning in a wealth of sensations. Her fingers trawled along the trunks of the plants, each touch filling her with visions. Hawkeye had opened her senses to this deluge but she fed the desire, her hands stretching out to each new plant or leaf.

Her companion stopped suddenly, and it was several steps before she realised that he was no longer walking beside her. She pulled her mind back slowly, reluctant to let go of her new vision.

"There are others in the library," Hawkeye said, worried. "That should not be."

Jenny looked at him without understanding. The words meant nothing to her at present. "Why not?"

"He will have closed it against the world when he came here. The garden is open and others must not be allowed to enter."

Jenny looked at him sharply, her understanding catching up with her hearing. "You said I had to come in here. Was that wrong?"

Hawkeye smiled and Jenny was reminded of the danger she had first seen in him. "No, you are needed. Not all are welcome. I must guard the gate." He turned to leave.

"Wait! What about me?"

"Find David," he said, slipping away between the hedges. "Look for the centre." His voice drifted back to her as he vanished. "Look for the fountain."

She was alone but it didn't seem to matter. She strolled on unheeding, her mind busy with the wonders playing out behind her eyes.

*

The fountain leapt and gurgled, a sharp sound after the quiet of the maze. Jenny emerged from the last twisting path onto a smooth green lawn which surrounded the chuckling water and the small summerhouse beside it.

Her step quickened; David must be here.

The stone glowed golden in the fading sun and the door stood ajar. She approached without caution, convinced he would be within and eager to ask him of all that she had seen. Out of the corner of her eye she thought she saw others walking within the garden but they faded and seeped away when she turned her head – another question for the librarian.

She pushed the door fully open and stopped in surprise. The building consisted of a single room, empty save for a large oaken table in the centre and a single, matching chair. Bookshelves lined the walls and a guitar lay in its open case in a corner, a music stand beside it, precariously situated amongst a pile of song books and folk tunes.

There was no sign of David nor any indication that he'd recently been here.

After a moment, she realised that there was something left on the table; pieces of paper or card spread on a linen cloth. Moving with more caution now, she stepped forward.

There were seven of them, lying face up in the centre of the table: tarot cards.

Six cards had been set out around a central seventh. This showed a Tower, forever falling. Jenny frowned, had David been doing this?

What did it mean? Curiosity made her look closer.

The cloth had a star marked on it and each of the cards was placed on a point of the star. They were marked in ink so ancient that it was barely readable; each point assigned a designation.

At the top of the star, labelled 'past' was a card with a picture of two walking sticks though it was upside down. Jenny absently stretched out her hand to turn it the correct way and images leapt into her mind, sweeping her away.

David, sitting in his office, a battered text before him. The viewpoint zoomed skyward, until she saw him from a bird's eye view. Around him lay the library and the town. People raced about, zipping and dashing like a manic army. And all the while, he sat at the centre, inactive.

"Two of Staves, reversed. An unpleasant situation due to bad judgment," a voice echoed in the back of her head.

Jenny snatched her fingers back. She let her eyes shift left to where the point was marked as 'immediate influences'.

This was walking sticks again – staves she supposed she ought to call them – and upside down – reversed – again. Jenny hesitated slightly but then once more stretched out a hand to touch.

A man strode the garden, violence written in his every movement. He was dark haired and dangerous looking, dressed all in black and possessing eyes of molten gold.

Jenny gasped as she recognised the stranger from earlier. Before she could react, the image shifted to show another man.

This one was taller, with greying blond hair fastened back in a leather band. His eyes were green and hard and filled with implacable purpose.

The image faded. Jenny blinked. Were both these men in the garden with her? Neither felt particularly safe. Perhaps the second was the one Hawkeye had said he had felt in the library.

Wanting to know more, she moved her gaze to the right where the point was labelled 'future influences'. Here the card was a picture of a jester, capering about in motley. Jenny laughed; it looked like the costume her dad had sometimes worn to play the fool for the morris dancers.

This time when she touched the card she gasped in surprise – the image was of herself moving through the garden earlier. So she was a 'future influence' whatever that meant. What was she supposed to be influencing? Hawkeye? A flush touched her cheek at the thought. In an attempt to avoid considering it further she turned to the bottom of the star —'long term influences'.

This was a grim card showing a man hanging from a tree by his neck. Feeling rather unsure, Jenny reached out to touch.

Darkness, emptiness, void.

She snatched her hand away.

She'd never felt anything like that deep cold; it had reached out, feeling its way deep inside. Moving on quickly, Jenny turned to the two remaining cards identified as 'present' and 'future'.

The present showed a Wheel of Fortune. Again she moved to make contact with the card.

The garden, not as she had seen it, but as it might become if neglected. Weeds ran wild everywhere; the gentle order was vanished. Spirits flitted in and out of existence: all was unkempt and abandoned.

Jenny pulled back, confused. This card was meant to be the present and the garden outside looked nothing like that. That didn't make any sense.

She shook her head and turned to the future: This showed a carriage.

She touched the card.

David was walking, deep within the garden. Forest rose all about him. Dark, moss-coated trunks lay to every side, their branches like fingers groping after his throat.

Jenny frowned, pulling her hand back. So David was further in to the garden, deeper. If, that was, the cards were showing what was real. She wasn't sure why they would lie but then, half an hour ago, she wouldn't have believed in tarot cards that showed films in her head or strange gardens behind mirrors.

As she hesitated, unsure what to do next, the cards and cloth faded out of existence leaving two cards on the wooden table.

Both cards showed old men, kings crowned and seated beneath ancient trees. As she touched the cards a blinding light filled her head.

The King sat in regal splendour, purple cloak and blue tunic hanging in rich folds. 'The King of Wands, Guardian of Knowledge, brings unexpected inheritances.' The scene whirled in her mind and she saw David sitting cross-legged and trapped within a circle of branches amongst dark, forbidding trees. A tall, ash staff lay beside him and he shuffled a pack of cards in his hands.

The vision faded and was immediately replaced by a second.

A different king, a different throne, this one carved from a living tree. 'The King of Coins, Energy of Earth.' Once more, the vision turned and she found herself watching a figure striding through the garden. Long hair tied back and eyes which glowed with a feral light. He moved through the maze with sure steps – the antlers crowning his head upheld with effortless grace. Except, just for a moment before the crowned figure reappeared, it looked like the Inspector who called on David sometimes, his face implacable.

Back in the summerhouse, a sense of foreboding filled her. Something was wrong, Hawkeye was right. David seemed to be trapped. Abandoning all caution, she knew she had to find him and free him. That much she did know was truth though how she could be so certain she couldn't have said.

She made to retrieve the cards from the table but they flickered and vanished.

Jenny frowned but then shrugged and turned away. Without stopping to think, she knew where she needed to go — further in, deeper.

CHAPTER 4

The lock finally splintered and cracked; it had taken some work. Ben dropped the ram that they had obtained from the boot of Marshall's car and pushed the heavy door wide. The library looked deserted. There was no-one at the front desk where the computer hummed gently to itself. Annie pushed past them and grabbed at the rucksack that was lying beside the monitor.

"This is Jenny's," she said. "She must be here."

Marshall nodded, trying to catch any sound of others in the high-ceilinged room. They had made plenty of noise breaking in. It was likely anyone present with ill intent had gone into hiding. David, on the other hand, should have come running. He had tried to phone again but David wasn't answering his mobile.

He realised Annie had set off into the gloom between the shelves.

"Where are you going?" He darted after her and took hold of her arm.

"To look for my daughter."

"We have no idea what we'll find," he said, as gently as he could. "I'm going to call the station to tell them what we've found so far – which was nothing – and then we'll take a look but you stay with us and let me lead."

He waited for her nod before letting go, pushing her gently towards Ben and speaking into his phone.

*

They searched every inch of the library. It had proved futile — as Marshall had expected. There was no-one here, nor any sign that there had been for some time. Now they had reached the office at the back. This was likewise deserted. They stopped at the door and looked in.

Marshall had been here a few times over the last year, always with David. There was a massive fire blazing merrily in the fireplace along one wall and a bed in the alcove at the back.

"Does the librarian live here?" Ben asked in surprise.

"I believe so," Marshall said. It wasn't something he'd ever really discussed with David. They were still working towards friendship and he had, probably deliberately, avoided pushing the bounds of credibility too far. If he wasn't sure he could yet cope with the answers, he hadn't asked the questions.

"Did your daughter know that, Mrs Williams?" Ben asked, obviously imagining different problems of a live-in librarian and a young girl.

When there was no response, they both turned to her. Annie was peering beyond them, transfixed by the doorway in the far wall. Marshall frowned, there was usually a mirror there. He knew it was more than that, but this was one of the things he had avoided going into in any depth so far. There were always reasons, when he came visiting, not to take the step into the garden that could now be clearly seen.

The three of them stepped closer, fascinated.

*

"There's no garden out there," Ben said flatly, despite the evidence. Annie gave him a doubtful look. "It's a painting or something," he added.

Marshall sighed inwardly; why couldn't people accept the evidence of their own eyes. He might not be comfortable with it and the step outside reality it boded, but at least he didn't go around trying to tell himself it didn't exist.

"Something's moving," Annie whispered.

At which point, to prove her words, a man strode into view. He was tall and slim with long, blond hair pulled back in a band and a trimmed beard. He paced quickly but without haste along the path towards them.

"Is that the librarian?" Annie asked.

Ben shrugged. "I've no idea. I don't think I've ever met him." He moved closer to the scene and to her. "If it is the librarian, he certainly has strange ideas about suitable office wear. And there's a car park on the other side of this wall," he added, his voice unsure.

"No, that isn't David," Marshall said.

A second figure appeared, running along a different path. He was dark and lithe and moved with unnatural speed. He also approached the doorway where the three of them were staring. He seemed not to have noticed the first.

"And neither is that," Marshall said, before either of the other two could ask.

"What's going on?" Annie looked around as if some sort of explanation might materialise within the library for all this.

Ben was also looking to Marshall as if expecting an answer. Marshall wasn't sure he could be any help, but it did look as if he was finally having to go in to the strange garden.

"I can't call this in," Ben continued as Marshall stayed silent.

"What would I say? I've seen a moving picture? Someone's stolen an entire car park?"

"Perhaps it's some sort of television?" Annie said.

Before Marshall could answer, the dark-haired figure arrived in front of them and stepped into the office; proving this was no television. He wasn't tall, but his presence dominated the room and his golden eyes were strangely hypnotic.

"Who are you?" He demanded without troubling to introduce himself. "How did you enter the library?"

"Well, we broke in," Annie said. "We're looking for my daughter."

Ben stepped forward to intervene. "I'm Constable Martin, this is Inspector Marshall. We are attempting to locate a missing person who we have reason to believe was in the library. Would you be the librarian?" He took another step towards the strange opening.

"No, he's not…" Marshall began and was interrupted.

"Do not enter the garden!" The figure said sharply, stepping back to fill the doorway. "You may do great damage. I am not the librarian and you should not have entered his domain without his permission."

"But my daughter…" Annie began.

Ben interrupted, touching her arm gently. "Allow me, please." He squared up to the dark stranger who blocked their path into the garden. "Mrs Williams' daughter was last known to be here. In fact, her belongings are still present. Please stand aside, sir, as I wish to satisfy myself that she is not within this garden." He spoke firmly but it seemed to have little effect. Marshall wasn't surprised. It brought back memories of the strange musicians from last Christmas who had also managed to avoid taking any notice of things they didn't want to hear. It seemed to be a characteristic of those he met through the library.

"You cannot enter," the stranger repeated, "but I believe I have met your daughter and that she is safe."

"Where?" Annie pushed past Ben's restraining arm. "Out there?"

"In the garden, yes."

"But," Annie stuttered, "But there shouldn't even be a garden there."

"What an interesting thought," the stranger said and Marshall heard corrosive amusement in his voice with an undercurrent of danger that increased the fear he could see in Annie's eyes.

"Indeed." The other, blonde-haired man had arrived without them noticing and now loomed behind the dark-haired man. "I agree; it is time the garden was elsewhere."

The dark stranger whirled on his heel and stepped back into the garden.

"Laodhan." He said, his voice cold.

"Wayland." The newcomer was taller and looked older; his blond hair and beard were flecked with grey. "You are in my way."

"I am in *their* way," the one named Wayland corrected. "They must not enter the garden."

"I agree," Laodhan said, "but you are also preventing me from leaving."

"Why?" Suspicion clouded Wayland's expressive voice. "Why would you wish to leave?"

"As I said, the garden should no longer be bound to mankind."

*

There was silence and Marshall tried to work out what was going on. Jenny did seem to be mixed up in all this, maybe David too. Neither of these strange men seemed remotely interested in finding her.

The one called Wayland suddenly lashed out, the violence in the move frightening. The other, Laodhan flew backwards landing heavily on the path.

"No," the dark-haired man spat out. "I see your intent. You mean to destroy the library. You would kill us all."

"I will save you all, fool." Laodhan surged to his feet. "You cannot stand against me."

"I will if I have to."

"You are blind, as he is. The old knowledge dies and lies forgotten. Our life is drained from us. We must cut this tie before it chokes us."

"He? Who, Laodhan?" Then, with understanding dawning in the smooth voice, "David? The librarian is in the garden. What have you done?"

Marshall echoed the question; this must have been the problem David had foreseen though what he was expecting Marshall to do about it was something the Inspector couldn't fathom.

"And he will stay here. We need the world no longer," Laodhan said.

"No!" Wayland straightened his shoulders and placed himself squarely in the doorway that led to the garden. "Without the world we will fail. You will not leave the garden."

"I am older and deeper," Laodhan said. "You cannot stand."

CHAPTER 5

The garden seemed to go on forever, the path winding deeper towards shadows under dark trees. Jenny felt as if she'd been walking for years, trekking towards the still distant fringes of trees. She knew she hadn't, but the illusion stemmed from more than just her state of mind. She could feel that she was travelling into older realms and darker places, toward knowledge forgotten or abandoned by the world outside.

She moved into the gloom between the trunks. They were slim at first – she recognised elder and hawthorn but still ancient and brooding. Their trunks were twisted and gnarled, nothing like the cultivated trees near to the entrance. There was plenty of undergrowth here to snarl her feet; tangled brush that tried to impede her progress. Jenny pushed her way through nettles and briars that twisted across the path. Some instinct within her halted the swing of the sword that she had started. The plants here were valuable, she mustn't clear the way in such a brutal fashion. Carefully, she used the flat of the blade to ease her way forward.

There was an overwhelming air of age to the wood. Trunks twisted and spread, their branches intertwining as they increased in size. Jenny struggled on, attempting care while her sense of oppression grew. She began to suspect that she was being watched. The air grew humid and she was sure she saw creatures out of the corner of her eye. If she did, they vanished as soon as she turned to look.

Just once she reached out and touched a towering trunk.

She stood in a black night. Arcs of lightning smashing at a lonely sky. Five men sheltered in the lee of a cave, hands held out to a meagre fire. They were dressed in rude skins. One, taller and older than the rest, chanted. Jenny didn't recognise the language.

She pulled back with a shudder: so old. The depth of hate and the sense of loss almost tumbled her from her feet as she snatched back her hand. Here knowledge lay lost and forgotten and the trees dreamed black dreams.

Eventually she reached a dead end. Strong branches lay tangled together into an impenetrable barrier she could neither move nor pass.

Through the twisted limbs she could see into a small glade. Verdant grass grew here, a circle bounded by ancient oaks and elms. At the centre of the clearing stood a tree older and taller than the rest. It was no species she could put a name to, possessing something of the look of an oak, but echoes of beech and elm as well. The wind whispered in its leaves: a mocking chuckle.

Jenny paused, unsure of what to do and reluctant to use the sword she still clutched. Her intuition had led her this far, no further. Steadying her breathing, which had grown ragged during her trek through the trees, she peered into the thicket.

"David?" She tried, her voice falling softly into silence and then, a bit louder, "David? Are you there?"

The librarian's head appeared within her view. He must have been sitting just to her left where she couldn't see.

"David? It's Jenny. I can't get out of the library." It was a stupid thing to say when he was obviously trapped worse than her. "Hawkeye sent me to find you."

"Who?"

"I don't know his real name. He has dark hair and golden eyes."

"Ah, the spirit, I saw him, in the cards," David frowned. "Why didn't he come to help? He shouldn't have involved you; it's not your problem."

"Spirit? Cards? The tarot? I saw it in the summerhouse but then it vanished." Jenny tried to follow what he was saying.

"You saw it?" David said, visibly shocked. "These?" He bent down and then straightened, holding a pack of cards.

"I think so."

"But they were with me. How is that possible?" A frown cut his forehead. "And you came all this way in on your own? Or did the spirit come with you?"

"He looked like a man," Jenny felt certainties slipping. "He came some of the way then he said there were others who he had to stop. He went back to the library."

"There is another, yes. He means harm."

"The man… spirit… with the long blonde hair, the other one who was in the cards?"

"Yes. You should go. I cannot guarantee your safety."

"Hawkeye gave me this." Jenny held up the sword so he could see it. "Could you use it to cut your way out?"

David blanched so pale she thought he might faint.

"I'm sorry," she said quickly, "it was only an idea, I guess you don't want to hurt…"

"Why, why did he give you that?"

"He said I might need it."

"And did this Hawkeye tell you what the garden is?"

"Not really. Just that it was knowledge and history, but also stories. I didn't really understand what he was trying to tell me. But he had me touch the plants..."

"And?" David was looking sicker by the moment.

"I saw things, wonderful things." Enthusiasm lit her voice. "How is that possible?"

"This, all of it," he waved his hand at the forest around them, "is spirit really. All stories, truth or fiction, have an essence, a passion at their core. Those exist outside the minds of reader and teller alike. They exist here. There is no time to explain it properly, not now but here is where the soul is."

"At least," he added, "they exist for the moment. But there is one, Laodhan, the blonde-haired spirit from the cards, who wants to change that. It was he who called me, imprisoned me here."

"Then let's get you free."

"It's too late for that. Here, pass me that sword."

She slipped the length of razor metal through the branches which writhed and twisted to avoid its edge.

"This is meant for me to use, but not on these bars. I am charged with their protection."

"Even when they hold you prisoner?"

"Even then. Here, take this." He passed a staff through to her. It was white ash, intricately carved and about six foot long. "You must go back. You must stop Laodhan."

"Me? But how?"

"It's easy. You go back into the library and use the staff to close the passage, the doorway you came through. Simply stand it in the doorway and the staff will do the rest. Laodhan seeks to destroy the library and the doorway that exists there. If he succeeds, he will break the link between this garden and mankind."

"What happens then?"

"To the garden? I'm not sure. Laodhan thinks it will be free from mankind's influence. That all the changes you make here with your new tales will stop."

"But you don't?"

He shook his head. "I don't believe the garden can survive without the link. But it doesn't matter. Even if it could, the price would be too great."

"What price?"

"Here is passion, here is spirit. Without the garden, every word written would be only that, empty facts devoid of any meaning beyond the dry letters on a page."

"But…" she began.

"You must stop him."

*

The wood crowded close about Jenny, its malicious whispering growing more frightening as she listened to the librarian. David wanted her to just abandon him here? David thought she could stop some spirit bent on destruction?

"I can't leave you here," she told him.

"You must. The role of librarian is a great honour, but there are responsibilities and trials too. I knew that when I accepted."

"Trials?" Like being trapped by the trees he was supposed to protect?

"Do you know how old I am?"

"Thirty?" she guessed. Truthfully, she reckoned him older – there was grey beginning to appear in the brown hair – but it didn't seem polite to say so.

"Three hundred and seventy-three."

"Impossible!"

"You say that, even after what you have seen?" He was laughing at her. "The librarian relinquishes mortality when he accepts the position. I am the guardian of the link that Laodhan seeks to destroy."

"Why not just kill you then?"

"There would be another guardian chosen. The library is the key – it is that he must destroy. I am just the face it presents to the world – its hands, its eyes. I can only die if the library is destroyed or when the task passes to another. But there are drawbacks. I can play no part in the wider world. I cannot even leave the library."

"Never?" she was horrified. Yes, the library was a haven, but to have no friends, no life beyond it. She couldn't imagine such an existence. Except, a treacherous thought whispered, isn't life here among the histories better than what you have at home? Isn't that why you come? What other life have you had for the past two years?

"Never." David was still talking. "Now, you have delayed here long enough. Go. You cannot free me without hurting these spirits, but you can save the library and all this with it. That is what matters."

Jenny turned away, impelled by the authority in his voice. She supposed that if he was immortal and imprisoned in the library, a few hours in this dank forest would be bearable. She didn't know how she could help, but she supposed if she found Hawkeye they could stop this Laodhan from his mischief. She gripped the staff tight and turned to face the dark trees about her.

"I'll come back for you," she said over her shoulder.

She never saw David's sad headshake.

CHAPTER 6

Annie watched as the blond man, Laodhan, walked slowly towards his attacker. He didn't seem troubled that Wayland was younger and faster. He just smiled. Annie felt it was a pleasant smile, despite the violence in the air.

"Are you sure that you want to do this, Wayland?" he asked.

"Of course I do not," Wayland sounded irritated. "But I will not allow you to leave."

"So be it."

Ben chose that moment to step up behind Wayland and reach through the doorway to grasp him by the shoulder. "There'll be no fighting here," he said. Wayland shrugged his hand away, but beyond that neither man paid the policemen any more attention, focused on their battle.

It was the strangest of fights.

Wayland planted himself in the doorway as if he was rooted there while Laodhan attacked with what Annie could only call magic. Gusts of fierce wind almost knocked her from her feet, but the dark man stood unmoved. Clinging vines sprang up to wrap him in a crushing embrace, but he tore them out as fast as they appeared. Lightning crackled from Laodhan's hands but was deflected with negligent grace.

The battle raged for what seemed an age, then Laodhan appeared to run out of patience and launched himself at the slim figure blocking the doorway. Wayland exploded into answering violence, using fists and feet to stop the other from accessing the office.

"Aren't you going to stop them?" Annie asked the policemen standing in amazement beside her.

*

Marshall had been watching in increasing horror; David thought he could be of use, and now Annie wanted him to intervene but this was nothing he knew how to handle. The feeling of futility he remembered from last Christmas's engagement with the gypsies crept up on him.

Ben glanced at Marshall and then squared his shoulders and nodded. "I'll try, though I think maybe I could do with back up." He stepped towards the scuffling pair and attempted to place a hand on Wayland's shoulder for a second time.

"Now then, that's enough."

The combatants seemed to pay him no mind but, either by accident or intent, one of Wayland's arms swung backward, his elbow striking Ben. The constable went flying across the office and landed in a tangled heap. There was no way a single blow should have done so much harm.

"Constable!" Annie ran to kneel at his side. Marshall followed slightly slower, torn between helping a colleague and watching the continuing fight in the doorway. There was a thin thread of blood snaking from Ben's temple but he seemed to be breathing.

"That's it," Annie said sharply. She got to her feet. On the desk set in the centre of the room there was a huge goblet — like something out of a medieval banquet. She picked it up by the stem, hefted it a couple of times as she headed to the doorway and, ignoring Marshall's strangled cry of protest, swung it back.

"Where's my daughter, you bastard?" she shouted as she struck Wayland's head.

She got no answer, but at least the fighting figures didn't ignore her. Wayland swayed and Laodhan's green eyes began to glow, like emeralds in the sunshine. He shot out a hand and grabbed Wayland about the neck. The younger man slumped, too quickly for it to be simply the effects of strangulation. Laodhan swung the limp form up and around, tossing him back through the doorway to lie crumpled on the grass.

Marshall got back to his feet and moved away from Ben towards where Annie still stood by the doorway. Nothing felt safer with the fighting finished.

"I thank you for your help." Laodhan smiled at Annie as he stepped slowly into the office. It was not a nice smile this time.

Annie backed slowly away towards Marshall.

"There is no need to be afraid," Laodhan said. "I mean you no harm."

"What about him?" Marshall asked, nodding toward the broken form of Wayland.

"He can do you no harm either, now. But this place is dangerous. What lies beyond that doorway should not be allowed to hurt your world again."

"Where's Jenny?" Annie demanded.

"Who?"

"My daughter."

"I know no Jenny."

"He said she was in there." Panic infused Annie's voice, sending it spiralling upwards.

"Then she is lost to you." There was no trace of regret or emotion on Laodhan's face as he spoke. "You must leave this place now. Take your friend and leave."

"I'm not going anywhere without Jenny."

Marshall stepped forwards, "Please, Mrs Williams, Annie, can you look after my constable and I can…"

"It is too late for her. Once a mortal takes on the library, there is no turning back."

"I don't believe you." Annie retorted but she was retreating from Laodhan back to where Ben lay slumped against the mantlepiece.

Laodhan only shrugged. "It matters not. I must complete my task."

"What task?" Marshall wondered what on earth he could do to stop events even if the strange man told them what he was about. The supernatural power already exhibited didn't encourage Marshall to confront him physically.

But Laodhan was no longer paying attention to them. He stalked towards the fireplace and scooped out a mass of burning wood – without a care for the flames that licked up his arms. He tossed the lot onto the librarian's bed — which burst into flame — and turned back to the fireplace for a second armful.

"Stop! What are you doing?" Marshall moved forward, torn between the lack of sense in trying to grab an armful of burning wood and the more practical, but less immediate, alternative of phoning the fire brigade.

Laodhan didn't answer, only marched to the door and threw his burden out into the library. Marshall compromised; moving to place himself between the man and the fire, he pressed his phone to his ear.

*

Jenny left the maze behind with relief. She was almost back now. In the distance, she could see the shimmering rectangle of the doorway that had started all this. She gripped the staff tighter and hurried forward. Then she noticed the lump in the grass.

Hawkeye.

She ran forward and rolled him onto his back. Should she have done that? Might it cause internal injuries? Could a spirit even be injured?

"Hawkeye?" He said nothing. He never even moved. She bent closer but found no sign of a heartbeat, no stir of breath.

Now what did she do?

She looked up at the mirror and what she saw made her heart lurch. David's office was on fire. Her mum was bent over a man Jenny didn't recognise while another figure — one she recognised from her vision in the summerhouse – tossed burning brands around with abandon. Hovering futilely was the inspector that had been visiting David regularly all year.

What were they doing here? What was her mum doing here?

Jenny almost sat down and cried – how was she meant to stop this? Why hadn't David given her better instructions? Close the passage? Stop Laodhan? How was she meant to do that? She'd relied on Hawkeye to help her and now he was dead.

Or was he?

If David was right, Hawkeye was a spirit: kin to the plants all around her. Slowly, she closed her eyes and reached out a hand to touch his forehead, concentrating on feeling just as he'd shown her.

Cold age. Deep anger and endless grief. Battle and rage. Hot metal folded into a blade of power. Here was an arms manual for a vanished age: a history of combat.

A blacksmith bent over an ancient forge. Muscles rippled in his arms. His chest was bare and covered by a constellation of burns. His fire glowed bright in the darkness of the forge. He pulled a line of metal free and set it on an anvil. His hammer rose to pound it into shape. It looked like the sword she had left with David. As his arm lifted, the smith paused, as if catching sight of her. His eyes caught the fire of his forge and burned a familiar gold.

"You have returned." It was Hawkeye's voice. "Have you freed the librarian?"

She shook her head, nearly in tears. "He said it wasn't possible. He gave me his staff and said to close the passage. But I don't know how and Laodhan is burning the library."

"David is dead then?"

"Dead? No. Why would you think that?"

"Only the librarian can use the staff. Only she can close the passageway."

Jenny snatched her hand back from the body on the grass.

She?

*

Deep in the garden David watched, dealing pictures with an endless snick of card on card. Card, card, card. Snap, shuffle. Then another set and another. The ten of swords, the four of cups, The Empress reversed. He shuffled quickly, then did another set; the three of cups, the six of cups, The Empress again, and again reversed. Another shuffle, another set of three. Sword, sword, Death.

There it was: time.

*

David had lied to her.

He'd let her think she could come back and free him. She remembered now the strange look in his eyes as he'd taken the sword and his words. *'This is meant for me to use, but not on these bars,'* and, *'I can only die if the library is destroyed or when the task passes to another.'*

The residue of the knowledge she'd taken from Hawkeye – Wayland, she knew his true name now – blossomed in her mind.

David meant to die so she could become the librarian: trapped in this one small building forever. She would not! She could not. Leave her mum? Abandon her degree? Give up everything to become – what? *'Librarian, gardener and guardian,'* Hawkeye's voice whispered in her mind. To be part of the visions around her and live forever. She raised tear-blinded eyes to the mirror and saw the fire growing on the other side. Her mum, oblivious, was still trying to rouse whatever companion had brought her here. The inspector looked dangerously close to being pushed into the fire he was standing in front of. She thought of a world with only dry facts, devoid of visions, of all the spirits Laodhan would condemn to extinction, of her mother trapped in a burning library.

What choice did she have? What choice had David left her?

*

David climbed to his feet and picked up the sword that lay on the grass beside him. It was short and made for suicide. He turned its point towards his breast, wondered how many other librarians had done this down the years. It needed to be right. The blade touched above his heart, he could feel the gap he wanted between two ribs. He closed his eyes. There could be no turning back.

He let himself fall forward.

*

Jenny walked towards the mirror doorway; the staff held loosely in her hand. As she stepped into the space – part entrance, part cold sheet of silver – she felt a link begin to form. And along that link came Spirit, Compassion, Intellect, a contract, a blending, and a responsibility. Jenny bowed her head, feeling the weight of it pressing her down. She was bound now, a part of this place, a part of the world but forever denied it.

Her mum was going to kill her.

CHAPTER 7

"No! You cannot!" Laodhan shouted. For a moment Marshall thought the man was still talking to him. Then he realised someone else was there.

Jenny.

The blonde girl stood just inside the doorway, a staff gripped in one hand, tears in her eyes.

"But I can," Jenny said, her voice strange. She shared a glance with her mother and then turned and touched the tip of the staff to the doorway. As she did, Laodhan started running towards her. Annie gasped and stood; the cup she'd used to hit Wayland still clutched in her hand. Marshall also began to move; she would never reach Jenny in time.

The space of the doorway rippled at the staff's touch, as if it was made from water. Silver radiated outward, solidifying as it went. In seconds, only a mirror remained. But a silver haze continued to ripple outwards, spreading and clinging until its misty tendrils touched everything in the room. As the magic blanketed the dancing flames, they stuttered and died. Laodhan gave a despairing cry and vanished with them.

"What did you do?" Annie demanded.

Jenny turned and stepped toward her. For an instant, Marshall thought he saw the glint of the silver mirror in her eyes. Annie obviously saw it too and her mouth twisted.

"Perhaps he wasn't so wrong about breaking the link to that place," Annie said. Turning away from her daughter, she threw the cup hard at the restored mirror.

*

Glass cracked.

Pain rippled across Jenny's mind and she toppled forward, clutching at the staff as she fell.

Visions flared; blazing through her in rapid succession.

A giant of a tree, ancient and brooding in the very heart of a dark forest.

A glade, open now and empty save for the sword planted upright in the earth beside a new sapling which pushed its way skywards.

A smithy, dark and yet full of heat and warmth. A pair of golden eyes reflected the dancing flames. "Welcome guardian," he said.

The scene fractured and disintegrated, the office swam back into focus, the pain fading.

Jenny looked up into the concerned eyes of her mother.

"It mended," Annie said, awe in her tired voice.

"Yes." Jenny leant on the staff to pull herself upright. An explanation could wait, she decided. New senses told her there were more urgent needs. "Call an ambulance," she said to Marshall. "Your policeman needs help."

As she turned away, she surveyed the office – her office. The logs scattered outside the door had scorched the floor, and her bed – she could see it properly now – still smouldered, but the flames were quenched. The library, the garden, it was quite willing to do whatever was necessary to take care of itself.

She thought of the golden eyes again and, ignoring the frantic phone calls going on behind her, her gaze was drawn to the empty wall above the fireplace where a sword should hang. Quite willing to take care of itself, whatever the cost.

Later, her new senses were telling her, she must retrieve the sword, ready for next time it was needed. Her mind shied away from such thoughts and she busied herself to avoid thinking.

She propped the staff in a niche beside the mirror that was obviously made for it, then picked up the cup and set it back on the desk where it belonged. As she did so, a tarot deck materialised. Absently she reached out and turned the top card.

The Fool, looking so much like her father in his motley. Her father also lost to her.

She closed her eyes and picked it up, reaching out with senses newly awakened. She saw herself, alone in the garden. Of course, this was her card.

Except that when she opened her eyes, what she held was the King of Wands.

The fool was no more.

CHAPTER 8

The ambulance arrived promptly and two burly paramedics stretchered Ben out of the library.

Annie fussed round them, urging them to be careful, while Jenny followed behind with the inspector.

As they neared the main doors each step became difficult and Jenny halted five paces from the opening. What if she really couldn't leave?

"Come on, Jenny." Annie was already hurrying after the stretcher on which Ben was beginning to stir.

"You go, Mum, I ought to tidy things up and…"

"That's the librarian's job and the inspector's, not yours."

"I told David I'd help," she said, not entirely untruthfully.

"You haven't even had tea." Annie said as the inspector said, "You know where David is?"

"I'll get some chips or something." Jenny said, ignoring the more awkward question. If chips was even a possibility now. "Don't worry."

Annie hesitated still. "I'm not sure…"

"I am. You go home and I'll… I'll see you later."

"I thought I might go to the hospital," Annie said, "It's my fault. I suggested he stopped them fighting."

"Mrs Williams, it is our job…" the inspector began but Jenny could tell her mum wasn't listening.

"And he does seem really nice…" Annie continued.

Jenny stared at her mum in amazement. Was she actually starting to notice other men? It would be a miracle if she was, however strange the time she was choosing to begin.

"Err… yes, I think that would be good," Jenny said before the inspector could interfere. If her mum was looking beyond the loss of her dad, even in a small way, then it was to be encouraged. If it gave her some breathing space to discover if she could leave the library then that would be an added benefit. Which meant she had to get rid of the inspector.

"Right, I'll do that." Annie followed Ben into the ambulance.

"I'll be all right, Inspector," Jenny said. "David asked me to sort things." The last thing she needed was to try and explain a dead librarian and a sword to a policeman, however much David seemed to have trusted this man.

"I'll come and check."

Jenny took a deep breath, she was going to have to push this; "Check what, Inspector? An empty office, a door that is now a mirror unless I choose differently, a library no longer burning. David has asked me to sort it. I am sure he will explain it to you soon." She wasn't, but that might get rid of the policeman while she attempted leaving the place. "Why don't you go and keep an eye on your colleague and I'll see you tomorrow, or David will."

The inspector hesitated but she had noted a certain ability to persuade against nature when David wanted people to leave and it seemed to be part of her role now. So, though he didn't look happy,

Inspector Marshall followed her mum and the constable out towards the ambulance.

Jenny pushed the door closed as the vehicle set off up the street and then headed back to the office. She might as well tidy up the mess before she tried to leave. That would give her time to work up the courage to make the attempt.

*

Out of curiosity, once the worst of the fire damage had been cleaned – not that there had been much of that – and to put off the moment of departure a little longer, Jenny picked up the ash staff and touched it to the mirror.

The silver flowed and vanished leaving the doorway into the garden beyond. Jenny wasn't sure whether to be pleased or disappointed at the sight. At least she wasn't going mad – it was still there.

Also still there was Hawkeye, standing in the middle of the lawn in front of her.

"You're dead."

"It is not that easy to kill me." He stepped through the mirror doorway and past her into the room.

Jenny did her best to ignore the magnetism in him. "Can I go home now?" She turned to follow his progress as he prowled around the office.

"The librarian doesn't leave the library."

"I'll starve."

He laughed at her and moved to open a small fridge in the corner of the cluttered room. "Lasagne or cottage pie? I think you'll find a microwave by the bed. Or you could phone out for something."

"But…"

"David coped and I can assure you that you have more familiarity with the technology."

"I don't want to cope. I didn't ask for this."

"You were chosen."

"By whom? You? I'm sorry but my mum needs me."

"No, the library needs you. Your mother is with her man, she will manage without you."

"Her man? But he…" Suspicions began to form. "What did you do?"

"Merely encouraged feelings that might have come in time. They have much in common and spaces to fill."

Jenny sat down in one of the armchairs by the fire as it all became too much for her. The world she thought she knew was vanishing as she watched.

"Lasagne," Hawkeye presented her with a heaped plate. "And then bed. It's been a long day."

The ease with which she gave in to the hypnotic stare in the golden eyes would have frightened her had she had enough will left to think for herself.

*

Marshall pulled up in his car at the Nightingale – as Fenwick's Hospital was familiarly known. He had followed the ambulance in his car though he wasn't entirely sure why he'd done so. Common sense told him he should have stayed in the library to take a statement from Jenny and yet here he was at the hospital having allowed himself to be dismissed, almost like a naughty schoolboy.

Having parked, he headed into A & E and gained directions to the small cubicle where Ben Martin was having his head seen to.

Annie sat outside the curtain, looking slightly uncertain as to what she was doing there either. Marshall nodded vaguely at her, unwilling to get into a discussion as to what they had gone through that evening until he was sure in his own mind. He pushed the curtain aside and stuck his head in. The doctor was tall, auburn haired and a welcome sight to Marshall.

"Alex!" Alex Ranald's daughter went to the same school as Sophie and Kate. His wife and Marian had made friends standing at the school gates each morning and evening. This had developed into the girls having sleepovers, followed by the parents managing occasional meals and evenings spent chatting when Alex and Marshall could synchronise their diaries to both have an evening off.

"John," Alex greeted him cheerfully, "getting your men beaten up, I see."

"How bad is he?"

"Not too bad," Alex patted Ben's arm, "bit of a knock but seems alert enough now. Keep an eye for concussion over the next day or two, maybe give him the weekend off, John." He teased and turned back to Ben, "Not sure I'd encourage driving for a day or two either just to be on the safe side."

"But Lucy, she's expecting me."

"Sorry, Ben," Marshall said, "Doctor's orders. Suggest you take it easy, okay? Better safe than sorry."

Ben didn't look happy about it but nodded, "I suppose."

"Mrs Williams is still here," Marshall said, "I think she might feel a little responsible for you getting hurt. Do you mind her coming in to see you are all right before she heads home?"

"No, that's fine," Ben seemed to visibly brighten, "send her in."

"I'll see you Monday," Marshall said as he left and held the curtain open for Annie to enter. Perhaps the widowed constable rediscovering an interest in the opposite sex might be an unlooked for bonus of this evening's strange occurrences. His daughter having to go to a ball on her own might also, in Marshall's view, be a positive side-effect.

*

A phone ringing woke Jenny. Her watch showed that it was half past eight in the morning. She stumbled from the bed and out into the library where her mobile phone was sitting buzzing on the issue desk.

"Are you still at that bloody library?" Her mum's voice shrilled out almost before she could get the phone to her ear.

"Err… yes… well, I…"

"What the hell are you doing?"

"I think you perhaps better come down so I can tell you about it." No point having this argument over the phone.

"I should come to you?" Annie sounded incredulous.

"It's important, mum. I… well, I think I've agreed to be librarian, so I have to open up, so you need to come here." It was the closest she wanted to get to the truth before she knew what the full reality of the situation was.

"What about college? Is it just Saturdays? Do you…"

"Mum, just come down and we'll talk."

"All right, I'll be there shortly."

"Can you bring some milk, please?" Jenny hurried on before her mum could interrupt. "There are coffee-making facilities, but I need some milk." It would go on the cereals for breakfast too, but she wasn't going to tell her mother that one yet.

Once her mum had promised milk and rung off, Jenny had a look round. There was a small, well-equipped bathroom behind a door at the rear of the bed alcove.

Once she was washed and dressed – she'd have to do something about different clothes at some point too – Jenny went to open up. The same reluctance dragged at her steps but less forcefully than last night so she made it all the way to the door where the damaged lock seemed to have achieved repair all by itself. An envelope addressed to 'Miss J Williams, Librarian' lay on the floor below the letterbox. With some trepidation she picked it up.

The letter inside was short and to the point. "Dear Miss Williams, we are delighted to welcome you to the post of Librarian for the Smith Foundation Library. The salary will be paid monthly straight into your bank account with the first deposit being made on 19 December. On the job training will be provided by your predecessor during the coming weeks. This is a permanent, lifetime appointment. We wish you every success." The signature was unreadable.

"Nineteenth December? That was yesterday. How did they know so fast?" She re-read the letter. "Predecessor? But he's dead what use is that going to be? On the job training? Yeah, right!" Jenny frowned and then phoned her bank.

"Hello, I wanted to check a payment. I believe that my first salary payment should have gone in yesterday. I wondered if you could confirm that?"

"Yes Miss Williams," the woman on the other end assured her. "Three thousand pounds was paid in."

"Three thousand? Err… right, thanks." Jenny stared, unseeing, at the letter for a long moment after ringing off. Obviously there were some bonuses to this job but…

A hammering came on the door disturbing her train of thought. It was the first of the morning's visitors and Jenny found herself rather busy with the administration of the library for the next hour.

*

By the time her mother arrived Jenny was starving. Annie arrived with the police constable in tow which was surprising and slightly worrying. She had thought it a good idea her mother showed some interest in the man but this development seemed excessively fast, particularly after Hawkeye's cryptic comment of the evening before.

They went through to the office at the back and Jenny tried to explain what was happening while she ate some breakfast.

"I've been offered the job of librarian here because… well, the man who was librarian here died last night while we were here and I said I'd take it on because… well, I've been helping out a bit. It's a… live-in post because there are valuable things here. They're going to pay me three thousand pounds a month for… for the inconvenience because I'm not supposed to leave the library at all."

That was almost the truth and still wasn't going to make her mum happy but saying that some spirit had told her she was physically incapable of leaving the place, not to mention David having killed himself to give her the job… she was having trouble with it, there was no way her mum would go for it, even after last night.

"At all? You are joking. I can't believe you would make up such a tale. You don't care about me, about what it means to lose you too."

"Mum, I'll still be here; you can come and see me." Jenny felt the familiar anger rising. "At least that way you might get out of the house for once."

Annie blanched. "How dare you? You never understood; he was your dad as well you'd think you'd feel something."

"Of course, I do but…" How had this become another argument about her dad's death. Except that everything these days went the same way with a dreadful inevitability.

"Not for me, you don't care what I'm going through." Annie burst into sobs and Ben put a comforting arm around her shoulders.

"Come on, Annie," he said gently. "I don't think we're getting anywhere here. Let's go." The look he shot Jenny was full of venom. "Hopefully your daughter will come to her senses shortly." The fact that he seemed to be reciprocating Annie's sudden desire to be a couple was, if anything, even more worrying to Jenny. Especially as he didn't seem to be sympathetic to her at all.

He slammed the office door behind them as they left.

*

The next visitor was the inspector. She had even fewer answers for him, so she purposely didn't invite him beyond the main desk. She'd read too many detective stories to suggest that trying to explain a suspicious death to a policeman was a good idea, particularly when she was fairly sure there would be no body.

"I'm sorry, Inspector, David isn't here this morning. He is in the garden," no harm in admitting that; the inspector had seen the place and may even have visited it before with David for all she knew.

"I need a statement about last night for the files," he said. "You were reported as a missing person and I need to close that down."

"I was in the library, in the garden, and didn't have my phone with me. I'm sorry if I worried people. David was showing me the other responsibilities of the librarian here." See how the inspector managed to write that down in any statement. He must know there was more to the Foundation Library, like she now did. So, let him think she knew about the strange side to things and he might give up and go away. "I really need to do my job," she turned up the persuasiveness, "maybe you could come back another time and we could discuss things when David is less busy."

Inspector Marshall hesitated but she stayed resolutely quiet and didn't move from the front desk.

"All right," he said eventually, "I'll be back." It sounded like a threat.

PART 2: THE WHITE STAG

Sanctuary.

It was quiet and dark and warm: like loam, fertile and rich. He nestled deep, resting, letting his essence spread like roots throughout this place.

He waited. He recovered.

Discontent grew, like a canker. This was not his proper place. He was outcast, abandoned. Hatred blossomed and with it a dark purpose. Once he had striven for a cause. He remembered that battle: he'd lost.

Now he wanted vengeance.

CHAPTER 1

Jenny looked out at the chaos of Christmas shopping. It might be a Sunday but with only four days to go most shops were frantically selling last minute bargains to desperate shoppers.

She stood on the threshold and held on to the massive door to keep herself upright. Her knees buckled with the effort of keeping her here in the doorway and her stomach felt sick and empty. The feeling was as bad as that which had assailed her on Friday night when she had tried to leave after her mother and the ambulance. She had had an uncomfortable feeling that she would have slipped into unconsciousness if she had stepped outside and she hadn't wanted to do that in front of her mother. Particularly as she had no idea what would have happened if the ambulance had tried to take her too.

Yesterday had been too busy with customers who showed very little curiosity about her appearance behind the desk but today was quiet, so she was going to attempt leaving.

The Christmas shoppers were paying her no attention and there was no sign of her mum who had threatened on the phone this morning to come again today – another row which had got them nowhere. Jenny caught sight of the small plaque by the door. The plaque which – mysteriously – now identified her as the librarian as it hadn't done on Friday. Well, Jenny decided, this librarian was not going to tamely accept being caged. She was going to attempt to lead a normal life.

Taking a deep breath, she stepped forwards.

Her hand on the door knocked it shut as she passed out.

*

The library was on Museum Street, which Eleanor felt was odd, as the museum was on Market Street and the market had long since migrated to the middle of the High Street. On Wednesday and Saturday afternoons it made the already crowded pedestrianised area virtually impassable.

Today was Sunday so Eleanor strode with less difficulty through the Christmas shoppers to where Museum Street went off to the right.

The library sat at the corner of Church Street with the vast wasteland of the pay and display car park behind it. This was overflowing with shoppers. Eleanor was pleased she'd walked down through the old manor grounds and past the children's playground with the ducks skating across the frozen pond. The avenue of old trees had been a fairytale glitter of frost in the December cold, even if the magnificent set of antlers had been awkward to carry so far.

There had been discussions started last year on moving the museum into the old manor but bureaucracy moved slowly. Eleanor considered it would likely be another year before the collections she tended so carefully were moved to their new home.

She wondered if they had once lived here on Museum Street, in what was now the Smith Foundation library. The building certainly looked impressive enough but the air of permanence inside gave the lie to that idea. The books felt as if they'd always lived here. That thought gave rise, as it had for the past two days, to thoughts of

David who she had felt had the same permanence and who now was gone. Without trace, seemingly, and his lack of farewell left an ache in her heart.

Stopping, as she did each time she came, to stare in appreciation at the ornately carved doors, she glanced at the bronze plaque on the wall. Perhaps she should contact The Smith Foundation, find out if they could tell her what had happened to their librarian – they'd been quick enough to change the name on the sign. Except that she was becoming less and less sure that whatever relationship she had shared with David justified her chasing him down. From this distance she wondered if she had imagined their closeness – something he obviously hadn't felt if he could simply vanish without a word.

Eleanor sighed. This argument had been running round her head for all the walk down and she was no nearer making a decision. As she pushed the heavy door open, she resolved that today – unlike yesterday – she would pluck up the courage to ask the new girl what had happened to David.

As the door creaked open it jammed on something piled on the floor. Eleanor placed the antlers down and peered round. The new librarian lay in a crumpled heap just inside the door, her chest rising and falling in time to ragged breaths.

"Oh my god, what happened?" Eleanor squeezed through the gap and bent down to shake the girl's arm gently. "Are you all right?"

Gradually Jenny Williams stirred and looked up at her. "I tried to go outside," she said so softly Eleanor wasn't sure she'd heard correctly.

"Outside?"

"I… I" Life gradually returned to Jenny's face and she pushed herself upright. "I didn't believe… I'm sorry, thank you… I ought to get back to the desk." She climbed to her feet, gave Eleanor a watery smile and walked away.

Eleanor was left staring after her in puzzled amazement. She hadn't even got round to thinking about asking for news of David.

*

Steve dragged the swords and doctor's bag from the back of the under stairs cupboard and took them to join the growing heap of props on the kitchen table.

It made quite an impressive display now it was all out. He had forgotten quite how much there was.

He checked his watch – still half an hour until the others would arrive for the last run through before they headed out; time enough to give the swords a quick polish. He grabbed a cloth and picked up the first, remembering the day Mike had first arrived with the sword. "Look what I found," he'd cried, waving it violently and nearly clearing the pub table of pints.

"I thought we'd be using wooden ones," Julian had protested although he'd obviously been itching to get his hands on a metal one too. He had insisted Mike find him one for the Turkish Knight saying that they couldn't have only St George with a real sword.

It made their mummer's play special, Steve always thought. The effort they'd put in to learning how to use those swords; proper choreographed fights which always looked spectacular. Mike had insisted they get it right. The fight and the death were so realistic that the doctor and St George's resurrection stunned the crowd. A real taste of magic.

Steve realised he'd stopped polishing, tears building. They hadn't bothered last year – the first time in ten years, but they hadn't had the heart.

Steve would have let it go but Julian had other ideas. "Mummer's play," he'd announced in October, "Ian says he'll take over as St George and Bob can take Ian's role as Father Christmas and now

Mark has joined us, he can take over from Bob." They'd stared at him in surprise. "Come on, this was Mike's baby. Do you think he'd want us to abandon it? There is no better tribute to him."

In the end they'd agreed – Mike would have wanted them to continue. Steve could still remember the fervour with which he'd sold it to them – arriving at morris practice with arms full of scripts and costumes. For ten years they'd celebrated the Winter Solstice with the words, 'In comes I' and for ten years they had walked back from the last spot at the Red Lion – he in front with the lantern, Mike at the rear in St George's bright, white surcoat with the red cross; all high on the success of another year's solstice play.

How anyone could not have seen them he could never fathom though the police had told him it had probably been a drunk driver – too many of those on the road at Christmas.

Mike had never recovered, died at the hospital – and the car hadn't even paused. Had mowed St George down and continued on, the white staring face at the wheel.

Steve would never forget that face. He spent the next months looking for it in every stranger he saw and fighting the guilt that he had looked so hard at the face and not the car or the number plate. But the compulsion to find the face, like the guilt, had passed as had the fear of walking at night. He was even going to walk the road home tonight with Julian, though not from the Red Lion – he'd been adamant about that. Tonight, they would finish at the White Hart – a slightly longer walk but less painful.

He looked at the sword, still slightly bent from its run in with the car despite their best efforts. He had a feeling Mike would be with them tonight. Julian was right – they needed to do this and not just for Mike. There were memories they all needed to exorcise, ghosts of the past to lay to rest. The relearning of roles and talking the new guy

– Mark – through it had already started the healing.

The doorbell broke into his reverie —it would be Julian, always early though more so than usual today.

Julian joined Steve in the kitchen. "I think he'll approve," he said.

"I was just thinking the same." Steve opened the doctor's bag and checked that the bottle was within. "Shame it couldn't really 'cure all ills'."

"Are you all right with this?" Steve knew his friend's extra earliness tonight was to ask this, to check for the hundredth time. "Still sure you want to walk home? We could take the cars."

"I'm fine," Steve smiled and replaced the bottle alongside the more modern first aid kit he had decided he would carry as well. "It's time to move on."

*

Lucy stared in rising annoyance at the rear of the driver in the car in front. Not that it was his fault that she was sitting, going nowhere, on a motorway sixty miles from home. That blame lay with the idiot ahead who had overturned his lorry and laid it sideways across all three lanes. According to the radio, the police were promising to have it clear in the next couple of hours but that still left Lucy a long way from where she needed to be.

Even if she had a free run all the way from here, she was still going to be late for dinner.

First time she'd seen her dad all term and the weekend ruined by some criminal deciding to brain him on Friday evening. She'd had to go alone to the Christmas Ball last night and it had taken her all day yesterday to pack her things for the break – a task which usually took half the time with his help. She'd promised to make it for a meal out tonight, particularly as he was bringing along a woman – someone he'd met on this recent case, but it was a start. She couldn't remember the last time her dad had shown any interest in a woman.

Lucy frowned. She had trouble equating the dad who'd been babbling about dates on the phone yesterday with the serious father he'd been. Part of her wanted to protest, claim he was trying to replace her mum. But that, she knew, was a childish part – a part that the university student should have left behind. The grown up in her could be happy for him after so long grieving. Though that wouldn't stop her vetting the new woman carefully. They had a long habit of protecting each other – her and her dad – and she would make sure this 'Annie' was good enough for him. Therefore, it was a shame that Annie's first impression of her was going to be her late arrival at the restaurant, totally annoyed from a difficult journey.

Lucy sighed and picked up her mobile. There was no way this was going to be a quick jam; she'd have to warn dad.

*

"That was Lucy," Ben called upstairs. He wondered if his daughter would approve of how he'd just spent the past hour. He smiled to himself – not bad considering Annie had merely popped in for coffee and to show him the new dress she'd brought for tonight. He'd seen her in it and then he'd taken her out of it. He felt like a teenager again. He couldn't believe he'd known her barely two days, they were getting on so well. She'd spent Friday night in A&E with him, holding his hand while the doctors patched his head. The concern in her eyes had been overpowering, more than he'd ever expected to see in a woman's eyes again.

"Is Lucy all right?" Annie appeared on the landing.

"She's stuck in a traffic jam on the motorway. Says she might be a bit late, but she'll meet us at the restaurant."

"Someone hit something?"

"Lorry lay down, she said."

Annie smiled. "Well, as long as she's all right."

Ben smiled back. He knew she was worried about tonight, feared what Lucy might think of her. She was concerned about Jenny too, though he had less sympathy about that —Jenny had made her choice and was stuck with it.

Ben frowned, a wave of anger, nearly hatred swept over him. Thinking of Jenny seemed to bring on this flood of feeling – almost the opposite of what he felt for her mother. He couldn't believe the girl was claiming an inability to leave the library. Obviously, her mother had – understandably – been a little overprotective after the death of her husband but this was a punishment too far.

Yesterday's meeting with Jenny had been a disaster. The things she had claimed about being the new librarian; it was beyond belief. She had flatly refused to come with them, and Annie said she hadn't come home all night.

"What's up?" Annie had joined him downstairs, her figure enhanced by the new black dress.

"Nothing. Just disappointed Jenny couldn't make it tonight too." He knew it was a mistake as soon as he said it. Her blue eyes clouded over and she bit her lip.

"Sorry." He put his arms around her and reminded himself to keep his feelings about Jenny under better control. "Forget I said it. I realise she's coping with… with this new thing. Maybe we can take Lucy round there tomorrow to meet her."

Annie nodded. "Okay, I'd like that."

Ben smiled, putting his anger aside forcibly. "Now, how about that coffee you came for?"

*

The garden lay peaceful in the sunlight. Jenny put the staff back beside the mirror and stepped out on to the grass. She guessed she probably shouldn't leave the desk unattended, but she couldn't just carry on as if everything was normal. She was going to find Hawkeye and get some answers.

Resisting the temptation to touch trees and plants as she passed, Jenny strode through the garden. She met no-one and the summerhouse stood empty.

She paused, unsure of what to do and then decided to retrieve the sword and put it back in the office.

The deeper parts of the garden seemed less menacing on a second trip though she still found the journey tiring and the thought of what she would find at the end of it made her feet hesitant. She needn't have worried; the sword stood upright beside a sapling. There was no sign of David's body.

Jenny slowly pulled the sword from the turf, unwilling to accept the future it boded, and turned to head back. Then she paused, remembering the letter she'd got yesterday. Hesitantly she reached to touch the trunk of the small tree. "David," she said feeling extremely silly, "is this you."

"The home of my spirit," he said from behind her.

Jenny dropped the sword in surprise, her hands coming up to cover her mouth. "I thought you were dead."

"I am." He smiled slightly. "The only way you can be librarian is if I'm dead."

"But... you're a ghost?"

"Something like that. A spirit."

"Why did you do this to me? I can't leave the library."

"I told you that."

"But you didn't ask me. You didn't say 'is this what you want?' or..." Jenny glared at him. She wondered if you could slap a spirit, he looked remarkably unconcerned by her distress.

"I didn't choose you, your Hawkeye did."

"I can't find him and I think he's called Wayland. He might be dead, I'm not sure." Jenny sat down suddenly. "I don't know what's going on."

"Wayland? Ah, that explains it." He nodded cheerfully. "I will help as best I can, have you shut the library?"

"No."

"Well, that's the first thing. You shouldn't come in here when there are people in the library. It's not really safe for them to find this place. Go and close up and then I'll try and tell you what you need to know." He handed her the sword he'd picked up. "Take this back while you go. It should be in the office."

CHAPTER 2

Jenny hurried back and began her rounds through the library shelves, greeting regulars she knew from her months of coming here and encouraging them that it was time to go home. The library was never too strict about closing time – if people had a need for the information or the solace to be found here then they stayed for as long as they needed. Tonight was quiet. Most people were too busy with last minute Christmas shopping to spend time in just sitting.

Jenny paused in her pacing, frowning at an occupied chair in the far end of the library.

It was the woman from the museum – a woman that Jenny had been doing her best to avoid all day after her collapse earlier.

It was a shame in a way. They would get on quite well, had similar interests. What kept Jenny away, in part, was the fact that she knew this. Realistically, she couldn't… shouldn't… know it. She had seen Eleanor in here regularly before but never to talk to, so how could she know they would get on or that the woman had interests akin to hers?

Jenny sighed. Her new senses were also telling her today that Eleanor was unhappy and unlikely to leave without bringing up the topic of David. The man she loved – though Jenny shouldn't know that either.

With reluctant steps, Jenny went to stand beside the table at which Eleanor was working.

"I was thinking about closing up soon," she started, "is there anything more you need?"

Amidst a supply of books and parchments Eleanor had set a rather splendid set of antlers.

"I'm trying to find out about these." She said. "They've been sent to the museum."

"A set of antlers? Why would you want them?" They did give off an aura of age though. What might she read if she touched them?

"Ah, not just any set. These have been dug out of a stone age grave at an archaeological dig in Yorkshire."

"Impressive!" Jenny smiled trying to keep the conversation light. "Have we got the information you need?"

*

Eleanor looked at her strangely. "This place always has the information I need. I don't know why more people don't come here. The county place isn't a patch on this."

Jenny nodded but didn't answer. She decided that saying the library chose who to encourage and who to give information to would just sound crazy and this woman was wary enough of her already.

"You're new here, aren't you?" Eleanor said, confirming Jenny's earlier suspicions that any conversation was going to head towards David.

"Yes," she agreed, "at least, new as librarian."

"I knew David, your predecessor."

"Yes, I know." Jenny waited for the inevitable question.

"What happened to him? I missed saying goodbye."

"Me too, sort of." Jenny agreed, without thinking.

The two of them looked at each other in silence.

"So, the Foundation put you in once he'd gone?" Eleanor tried, obviously thrown by Jenny's cryptic utterance.

"Sort of." Jenny prevaricated, doing her best to avoid an outright lie.

"You don't know where I could contact David now, do you?"

Jenny thought of the sapling growing in the garden and the long chat she had planned with the spirit she'd called forth. It would be strange to sit and chat with the ghost of someone she knew was dead, but she needed more information after her failed attempt to get out and she obviously couldn't rely on Hawkeye.

Something of her thoughts must have shown in her face because Eleanor continued, "You do know where he is, don't you?"

Jenny sighed. "I'm sorry; I really can't talk about it."

"You're quoting confidentiality at me?" Eleanor was incredulous. "He's a friend."

"I know. Truly, I'm sorry. I need to close up."

Eleanor glared at her but Jenny wasn't going to give anything else away. She watched in silence while the other woman gathered her things together and then the two of them headed for the exit.

*

Rick looked around the circle of faces with something akin to contempt and wondered where he'd lost his respect for those who'd been friends. Probably somewhere in the heated deserts of Afghanistan or its blood-soaked streets, he reflected. Now his old mates looked soft from too much good living. A couple of them had even succumbed to middle class harmony and were on their way to two point four children. Joe had brought his wife along and had spent the evening so far worrying about the babysitter.

Rick smiled to himself. His gran was forever going on about his single status. 'In my day,' she told him every time he went home on leave, 'everyone was married by your age.'

"In her day," he'd told his mum last time, "half the male population was dead in French ditches by my age." This, of course, had set his mum off about his choice of career and how much she worried, so he might as well have kept his mouth shut.

Running his hand across his shaven head, he tried to remember why he'd thought it would be such a good idea to come out tonight – all these shop assistants and bank managers with their tales of small town life. It had seemed like such a great suggestion when he'd met Matt in town; come out to their old haunt and have a few beers. Catch up on old times. Except you couldn't go back. What worth were memories of school playgrounds? He could tell some tales of school children – with rifles and petrol bombs and faces full of hatred.

"You're quiet, Rick." Matt set another pint down in front of him. "No tales of heroics? You must have some, surely."

"No." Heroics? Heat and dust and hate until it seeped inside you and clogged every sense. "It's not that exciting."

"Dangerous, though," Cara said, "compared to what the rest of us do?"

"Crossing a road can be dangerous." Mel pointed out, forever contrary.

"It's all so pointless," Ryan said, "we didn't need to go to war at all. I mean, there weren't any weapons of mass destruction, were there?"

"Don't look at me." Rick shrugged. "I just follow orders." A half truth at best. "I came home to escape the war."

"But surely you've got an opinion on it?" Ryan never had been one to let things lie. Rick could remember smashing that handsome face into the playground... or was that just wishful thinking?

Sometimes the violence all ran together and he couldn't be sure which memories were true and which were the result of too little sleep and too much pain.

"I don't want to talk about it, okay?"

"Leave him, Ryan." Matt came to his defence. "We can't imagine what it's like out there."

"But it's not proper war though, is it?" Cara said. "Not like our granddads went through."

"Try telling that to the lads out there." Rick snapped. "I sometimes think I'd prefer to lie in a ditch knowing that the enemy is the one twenty yards away firing at me. I don't know if today will be the day when the woman with the pram is pushing a bomb, or someone who cheered me yesterday will try and kill me. All the time, you're aware that if you even think of putting a foot wrong or retaliating, then it's your own countrymen who'll turn on you and portray you as some sort of villain. The stress can send you mad out there."

His friends stared, open mouthed, and an awkward silence developed until Matt said, "Game of pool, Rick?" Conversation gradually resumed as Rick picked up his glass and followed Matt into the back lounge.

"I'm sorry. I probably shouldn't have come." He picked up a cue.

Matt shrugged. "Needed saying. Cara has no idea, none of us do. Besides, in a way this was a damn good idea – shows you can't go back, doesn't it? Put all the childhood fancies away for good and move on."

Which was what Rick had been feeling all night.

"I can't believe," Matt finished, "that I used to fancy Mel. God, I was blind. You break, best of three."

Rick nodded, laughing. Some friends, he thought, might be worth keeping.

*

"So what happened to Marianne?" Rick was feeling mellower. Three more beers and two pool wins had improved the evening.

"Did a degree and gone on VSO, last I heard." Matt re-set the balls on the table. "Another one?"

"She was always good for a laugh." Rick put some more money into the table.

"Engaged to one of the other volunteers, I think Ryan said."

"How about Lucy? She was a looker."

"University."

"Still? That's years."

"Done Chemistry, something medical, I think. I saw her Christmas last year." Matt paused and thought. "No, must have been two years ago now. She's aiming at doing some doctorate thing. I got the impression she's still trying to save her mother."

Rick blinked. "I remember her dying, vaguely. Cancer, wasn't it? We must have been… ten?"

"Yeah, about that. She spent most of the year we had Miss Walters at the hospital."

"I used to feel sorry for her." Rick surprised himself; it seemed years since he'd felt pity for anyone, even longer since he'd admitted it. Too many of the finer feelings were buried under the hard shell he'd built.

"I think Charlene had Chemo for cancer last year," Matt said.

"Really? Didn't know her as well, wasn't she the year below us?"

"Yeah, Mel said something about it; she's going out with Charlene's brother."

"Mind you," Rick recalled standing outside the school gate at lunch times, "I think she started smoking about twelve."

"Were you there the day Lucy flipped at her?"

Rick laughed. "Oh God, yes. If her dad could have seen her."

"I suppose her mum had died by then."

The two of them continued their game, engaged in pleasant reminiscences about a childhood they had left behind. Through alcohol-tinted spectacles, it seemed a simpler time of laughter and joy. Rick revised his earlier thoughts – perhaps it hadn't been such a bad idea to come. You couldn't go back but at least you could forget the present for a while.

*

Annie flushed the toilet and headed back down to the hall.

"Ben?" she called. "Time to go."

She liked Ben's house. She smiled at that thought, she liked Ben too. But the house had a comforting sense of history to it, of a family raised. She didn't feel that she was competing with Ben's lost wife – Sarah had been gone longer than her Mike and Ben had moved past that tragedy; there was no threat in the solitary picture propped on the mantelpiece. Perhaps that was a part of his attraction – he gave her hope that she could come to terms with her loss too, with what had happened two years ago. Maybe he could replace Mike; give her someone to hold to. Perhaps, one day, her own relationship with Jenny would settle as well as Ben's seemed to have done with his daughter. She frowned. She wasn't going to let thoughts of Jen messing in that damn library spoil this evening. Tonight was about fresh starts.

"Ben?"

Where was the man? Honestly! You'd think a policeman would be less absent minded. She stuck her head into the sitting room. There he was, staring blankly at the dark beyond his window.

"Ben!"

"What?" He twisted with a start, smiling at her in a way calculated to wash away her exasperation. "I'm coming, I'm coming."

"We don't want to be late – the restaurant's bound to be busy and parking will be murder."

"And who's driving?"

She slipped an arm through his and towed him toward the door.

"And very gentlemanly it is of you to offer." She hated driving in icy weather, hated driving at this season at all, particularly after… no miserable thoughts, she reminded herself. This was their first real meal together, with dressing up and such. A date of sorts! She wasn't going to let anything spoil it, even if Lucy was going to be late. Never mind what the doctor had said on Friday night, Ben had been fine all weekend, so it wasn't an issue him driving.

She just hoped Lucy liked her.

Ben took his time locking the door, keys and bolts clunking into place. "In my line of work, you get wary about these things," he told her. Once he was done, he held the passenger door of his car for her to climb in.

She settled back into her seat and watched Ben walk round the bonnet. He still wore an abstracted air. She'd seen it a few times today, that and the blank look. Well, the doctor had said there may be headaches and dizzy spells from the blow to his head and there hadn't been. This abstraction was the only symptom.

Nothing to worry about, she told herself, nothing to trouble over.

*

The two women walked the length of the library in silence, lost in their own thoughts. Jenny did her best to stifle the twinge of envy as they approached the door. The last two days had been challenging in many ways but this inability to step beyond the confines of the library was the hardest thing. Somewhere outside were her mother, her friends, the life she had left behind and, despite the promised wonders of this new existence, she missed it.

In a funny way, she had begun to realise that what she missed was the life of two years ago rather than the one she had walked away from on Friday. She had wasted two years… or her mother had wasted them for her. Tonight, the mummers would be out, singing and playing until late, sitting around at Steve's until the early hours with mulled wine. She'd learnt all the folk songs she knew with those men and then her mother had decreed they were almost evil, at fault for the loss of her husband.

She hadn't been allowed to go to the music sessions or the ceilidhs. There were friends she had last seen at her dad's funeral because her mother had shut them all out, holding tight to Jenny for fear of losing her. Only now she had moved out of such a shadow could Jenny see what she had been missing.

Pulling wide the door for Eleanor, she stopped in delighted surprise and the two women stared in wonder at the swirling snow which was blanketing Museum Street.

"Oh wow!" Jenny's bitter thoughts gave way to a childlike awe. "It's settling too."

Eleanor gave an answering grin. "We may actually have a white Christmas." She made to step forward and only then did Jenny realise what she was looking at through the snow.

She grabbed wildly at Eleanor's arm. "No! Stop!"

"What?"

"Look." Jenny pointed. "Where's the bank? And Benito's? And the lights?"

Looking properly, there was no sign of any building she recognised. Across the street lay a row of wattle and daub cottages with thatched roofs and, in places where the snow had not yet settled properly, the tarmac of the road had been replaced by uneven cobbles packed into hard earth.

"What the hell?" Eleanor gaped at her. "What's happened?"

"I'm not seeing things then?" Jenny took a step back from the yawning doorway. "There are thatched cottages and cobbles?"

"Yes." Eleanor nodded. "That's what I'm seeing."

"Let's shut the door and try again." Jenny wasn't really sure this would help but it was worth a try, a bit like turning the computer off and on again often worked.

The two women pushed the door to and exchanged nervous glances.

"Ready?"

Eleanor nodded. "Okay, let's see."

They pulled the door open once more. Dancing white flakes littered the dark sky and settled on the unlit street. All signs of Museum Street, its Christmas lights and the crowds of late-night shoppers had vanished.

"I don't know what's going on," Jenny said slowly, "but you can't go out there." So much for talking to David, just when things had got even stranger.

"No." Eleanor agreed.

They shut the door and moved back into the warmth of the library.

"Come back to the office." Jenny offered. "I'll sort us something to eat." The supermarket had delivered a load of stuff this morning including new clothes and food to keep her going all week.

"Then we ought to work out what's going on." Eleanor said.

"If we can." Jenny's heart sank. She was sure there must be an explanation and she knew where she needed to go to find it but that would not be possible with Eleanor in tow, without all sorts of awkward explanations.

It looked like being another difficult night.

CHAPTER 3

His strength had grown and with it his control of this sanctuary. His roots ran deep, piercing every corner.

He used the eyes and hated what he saw.

He had no business here. It was filled with chaos. It stank of waste. He stayed quiet, holding himself close. The enemy would be watching. He needed complete control before he challenged. He observed and he waited, biding his time. Time slipped by, his sanctuary undiscovered.

Then the solstice dawned: a day of power. The world trembled at the heart of winter. He stayed still. His time would come soon enough.

He felt the shift. He knew what had been loosed, but there was nothing he could do. Only wait, watch and stay away from the centres of power.

Only hope the blood about to spill might aid him.

*

Dinner lay in ruins around them. Ben settled back in his chair, his pleasantly full stomach an uneasy contrast to the worry and anger churning inside.

The worry was reasonable enough.

He glanced at his watch again. Gone nine. Lucy should have been here by now. He'd hated starting without her, but the restaurant had given them no choice. Start or try elsewhere: it was almost Christmas and they had customers waiting. He'd bowed reluctantly to their pressure. It had never occurred to him that they'd finish before she arrived.

"Would you like anything else?" Their waiter had been busy throughout the meal, but now he was hovering, sensing another table about to become available.

"Coffee." He didn't need it, but it would give Lucy another ten minutes.

"Yes please." Annie smiled up at the waiter, softening Ben's abrupt tone.

His anger at the staff was misplaced, he knew it. They'd a job to do – Christmas crowds were not their fault. The clink of glasses and the buzz of happy conversation surrounded him. Across the table sat a beautiful, mature and passionate woman. He had no excuse for the anger which had been growing all evening.

"Are they worth a penny?" Annie's hand closed about his on the white tablecloth, breaking in on his thoughts. He summoned a smile.

"Hardly. I'm just worried about Lucy."

"I'm sure she's fine. You could try calling again."

He supposed he could. He pulled his mobile from his jacket pocket. The call went straight to voice mail.

"She must have switched hers off," he told Annie as the message played. Now why would she do that?

"That's good. I never leave mine on when I'm driving. It probably means she's out of the jam."

"Maybe, but what are we going to do if she hasn't arrived by the time we've finished coffee?"

Her foot toyed with his leg below the table. "Go back to yours, I guess, where she can find us." Her smile offered other reasons for following that course.

The waiter arrived with the coffee and they sipped in silence awhile.

*

Lucy groaned as the snow began to fall. That was all she needed when she was already running late. She switched the wipers on with a sigh. As if on cue, Runrig blasted out the first bars of 'Going Home'. They were rudely interrupted by a traffic report telling her all about the jam she had just cleared. Pointless really, why couldn't they have mentioned it two hours ago? Lucy switched off the Traffic Master and Runrig returned at full volume.

A crossroads sign flashed past and Lucy slowed. Left was her usual choice. It was longer but the roads were bigger, better lit and more likely to have been gritted. On the other hand, if she went straight on she could cut the time in half. She normally avoided the narrow, twisting lanes through West Cross that led to the back streets into town, but they would be traffic free and avoid all the lights and roundabouts of the ring road.

She realised that a small queue had formed behind her as she hesitated.

Slamming the gear stick into first, she let the clutch out and the car leapt forward into the narrower road ahead. No-one followed.

The snow stayed relatively light as she negotiated the S-bends through the middle of West Cross. The hamlet sparkled with Christmas Lights which twinkled amidst the falling snow.

Standing under lamp light on the small green in front of the church, a group of carol singers dispensed festive cheer.

Lucy spared them a brief glance. She remembered coming out here to midnight mass during her mum's final Christmas. It was a beautiful stone church, even more so when lit only by candles. They had huddled in coats and hats, warmed more by the friendship around them.

Too many memories.

It was another reason she usually took the long road home.

The Red Lion came into view on the left; its car park crowded and light flooding out across the lane.

She was in the outskirts, soon she'd reach Five Oaks junction, then on through Manor Estate, and past Old Manor Park. She should make it in fifteen minutes. She just hoped she could find a parking space near the restaurant.

The snow thickened. She put the wipers up a speed and eased slightly off the accelerator, her hands gripping the steering wheel tighter.

Five Oaks loomed through the dark. Except there weren't five any more. Ever since the big winds of '87, three stumps had squatted on the corner beside the two remaining oaks. There had been attempts to replace them, but harsh winters and autumn gales had done for all the saplings.

Lucy slowed for the junction and her left turn towards the town centre.

Something crashed violently into the bonnet. Something white, leaping from between the oaks.

God, she'd hit someone. For a sickening moment, a man seemed to hang in the air before her – bearded and dressed in armour with a bright red cross on a white surcoat. No, not a man, it was a white stag, falling away from the car in the swirling snow.

Lucy slammed her foot on the brake making the car slide to a halt and stall. She sat there, shaken, for several long seconds. Eventually she clambered out into the cold to see what she'd done.

There was nothing in the road.

No stag.

No man.

No sign that either had ever existed, not in the snow or on the car.

Lucy looked around slowly but there was nothing to be seen and the only sound was Runrig singing 'Loch Lomond' from within the car.

She took half a dozen deep breaths of the crisp, cold air and then returned to the driving seat. She turned the key in the ignition.

Nothing happened.

After several attempts, listening to the impotent whirring as the engine turned over and over without firing, she gave up and sat back. She pulled her handbag on to her lap and removed the phone. This was really going to mess up her dad's evening — dragging him out to pick her up or tow her in. She flicked the phone open.

No signal.

She stared in amazement and then shook it slightly. As that had no effect, she turned it off and then back on again. It still resolutely showed no signal. Lucy hit the steering wheel in frustration. What a bloody awful day. What was she going to do now?

"Well," she said aloud, "I assume the Red Lion has a phone."

Grabbing her bag, hat and gloves, she got out, slammed the door and locked it. The phone showed no change, so she set off back the way she had come. The snow was settling and she already had to stomp through a half inch layer.

Having spent the past hour and a half wishing she'd got ready for the meal before she'd left as she wasn't going to have time to change, she was now perversely grateful for the jeans and trainers she was wearing.

After a hundred yards, she tried the phone again, but it was as dead as the proverbial doornail. She thrust it away in her bag and strode on. The pub was just round the last bend and at least she would be able to wait for her dad in the warm with a drink. She could definitely do with one just now.

She strode round the corner, her face already stinging with the cold, and stopped dead.

There was no pub.

The cars, the lights, and the entire sprawling red brick building that was The Red Lion had vanished as if they had never been.

*

When he could stretch his cup no longer, Ben drained the last dregs and got to his feet. "I'm going to the toilet and then I'll pay the bill. If Lucy isn't here by then, we'll leave a message on her phone and head home." Annie nodded consent, though it wasn't the way they'd planned to end their evening.

When he returned, she was still alone at the table. She looked up and smiled. "Ready to go then?"

He nodded, helped her into her coat and led her to the door. As he followed her out into the street, he was hit by a wave of dizziness. White snow swirled about him. Shadowy cottages seemed to hover on the edge of perception. The road was uneven beneath his feet, the night dark and cold.

"Ben?" Annie's worried tone penetrated his confusion and he blinked at her. She stood beneath a streetlight, the snow dancing in its bright glow. Solid pavement lay underfoot.

"I'm fine," he told her. "Just a dizzy spell."

They started walking towards the car, but with his first step the dizziness returned. Merchant Road seemed to fade, replaced by a tunnel of darkness. He smelt a wash of sour manure and garbage, his foot landed in something that squished, half frozen beneath the snow. He glanced down and saw mud. When he looked up, for a moment he recognised nothing.

Pain brought him back to himself. He blinked. He'd walked into the lamppost. He shook his head, trying to drive the bizarre hallucinations away with the hurt.

"Ben?" Annie asked again.

"I think maybe you'd better drive."

"I can't. I had two glasses of wine."

"Trust me, you'll be safer than I will."

"What's wrong?"

"I don't know."

"Maybe we should go to the hospital instead of home." Her voice faded out, then steadied again. Accident and Emergency would be a nightmare four days before Christmas – Friday had been bad enough. Besides, he hated hospitals; he didn't want to go back again. He shook his head.

"Just get me home."

She took his arm, steering him towards the car while he concentrated on putting one foot in front of the other. His vision wavered between the familiarity of Merchant Road and a surprisingly squalid scene from a Christmas card.

"I'll phone the doctor tomorrow. There's nothing to worry about. I'll be fine."

CHAPTER 4

The door swung open letting in a flurry of snow. With it came a group of oddly dressed men carrying swords, bags and musical instruments. Matt looked up from his shot and grinned. "Entertainment's arrived."

Rick was watching the door in surprise. "What are they going to do?"

"Forget what they call it, but they do some sort of play with sword fights and things. Saw it a couple of years back. It was quite fun actually. They don't hold back with the violence."

"What's it for?"

"God knows. Bit like pantomime, I suppose, but taking it out to the people."

They finished their game but with one eye on the front bar where the players were clearing an area to perform amongst much ribald comment from various drunken parties.

Once the seven men were sure they were ready, one got out a concertina while the others lined up and began a song, demanding the attention of anyone who might still have been unaware of their presence.

"We are six actors bold
Never come on stage before
And we shall do our best
And the best can do no more."

Rick and Matt moved forward, clutching their pints, to get a better view.

*

Marshall grinned at his wife, "This should be fun."

"Which one's Mark?" Marian peered past Marshall's shoulder at the group lined up against the bar.

"The one in the black cloak. I think he said he was doing Beelzebub. Didn't quite follow how the play went but got the impression that it wasn't supposed to make a lot of sense."

"And he does morris dancing?"

"I don't think they do any of that tonight. Think Mark said this is something different that they just do at Christmas."

Marshall had got the impression that Mark was quite proud of his hobby but aware that Marshall might not approve. He had been a bit reticent and Marshall wasn't totally sure how welcome he was here tonight, but it had seemed like a good excuse for a date night with Marian. The steak at the White Hart had been good and his wife looked beautiful in a new brightly coloured dress.

He caught Mark's eye and raised his wine glass in salutation. Mark grinned back; he seemed to be enjoying himself and not at all put out by his superior's presence. Marshall shuffled round to sit closer beside Marian, pulling the table further out of the way to give the group of performers extra space as they spread out to begin.

*

Steve nodded to himself. The White Hart was packed and a huge ring of faces now watched the mummers. They all still wore the slightly amused expressions of people who were embarrassed on another's behalf. That would change. The applause they'd achieved at The Red Lion half an hour ago had been the loudest they'd ever garnered. Ian had thrown himself into the part of St George and the addition of long swords instead of sticks to the dance at the end had been an inspired idea from Mark. Skirmish was made for the whirl and clash of swords in the chorus; it looked and sounded like a full-blown melee.

Ian finished declaiming that he was St George and Julian strode on to do his bit as the Turkish Knight. Steve led the booing, encouraging the audience to do the same. The crowd, already into the spirit of the thing, joined in with gusto, almost drowning out the words but Julian let rip and his deep voice roared out.

"In comes I, a Turkish Knight
Come this way St George to fight"

Then came the sword fight, the clash of blades shockingly loud in the sudden silence. Steve looked round. No-one was laughing at them now. This was the true power behind the mummer's mask of foolery. Their dedication to making the sword fight real paid off every time. Here they earned the respect of the audience who watched wide-eyed and flinched back if the fight came too near. Drinks were forgotten for a while. Even breathing seemed to wait, suspended while the battle raged.

With a last ferocious blow, the Turkish Knight sent St George crashing to the floor, dead.

Steve felt the combined intake of breath. The crowd, caught now, looked for a solution to the death of their hero.

"Is there a doctor in the house?" Tony said, on cue.

Taking a deep breath, Steve stepped forwards.

"*In comes I, a doctor.*"

*

Marshall picked up his drink, slightly dazed. The policeman in him had wanted to stop the fight; he shouldn't be encouraging two men to hack at each other in that ferocious way with swords. He had had to keep telling himself that it wasn't real; he had to applaud the acting. He caught Mark watching him and raised the glass slightly with a nod of his head. 'Brilliant,' he mouthed and Mark grinned back.

Marian was engrossed, her drink forgotten on the table. Marshall tuned back in to the guy being the doctor telling the pub a list of just what he thought he could cure.

*

Moving fast, Lucy headed back to where she had left the car, her heart pounding in her throat. She rounded the bend and stopped for the second time that night in stunned surprise. Five Oaks now thoroughly deserved the name. Five majestic trees, their bare branches glittering with fallen snow, rose before her.

Lucy set off again, her steps slower, dreading what she would find. Past the oaks she stopped for a third time.

The car was gone.

She stood, caught by indecision. What should she do now?

Well, there was no point going back. She knew the pub had gone. It had to be forward. She really couldn't believe that an entire town would have vanished. There must be someone else ahead.

Lucy set off at a brisk pace in an attempt to stay warm and keep panic at bay. She headed down what should have been a shop lined road through the middle of Manor Estate but was actually little more than a muddy lane between high hedges. Fields stretched away on both sides and the usual orange glow of the town was missing from the night sky.

Lucy marched on, resolutely trying to ignore the gnawing terror growing inside.

*

After a while, the hedges disappeared and the fields were replaced by rolling park land. She realised that she was now walking through Manor Park itself, having gone through where the current Park Road entrance was.

She approached where the Old Manor should be.

Where it still was.

The large, gabled building stood, dark and brooding, in the open land. No sign now of the children's playground where her dad used to bring her or the public toilet block, though the avenues of trees still ran down from the front entrance of the manor towards the main town gate.

There was no light in the old building, no sign of habitation. Lucy hesitated. In her reality the manor stood empty. Would it be any different in whatever existence she now found herself? Lacking the courage to approach and find out, she headed for the avenue of trees. If the manor was still here, then surely the rest of the town would be.

She followed the avenue down towards the centre, expecting to find the row of large town houses that lined Westgate Road from the town gate of the park to the High Street.

Instead, a muddy, snow-covered track led on into town. A few thatched cottages stood along its length but all were in darkness.

Lucy paused. She was very cold now, inside and out, but what else could she do but go on? Her imagination peopled the Manor and these silent cottages with ghosts and ghouls and unspeakable things of nightmares. Hurrying past, she headed for where a last, forlorn hope told her the restaurant might be.

*

Eleanor looked round in surprise. The librarian's office was almost more of a museum than some parts of her actual museum. A fire burned in the huge grate and shelves around the walls held a variety of ancient books and odd objects — coins and pots and a beautiful gold chalice. A rather lethal looking sword hung above the mantelpiece.

Surprisingly, there was a bed in the corner and a small fridge – looking distinctly out of place – stood just inside the office door with a kettle and microwave on the small table beside it.

"You live here?" She looked at Jenny in surprise.

Jenny shrugged. "Part of the job."

"So did David live here? Before you did?"

Jenny nodded and began to bustle about, putting the kettle on and getting some rolls out. Eleanor watched her in silence for a while, recognising the distraction tactics.

"Why don't you want to talk about him? What are you hiding?"

Jenny stopped moving but remained staring at the rolls she was buttering. Eleanor had a sense that some sort of inner argument was going on. Then the younger woman shrugged and continued with the tea. "You wouldn't believe a word of it. So why bother?"

"What do you…?"

"So, let's try and figure out what's going on outside, shall we?" Jenny steam-rollered on.

Eleanor laughed briefly, without humour. "Someone or something has nicked the entire town centre and all the people and you expect me to believe that but not an explanation as to what happened to David?"

"You can see that."

"I'd prefer to see David."

"Well you can't. He's dead."

Eleanor stared at her in horror and then stumbled blindly towards the bed so that she could sit down. Her legs no longer felt up to holding her. How could he be dead? He couldn't have been much past forty.

"I'm sorry. I didn't mean to tell you like that." Jenny put down the butter knife and came to sit beside Eleanor on the bed, though she didn't presume to try and offer a comforting arm for which Eleanor was grateful – she wasn't sure she trusted this young woman. "I thought if I said nothing then you'd eventually forget him and move on. I know what it is to lose someone you love."

"Is it that obvious?"

"What?"

"That I love… loved him." It had never seemed to occur to David.

Jenny bit her lip, frowning. "I just assumed." She looked down, staring at her hands, linked on her lap. "I… I don't know why."

She's lying. Eleanor looked at Jenny in surprise. Not about David being dead, that had contained a ring of truth, but she was lying about this; about how she knew Eleanor's feelings. Eleanor couldn't fathom why the young librarian would lie about such a thing. She wasn't really sure it mattered except that it was odd; another thing which made no sense.

"How did he die?"

And again she felt the hesitation there, another lie on the way.

"Don't tell me if it's not going to be the truth!"

Jenny nodded and got up abruptly. "I'll make the coffee."

Eleanor wiped her eyes. Everything felt wrong. There were too many secrets here; she could feel them closing in.

"I'm going to check outside again." She pushed herself off the bed, fully expecting Jenny to argue that there was no point, that nothing would have changed. Jenny merely shrugged, perhaps appreciating her need to get out. "If you like." She gave a small smile, an offer of peace. "Then, perhaps I could help you find out about your antlers. It looks like we're stuck here."

*

By the time Eleanor returned, a plate of rolls and crisps awaited her beside a steaming mug of coffee. Nothing had changed outside; the snow still fell on a scene she didn't recognise. But the walk through the library and back had allowed her to calm down. If she was stuck here with Jenny, then they had to get along, whatever the truth about David and his death.

"The same." She sat down across the desk from Jenny. "Would make a lovely painting. Shame I can't draw."

Jenny didn't seem surprised by the news. "Looks like we're stuck here then. I've got a TV though I don't know as that would help. We could try the internet and see…"

Jenny tailed off. Eleanor could almost read the thought there – what would they find on the internet about disappearing towns? It was hardly an everyday occurrence. She agreed anyway – some action was better than nothing.

It was also pointless; the internet was down and the phone no longer seemed to work. Neither of which was surprising considering that the whole town they were connected to had gone.

"We're stuck," Jenny said, shutting her phone.

"But the library does have information on just about anything as far as I can tell." Eleanor said. "There might be something about this phenomenon."

"Wouldn't you prefer to research your antlers?" Eleanor had the same feeling of evasion from the other woman as before. "I don't mind giving a hand."

Eleanor shrugged. "Well, we could do both." No point in arguing. "Who knows how long we're going to be here."

Jenny looked distinctly unhappy at the thought.

CHAPTER 5

Annie pulled the car slowly into the A & E car park in the thickening snow. Ben sat beside her, his eyes unseeing, his hands crushing the seat.

"We're here," she said, "can you walk?"

He shook his head and rubbed hard at his eyes. "This isn't home."

"Ben, I've just driven the entire length of Northgate Road with you yelling at me that I'm hitting trees that weren't there. You need to see a doctor now, not in the morning."

"This is the hospital?" He looked round as if trying to see something that wasn't there.

Annie nodded, desperately worried now. "Where did you think it was?"

Ben kept searching. "I… I can see it now… but like a… a ghost. I can see through it."

"See what?"

"Fields. Trees. Snow"

"Let's get you inside." Annie leapt out and made her way round the car to help Ben out. She held his arm tightly as she steered him towards the entrance doing her best to ignore the way he was picking his feet up as if it was a muddy field he crossed instead of a tarmac car park.

*

She recognised the woman on the desk. It was the same receptionist as two nights previously though that time they had arrived in the back of an ambulance.

"Can you help me please?" Annie dragged Ben towards the desk, past the rows of plastic chairs and the blaring television screen.

"What seems to be the problem, madam?"

"He was hit on the head on…"

"Ah, yes." Recognition dawned in the woman's eyes. "Policeman, yes?"

"That's right. Well, he's started seeing things that aren't there and not seeing things that are."

"Hallucinations?"

"I don't know. He just said that he thought I'd brought him into a field, he didn't know it was the hospital. I'm really worried."

"All right, give me some details please and then take a seat. I'll get a doctor to see to him."

"How long is the wait?" Annie looked up at the LCD display and her heart dropped to see that the waiting time was currently displayed as two hours.

"The doctors prioritise," the receptionist reassured her, "so it shouldn't be too long, not for a head injury."

*

It was barely fifteen minutes before Doctor Ranald called them through.

"Mr Martin, Mrs Williams, I hadn't thought to see you back. How can I help you?"

He was clutching a large buff folder with Ben's notes in.

"He has no idea where he is, keeps seeing things that aren't there. He spent the journey here yelling at me about things I was hitting when I obviously wasn't."

"Mr Martin? Ben?" The doctor prompted.

Ben rubbed frantically at his eyes, shaking his head violently.

"No!" Doctor Ranald grabbed his head and held it still. "That's really not a good idea. If you've got a problem, then we need to keep your head still, not shake it about. Is there any pain?"

"No." Ben held still. "Nothing hurts."

"But your vision is affected?"

"Yes."

"Spots? Lines? Blank patches? Can you describe what the problem is?"

"I can see through you."

There was a small silence and then the doctor said, "Can you explain that a little further?"

"It's like I'm seeing two things at once. Well, if I concentrate, I can see what's really here, but I can see another scene at the same time."

"Double vision?"

"No, not two of the same thing. Two totally different scenes one on top of the other."

"And if you don't concentrate?"

"What I know is really here vanishes and I just see the other scene."

"Which is?"

"A field at the moment."

"Just a field?"

"Yes, a very boring, muddy field where it's snowing."

"And how long has this been going on?"

"Since we came out of the restaurant about forty-five minutes ago," Annie said. "I don't think it was a field then though because he kept yelling about trees and he walked into a lamppost."

"It was a street of thatched cottages and then a very narrow lane with trees and hedges down both sides and you spent the entire way driving through the hedge." Ben sounded despairing. "I'm sorry. What's happening doctor?"

"I think we need to get you down for a CT scan. Nothing showed up last time but I think we may have missed something, so I want to double check for delayed bleeds or swelling."

"And that would cause this?" Annie asked doubtfully.

"Possibly." The doctor, Annie felt, didn't sound at all sure.

*

Annie sat in the quiet corridor watching the light telling her that she couldn't go in. It all seemed peaceful, just half a dozen people sitting silently waiting for their turn. No-one was yelling or screaming, no doctors charging about. It was all so different from the nightmare of panic of two years ago. Then she'd paced, her heart in her mouth, while whole battalions of doctors and nurses had flocked round Mike's still form. Machines had constantly bleeped and whirred and she'd been stuck behind a closed door watching all the activity beyond it and feeling totally helpless. That helpless feeling was back; she was stuck outside unable to influence whether a man she loved was going to live or die. Though she mustn't think like that. Hallucinations weren't life threatening, were they?

Annie caught herself. A man she loved? What was she thinking? She'd only known him two days and here she was dreading the thought of losing him. Of losing Mike all over again. Perhaps it was Mike in there and…

The light went off and the nurse wheeled Ben out on the bed they'd laid him on.

"Is it okay?" She leapt up, glad to escape her thoughts.

"They're sending me back to a cubicle and then Doctor Ranald will be along with the results in a little while." Ben was obviously still struggling to see as he was squinting furiously at her.

"All right." She walked beside the bed as they headed back to A&E.

"Will you do me a favour?"

She nodded. "Of course."

"Will you go and try Lucy again. She's going to be frantic when we're not at the restaurant and not at home either." He handed her his phone. "The number's programmed in there somewhere."

She wandered outside to stand in the dark and the falling snow. There was still no answer from Lucy's phone, just the voicemail asking for a message.

"Hi, this is Annie, your dad's... friend. I'm with your dad. He wasn't feeling too well so we've come to the hospital. Hope to see you soon." It sounded trite and, once she'd finished, she realised that she should probably have told Lucy whether to go to Ben's or to come to the hospital but she felt rather uncomfortable talking to this woman she had never met – even if it was just the answerphone.

She pushed through the doors back into A & E and then went in search of a toilet, she felt in need of freshening up. Actually, what she realised she needed was a good cry. She'd retreated in this way two years ago; sat hunched in a cubicle sobbing her heart out as her world crashed down around her. Now irrational fears had her seeing it all happening again and the tears came.

*

After a while she scrubbed at her eyes, telling herself this wasn't going to be the same; Ben was going to be fine and was probably worrying about where she was and – as she kept telling herself – she barely knew him; it was nothing like the same as Mike.

She left the toilets and her feet took her, without thought, to the small morgue room where she'd gone after saying her goodbyes to Mike. She stood outside, looking through the small window. The room was empty tonight but she saw it as it had been; Mike laid out under a crisp white sheet that hid the worst of his injuries, his eyes closed and his face at peace. Annie bit back on the sob that threatened to escape and turned away.

Then she realised that she was rather a long way from where she should be. She set off, looking for the signs directing her back to A & E, getting progressively more annoyed with herself.

It was just as she discovered that she now recognised the corridor she was walking down that she heard a voice in the room she was passing say Ben's name.

"Ben Martin? The constable?" It was a man's voice.

Annie paused, curious.

A second voice which she recognised as Doctor Ranald's soft Scottish burr replied. "That's right, brought in a couple of nights ago after a blow to the head."

"I remember." The first voice was deep with a slightly foreign hint to it. "Nasty blow but no cause for concern."

"Well, he's back. Suffering severe hallucinations." Doctor Ranald said.

"Interesting."

"Was there anything… the notes suggest…" Doctor Ranald left it hanging a moment. "There were a couple of occasions, just a couple, where he spoke to me almost as if he didn't know me. A certain violence to his speech and demeanour. Spoke once of an enemy though it didn't make much sense."

"Hmmm, you know what that says to me?" The other voice mused.

"Psychotic episode. I suppose a blow to the head could do it. Hallucinations, suggestions of paranoia, disorientation, yes something worth watching for, though I think it is a long while too early to leap to conclusions like that."

Annie staggered and then fled though she faltered as the cubicle approached where she'd left Ben – how on earth was she going to tell him this?

*

Doctor Ranald followed Annie into the curtained cubicle. Ben recognised the soft Scottish lilt from last time he'd been here even though he could barely see the man himself.

He smiled at Annie and held out his hand, forcing himself to focus. She had obviously been crying which explained what had taken her so long. "Hey you, it'll be fine."

The doctor sat down on the end of the bed. "I have your CT scans back, Mr Martin, and there don't seem to be any problems showing."

Ben nodded. "That's good, surely?"

"Certainly." The doctor nodded. "I would, though, like to keep you in for observations. Something is causing these 'hallucinations' and we would like to work out what."

"What would do this?" Ben sat up and rubbed at his eyes. "It's like I'm seeing two places at once."

"Damage to the head can cause all sorts of problems with vision and…"

"Psychotic," Annie snapped. "That's what you were saying to that other doctor. You think Ben is psychotic."

The doctor sighed. "It's just one of many possibilities that need watching for and is much too early to say. Have you noticed any other periods since Friday where you are hearing or seeing things that others can't or any unreasonable anger or paranoia?" The doctor seemed to be looking to Annie for answers as much as to Ben.

"He does seem to stand and stare into space regularly and I have to say his name several times to get his attention." Annie frowned and then said loyally, "But I didn't know him before he got hit on the head so he may have done that all the time before as well. You did get very cross about Jenny, I suppose."

Ben swung his legs off the bed. "That's just because of the way she's treating you. It's nothing to do with being hit on the head."

A white stag leapt across the field he could see through the doctor and stood proud and challenging before him. Ben lost concentration; he was standing in a field, an antlered deer just in front of him.

"Ben! Ben!" the voice seemed to come from a distance and he forced the image away. Gradually the hospital swam back into focus but, just as it did, Ben felt a tug, almost as if something else was trying to hold on to his vision.

"What happened?" Annie sounded scared stiff. "You faded."

"Now, now madam, that's just not possible." The doctor sounded stunned so Ben assumed that he must have faded out briefly.

"There was a stag." Ben looked round but he couldn't see the animal in either vision now. He clutched his head. There felt like a tug of war going on behind his eyes and the picture of the field was strobing in and out of focus through the doctor.

"We need to get you to the ward." Doctor Ranald stood up. "Something is very wrong."

"No!" Ben shook his head vehemently. "I can't stay here. There feels like something in my head trying to look at… I've got to get out."

"Ben," Annie reached out to him. "Surely you'll be better here."

Doctor Ranald also reached to take his arm. "Seriously, Mr Martin, I'd like to offer you something to calm you down."

"No!" Ben had a sudden insight into what would happen if he was drugged. Unable to fight to hold on to what he could see, this other vision would take over his sight. He would be stranded in the field, unable to get back. A shiver ran through him; echoes of icy ages and deep roots and a flash of understanding which eluded him even as he chased it. He felt a deep hatred which echoed within his skull, pain constricting his mind as if someone squeezed it in a giant fist. Ben threw his head from side to side, trying to dislodge the other vision. *"Fight, don't get dragged in."* It felt like a voice right inside his head. *"Leave the smith to it."* Ben had a sudden picture of the golden eyed man from the library though he was unsure where it came from. "I have to get to the library." He knew it, wasn't sure why. Even as he spoke, he felt the struggle in his head intensify and was sure that whatever was in his head didn't want this either.

"Annie, get me to the library. Get me to Jenny." If whatever was trying to hijack his vision wanted to avoid the place then that was where he would go, whatever his feelings about Jenny.

"I really think, Mr Martin, that you should stay here." Doctor Ranald tried to make him sit down on the bed.

Ben pushed violently at the doctor, exulting in the force used as the man went crashing to the floor. Grabbing Annie, he headed for the ghost of the door. "Lead me," he insisted. "I can't see. I've got to keep fighting."

"Fighting?" Annie hesitated.

"Something's trying to take control of my sight, of my head. I don't know. It's all the fault of that bloody library. What happened on Friday. Got to be. Get me back there!"

CHAPTER 6

Rick and Matt went back to the pool table though they kept one ear on the music coming from the corner of the front bar.

"That was bloody good." Matt sounded surprised but Rick had to agree. The mummers had given an awesome performance. It wasn't easy to impress a crowd full of drunken youths with something so obviously 'untrendy', but Rick thought the mummers had really pulled it off. The dance at the end with the six whirling sword blades had had the whole place gasping and roaring applause.

"That was Mr Hood as the woman wasn't it?"

"Yeah," Matt laughed. "Can you imagine his history lessons if we'd realised he dressed up as a woman every Christmas?"

Rick laughed. "Should we go and say hi? Do you suppose he'd remember us?"

"Probably wouldn't want to. We never were that keen on why Henry the Eighth had seventeen wives or whatever it was. Anyway, they're busy playing."

The mummers had taken over a table and were playing sets of fast folk tunes on a wide variety of instruments interspersed with songs and Christmas carols.

The entire pub had spent the last five minutes belting out Good King Wenceslas and had now started in on We Three Kings.

Rick potted the black and re-set the table. "One more and then I think I'll call it a night."

"Want a lift home?" Matt offered.

"I thought I'd walk. It's not that far and I miss the exercise when I'm home." Rick smiled. "You could join me."

"Oh, don't do that. I'll drive. I've only had a couple and you're on my way."

*

Marshall found he and Marian had become part of the group gathered to sing as Mark had joined them when the play finished, and the rest of the group had also migrated that way. Mark was grinning widely and slightly flushed from his exertions.

"Absolutely amazing," Marshall said while Marian clapped. "Those swords look dangerous though."

Mark's grin became even wider, "My idea that. They had the metal swords in the play. I suggested they use them in the dance too. Looked good?"

"Really good."

"Glad you came," Mark said. "We'll probably sing and play now, do join in."

"What do you play?"

"Penny whistle," Mark drew a couple of thin tubes out of a small bag. Marshall realised they had mouth pieces on and holes at intervals.

"Don't let us stop you," he said, "maybe we shall sing along."

As the group of mummers struck up with their music, mainly carols, Marshall was soon joining in.

At one break, while various glasses were filled, Marshall let his policeman side get the better of him briefly. "How are you all getting home, Mark? No-one's sober enough to drive."

"Walking," Mark said cheerfully. "It isn't too far through the lanes and it seems to be traditional. We all go back to Steve's," he pointed out the man who had been the doctor, "and sleep over there."

"You as well?"

"Morris is family," Mark said, "not easy to explain if you've never been part of it but it's like I've known this bunch for years because I've belonged to other groups, if that makes sense."

"No, not really. What does Lily feel about it?"

"She's at Steve's already, spent the evening with the other wives, will be there for me."

"Okay, well enjoy the walk. Looks like it started snowing out there. We ordered a taxi."

*

Steve grinned at Julian who raised a finger. "One more."

They'd agreed that they would try and leave before closing time. That way they'd be back on roads with footpaths before the drunk drivers left the pubs.

"Rolling Home?" The John Tams song was their traditional end to an evening.

They set off into the rousing anthem and soon had the rest of the pub joining in on the chorus.

"Rolling home, when we go rolling home
When we go rolling, rolling
When we go rolling home."

"Good night." Julian yelled over the applause. "See you next year."

They packed up and distributed the swords before heading out into the night. All still in full costume with added coats, hats and gloves and with each carrying a sword plus an instrument, they made an interesting sight.

At the door they met two young men who were also leaving.

"That was brilliant," one told them.

"Thank you." Julian grinned. "It was a good year."

"Are you walking?" The other looked at them in surprise as they set off across the car park.

"All part of the tradition," Steve assured them. It was and that had been Mike's idea too. "Mummers used to walk the play around the village," he had told them so they had used two pubs they knew on the outskirts of town which just about counted as 'country pubs' and were close enough to walk between them. They cheated slightly in that Jill and Diane – Steve and Julian's wives – dropped them all off each year at the first stop but then they walked from one pub to the other and then home at the end of the night. All back to Steve's to sleep on his lounge floor. Well, that was the aim but quite often the playing and singing lasted until nearly dawn.

"Rather you than me in this weather," one of the youths said.

"Doesn't surprise me." Tony waved his hand. "Matthew Cork and Spiller, err, Richard Spiller. Form 5B. Yes? Never keen on effort, were you?"

The one identified as Matthew nodded. "Rick and Matt, that's right. Evening, sir." The two young men passed and headed for the car park leaving the mummers to continue their walk.

They fell into their accustomed line and soon their voices rose in a rendition of 'In the Bleak Midwinter' which seemed amazingly appropriate in the whirling snow.

*

Marshall yawned and stretched. "One more drink and I think we'll call it a night, sweetheart," he told his wife. "I think the lates on observation and then all the paperwork is catching up with me." It had been a long week tying up all the loose ends from the drug case though slightly depressing; the street value of what they'd collected was more than he could earn in a lifetime.

Marian grinned, "You're getting old! Want to..." she began when Marshall's phone rang.

Marshall flicked it open. "Yes?"

"John? It's Alex." The Scottish accent was instantly recognisable.

"Alex, what can I do for you?"

Marshall waved for Marian to stop her advance to the bar as the voice on the phone continued. "Problem, John. One of yours."

"Go on."

"Well, it's odd. Ben Martin, the guy who you came in with the other night?"

"Yes, is he all right. I thought it wasn't too bad."

"He seemed all right on Friday but came back in tonight and he's in a really bad way. Hallucinations, paranoia, talking absolute gobbledygook." Marshall waited. "I wanted to keep him in, John. I'm thinking something serious caused by the blow to the head. But he left."

"Who did he hurt?" Marshall was no fool.

"Me. But my pride mainly. I'll have a couple of bruises, nothing serious."

"But you think he's dangerous?"

"I think there is the potential for more violence, he's disorientated and unhappy. I do know where he's heading."

"Go on."

"He seems to be blaming his problems on the people at the library where he was initially hurt. I think he's heading there and he's got some woman in tow."

"Hang on a sec, Alex." Marshall held the phone away from his ear. "Sorry, Marian, looks like I may have to deal with this."

Marshall frowned, "I suppose I've been caught up in this drug thing, or relaxing after it anyway, haven't really given Ben any thought." He considered briefly. "Okay," He spoke into the phone again. "Foundation Library in Museum Street, Alex. I'll see if I can find him for you. Do you want me to send him home or get him back to the hospital?"

"Shift ended five minutes ago, John. I'll meet you there."

Which meant, Marshall thought, that it really was bad. Alex had long since been promoted past the need to make house calls. He flipped the phone shut as his wife picked her coat up.

"Assume you're taking the taxi and I need another one?" she said.

"I'm sorry, sweetheart, but Alex Ranald doesn't jump at shadows. If Ben Martin has gone AWOL with a bang to the head then who knows what might set him off."

"We've done amazingly well this year, John, and I knew what I let myself in for when I married a policeman. I'll get home to the girls and see you when I see you." She gave him a quick kiss and a push towards the door.

*

After half an hour Steve began to worry. His steps faltered and he eventually stopped. The rest of the crocodile caught up with him as he stood in the deepening snow.

Feeling slightly silly he turned to Julian. "This is the way, isn't it?"

"Of course." He and Julian had driven this way home on the first Wednesday of every month for years. Folk sessions in the White Hart on the first Wednesday and the Red Lion on the third Wednesday had made the two pubs the ideal choices for the mummers.

"So where are the houses?" By now they should be walking into the far reaches of Manor South but they were still in a country lane. There was no sign of streetlamps or pavements.

"Good question." Julian obviously didn't have an answer.

"Do we carry on?"

"Oh, come on," Bob butted in, "we've obviously just misremembered the distance. Keep going."

"It's probably just the snow," Ian suggested.

Mark nodded, "It's taking longer than we expect and making things look different."

Steve exchanged glances with Julian who shrugged and then indicated that they should carry on.

They set off again, Steve forging a path through the snow.

*

Matt had a small coupe which wasn't really designed for driving in the snow. He drove carefully, navigating the twisting lane back towards Manor Estate with exaggerated caution.

Rick was just feeling that Matt really had drunk too much to be safe and that he might have managed faster by walking when a huge white shape hurtled from the hedge. It slammed against the bonnet and flew gracefully through the air. A man in white hung suspended for a moment, his red cross livid in the headlights, and then a white stag crashed against the windscreen.

Matt slammed on the brakes and the two of them leapt out and raced to the front of the car.

"I thought..." Matt said, "I mean... it looked like..."

"... one of the players?"

"But it was just a stag."

"So where is it?" The two of them stared ahead at an empty road.

"That was... awful... weird..." Matt took a couple of steps

forward, peering ahead.

Rick joined him. "There's nothing…" He trailed off. Ahead had just got darker and there was a sudden disquieting silence behind them.

They whirled round.

The car had vanished. The road behind them was now as empty as that in front. Except it wasn't much of a road any more.

"What the fuck?" Rick glared at the track they now stood on.

"I see a light," Matt said. He was looking the other way.

"Where? Oh yes, looks like a lantern of some sort. Come on."

"But what if…" Matt struggled to keep up, "I mean, we don't know what's out there."

"I'll deal with it. We need a light."

*

After a further fifteen minutes, Steve stopped again. The hedges along the lane had given way to rolling parkland dotted with vague silhouettes of trees against the night sky. For as far as they could see there were no houses, no streetlights and nothing they recognised.

"Now what?" Steve heard the shake in his voice. "Anyone still think we've misremembered the distance?"

Various heads were shaken as the seven of them looked round in bewilderment.

With sudden violence a huge shape leapt on to the road ahead. It was a majestic white stag with towering antlers. It stood there for three heartbeats before turning and galloping off along the road away from them.

"Shit!" Julian exclaimed. "My heart nearly stopped."

"Oy! Ahead!" The cry came from behind them. "Wait up!"

"It's those young men," Julian said, "the two you knew, Tony."

"Rick and Matt? I thought they were driving."

The two men strode up looking out of breath.

"Decided to walk after all?" Steve asked.

"No, but then we thought we hit a stag thing and the car vanished," Matt said. "Any idea what's going on?" He sounded rather more sober than when they'd left the pub. Steve felt sure they could probably all do with another drink.

"I wish I knew," he said. "There's no way a whole town can just vanish."

"Or people?" Ian sounded slightly sick. "Where's Bob gone?"

"What?" Steve looked round and realised Ian was right, Bob had totally disappeared. There was no sign of him, his accordion or his sword. "Where did he go?"

"I don't know. One moment he was here and then that deer bounded out. When I looked again, he was gone." Ian continued to look around as if a large bearded man carrying a piano accordion on his back might suddenly materialise out of the snow. "Bob!" his voice vanished in the echoing dark. "Bob!"

"He's gone," Mark said.

"We can't just stand here shouting," Julian said, "or we'll develop hypothermia."

"Well, yes, but on or back?" Steve could see nothing to give him a clue. "And what about Bob?"

"Perhaps he's gone back to where we should be," Julian suggested.

"Where we should be?" Rick asked.

"Oh, come on, young man, you're not telling me you think this is really the road through Manor Estate?"

Before Rick could answer, a sudden baying sound, as of hounds in full tongue, came from behind them. Harsh and strident it rang out and then, just as quickly, was gone.

"On, and hope Bob is back home," Julian said with a shudder.

"But Bob…" Ian peered behind. "What if he's back there?"

"How the fuck would he manage that if he was with you?" Rick demanded.

"I don't know," Ian said, "but then none of this makes sense."

The sound came again, hard and cold.

"I don't think we want to go back to look for him," Steve said, "and I don't see that he would be. We'll hope he's ok but let's go on." This time no-one disagreed though the strange sound wasn't repeated.

As they walked, Steve's mind churned through endless possibilities. Perhaps Bob had arrived back where they should be to find himself all alone, or perhaps something worse had taken him. Except his mind struggled to believe that he was seeing the suddenly strange world around him and it just couldn't grasp the thought of further impossibilities. He firmly reminded himself that there really seemed nothing any of them could do about whatever had happened to Bob and trudged on through the snow.

*

A shape gradually appeared among the trees, gabled and dark. As they got closer, recognition dawned.

"That's the manor." Tony eventually put it into words. "We're in the park."

"Just how did we get from The White Hart to the park without going through the estate?" Ian looked round.

"And where's the kiddie's playground?" Julian pointed to the right, away from the old house. There were no swings, no slide and no climbing frame to be seen.

Something else gradually dawned on Steve. "Not to mention Colin," he said, his heart sinking.

They looked at each other.

"Perhaps," suggested Julian, "we're all going home one by one and this will just be a bad dream."

"God, I hope you're right."

Tony obviously hadn't been listening. "Do you know, this is almost as if..." he paused as they all swung to look at him.

"What?" Steve prompted.

Tony hesitated and then shrugged. "This is what the landscape must have looked like when the manor was first built." He rushed on once he'd begun before anyone could speak. "I'd say this was before the new wing was added to the house in the seventeenth century and the gable there was actually knocked off by the roundheads so..."

"I'm not sure now is quite the time for a history lesson, Tony." Ian said and vanished.

The six of them who were left looked at the spot where he had been standing for several long moments and then Julian said shakily, "So is this the manor or not?"

"Oh yes, I'd say so," Tony said, "just not as we know it. I've seen the old plans when I researched it for *Fenwick Through the Ages*." This sold limited copies each year from the local bookstores.

Rick laughed. "You're saying we stepped into the past? Funny, I don't remember going through any wardrobes."

"Do you have any better ideas?" Tony snapped.

Rick bristled. "Better than assuming we've all stepped back in time?" The young man's fists had balled as he faced the teacher who had once taught him history.

Mark stepped between the two of them and Steve remembered the new man was a policeman. "Look round." Mark said, "I don't believe what I'm seeing but something has happened to the town we all know. Let's not discount anything."

He waited until both men had visibly relaxed before turning to

Julian and Steve.

"What do you think we do now? Shall we keep going?"

"Might as well," Steve said.

"Where?" Julian waved his hand around. "Everywhere's gone."

"The manor is still there," Tony pointed out.

"All right, how about we go and see if anyone's in." Steve, quelling his own fears, set off towards the building.

*

The manor was in darkness and had an abandoned feel to it. There was no sign of light or life as they approached. They huddled together, five yards from the door, hesitating over the final move. They were still six; whatever had been vanishing the members of the party seemed to have stopped.

Rick, exasperated, strode forward and hammered on the door. He had a feeling of being stranded in an alien landscape which reminded him strongly of his first few months in the desert. Except that here all he had to rely on were a bunch of soft, middle-aged men who were going to be absolutely no help if it came to a fight despite the swords they carried, and Matt.

There was no response to his hammering, so he braced his shoulder against the door and pushed. Nothing happened.

Rick stepped back and tried slamming his heel against the lock. The door resolutely refused to budge. He hadn't really expected it to. This sort of place was built to last and the door had to be several inches thick.

"I could try a window," he said to the group who now crowded behind him, "but there's no-one here so I'm not sure why we would want to go inside."

"Stop ourselves developing hypothermia," Matt said.

"It depends whether we think it's more important to set up a camp or to see if we can find other people." Rick decided that someone ought to take charge if they were going to be stranded here.

"I would say," Julian offered, "that we know this place is here and we could get in if we wanted to so let's go and see what we find in the town centre. If there's nothing there, then we can come and set up camp here."

There were general murmurs of agreement.

Steve turned to Tony. "If you're right…" He held up his hand to Rick. "I'm saying we need to consider this, Okay?" Rick nodded. At least they were deferring to him which seemed to suggest they would accept his leadership if that became necessary and he wasn't stupid; however daft it sounded, he didn't have any better ideas than Tony's.

Steve continued. "If we accept Tony's premise for now, what other buildings might still be there that we would recognise and that might be of use to us?"

"Nothing, the manor is the oldest…" Tony paused. "Actually, no, that's not right. Do you know that big stone place on Museum Street, a library of some sort?"

"Yes, run by some foundation or other," Julian said.

"Smith Foundation," Mark said, he sounded suddenly interested.

"Well, that's actually mentioned in all the old documents, seems to have stood there forever, though I can't remember what it used to be."

"Abbey building of some sort?" suggested Julian.

"I don't think so but I can't remember, off the top of my head."

"Shall we go and see?" Steve looked round.

"I don't think there will be anyone in a library," Rick pointed out as Mark said, "Definitely."

"But it probably wasn't a library back then… well… now…" Tony said.

"I still don't see…"

"I don't see anything, young man. Or, at least, nothing I recognise. I think we ought to try anything that might be remotely possible."

Rick recognised that tone from history lessons; it still made his hackles rise. He forced himself to relax. "OK, fine! Which way?" There would be plenty of time once they'd finished this wild goose chase in search of a library for him to organise them and get some form of discipline.

"Down the avenue of trees," Mark pointed away from the manor's main door, "and that will bring us out almost opposite the High Street." He was already walking.

"Come on then." Rick set off, determined to be in front. "Keep moving or we're going to catch cold."

CHAPTER 7

Lucy pushed on down the High Street, wading through snow which now lay several inches deep. She was cold and scared and kept moving simply because if she didn't she knew she would sit down and cry and probably never get up again. She recognised nothing – no Marks and Spencer, no Boots, no Wilkinson, no post office. There was a low thatched house with a swinging pub sign that claimed it was the 'Market Tavern' in the place where, last time she had walked down this street, there had been a rather posh glass building housing the HSBC bank.

She knew there would be no restaurant and wasn't really sure why she kept going, except that there was nothing else to do. Gradually she realised that the dark shadow looming behind the row of cottages to her right was a larger building. She moved faster until she reached the junction where Museum Street – what she knew as Museum Street – met High Street. There she stopped in surprise. The dark mass was the library, looking as it ever did, including the discreet lights in the door alcove.

Small round lights were set around the massive door at twelve-inch intervals.

Small, round *electric* lights.

They glowed out along the street like a beacon of hope.

Stifling a sob, Lucy set off at a half run down the street and hammered on the library door.

"Help, help me, please. Is there someone here? Please be here, please let me in."

*

Eleanor raised her head. "Do you hear that?"

Jenny was already moving. The two of them had been getting on surprisingly well discussing various theories as to how the magnificent set of antlers might have come to be in a Stone Age burial. Jenny found she was learning a huge amount about rituals and horned gods from Eleanor as well as from the various books they'd found on the shelves. As long as they kept to the topic under research, they'd managed to steer clear of any further upset. Jenny could still feel Eleanor's reserve, but she could also see that the other woman was edging closer towards friendship. She wasn't really sure whether that was a good thing or not; didn't think the feeling would survive the night as she was fairly convinced the strangeness outside wasn't just going to give up and go away. Sooner or later she was going to have to make a decision about entering the garden – with or without Eleanor. She dreaded to think what might happen if David got fed up waiting for her in the garden and came to find her.

The banging on the door had her leaping to her feet. Perhaps the world outside had re-asserted itself so saving her the dilemma.

"Maybe we're all right," she said over her shoulder as she headed for the door.

"Or maybe this is some new weirdness." Eleanor caught her arm as they reached the door. "Take care; it might not be something we want to let in."

"Please let me in." The voice beyond the door was young, female and frightened.

"It doesn't sound like a threat," Jenny decided. She half wished she had thought to bring her staff or the sword from the office but couldn't really believe the need for caution. Taking a deep breath, she dragged the door open and then caught the young lady who almost fell through it.

Eleanor leapt forward to shut the door. "Still the same," she said as she pushed it to. "No sign of shops or lights."

"It's all like that." The new arrival was shivering uncontrollably. Her dark hair lay in damp strands and her lips were blue with cold. She wasn't much older than Jenny, slightly shorter, her slim frame not really dressed for tramping about in the snow.

"All?" Eleanor slipped her arm around the girl too as they headed back to the office.

"The town's all gone and I couldn't find anyone and…" the voice spiralled upwards.

"Hush, you're here now." Jenny heard the hysteria under the words and moved to deflect it. "Let's get you warm and then you can tell us all about it."

Once in the office, Jenny pulled one of the chests from under the bed where she'd piled her new things and found a longish skirt and a thick jumper.

"Get your wet things off," she ordered. "You can borrow these while yours dry."

Eleanor made them all a coffee and they settled the newcomer into one of the chairs by the fire, once she was changed.

Eleanor paused as she came to sit down. "I'm sure there were only two armchairs before."

Jenny shrugged and then decided to ignore the implied question —

something else she couldn't explain. She focused on the new arrival instead. "I'm Jenny, I'm librarian here, and this is Eleanor. We seem to be trapped here because Museum Street has vanished. Do you think you are up to telling us what's happening out there?" Jenny spoke as gently as she could.

"I'm Lucy, Lucy Martin." Jenny blinked in surprise but said nothing. "My car broke down by The Red Lion. Well, out by Five Oaks. I thought I hit a stag except it vanished and then so did everything else. The pub went and then my car and then the town." Jenny reached out and took the coffee off her as Lucy began to shake again.

"Everything's gone?"

Lucy struggled to control herself. "The manor was there and there's thatched housing on some streets but everything else is just fields and trees and dark."

Eleanor dragged one of the blankets from the bed and wrapped it round Lucy's shoulders. "I'm not surprised you're cold if you've walked all the way from Five Oaks in the snow." She looked at Jenny. "I don't suppose you've got anything we could put in this coffee for her?"

Jenny nodded and took a bottle from the desk drawer where she'd discovered it earlier. "Whisky?" Single malt had been her dad's favourite nightcap and David, it seemed, was also fond of a glass.

Eleanor put a large shot in Lucy's cup and a smaller one in her own and then helped the other girl to hold the cup to drink.

"I was supposed to be meeting my dad and his new girlfriend for dinner," Lucy said once she'd finished her coffee. "He's going to be worried sick about me."

Jenny sighed. "Oh dear. I had a feeling that's who you might be when you told us your name and your dad's already not very happy with me." At Lucy's puzzled look she sighed again. "I'm Jennifer Williams. I think your dad is out with my mum. We didn't meet in the best of circumstances, your dad and I. I hope he doesn't assume that what's happening tonight is my fault."

"Your fault? Of course it isn't." Lucy looked amazed.

"Maybe not, but I think you know more than you're telling," Eleanor leant forward, "and I think you ought to share what you know."

CHAPTER 8

Marshall watched the snow fall as the taxi headed towards the centre of town. He had considered phoning Mark but didn't want to disrupt his sergeant's evening, he and Alex could probably manage Ben Martin. On the other hand, the constable had been Helen's partner, so maybe she could give him some advice.

Helen Lovell answered her phone almost immediately.

"Sorry to disturb you on a Sunday evening," Marshall said, "just I've had a call about Ben; he seems to be suffering from the bang to his head on Friday. Would you say he was the violent sort?"

"Not really," Helen said, "what's he done?"

"Well, hurt one of the doctors and has rushed off to the library and seems to be rather angry about it according to Alex."

"Have you warned David?"

"Tried, he still isn't answering his phone," He hadn't been all weekend which was another thing worrying Marshall. "Wondered if you might have success talking to Ben as you were his partner. If you wouldn't mind joining me at the library. Don't worry if you're busy, I'll deal with it."

"No," Helen said immediately, "I'll come down, been drinking with a couple of the girls so I'm almost there anyway. He knows me so hopefully I can get through to him."

*

Museum Street was barely two minutes drive. The taxi dropped Marshall in front of the Smith Foundation where Helen Lovell was already standing on the steps.

"Evening, John." She was dressed in jeans and fleece with her hair pulled back into a severe bun at the nape of her neck. "No-one around except the odd drunk. Pubs have all turned out now and it'll be a couple of hours before 'Legless' shuts down and fills the town centre with idiots." Legless was the night club on Merchant Street outside which, Marshall suspected, a lot of the night shift were probably being kept busy with queue control this close to Christmas.

"Anyone in the library?"

"Not as far as I can see. It's all in darkness. I was just about to check round the back for any signs of disturbance."

"Backs onto Church Street car park," Marshall frowned; some of it did, at any rate. Some of it backed onto something else entirely. "If Ben drove down then he may well park there. Maybe we ought to go and check round the back but from the hospital he'll have to come past here." He turned to Lovell. "First, you can tell me everything I need to know about Ben Martin and possibly should have asked a while ago." Though he had had no reason to.

"He's late forties and a widower with an only child, a daughter, Lucy. His wife died years ago. Cancer, I think, though he doesn't really talk about it. He's very good with victims, could always get more out of them than I could. He's very gentle, would always go that extra mile for them, work the extra hour."

Which didn't tell Marshall much he didn't know and he had no idea what else he needed to ask. He looked round, trying to work out what steps to take next.

Helen suddenly gasped, "Look at the plaque." She pointed to a small bronze board beside the massive wooden doors. It read, 'Smith Foundation. Librarian Miss J Williams.'

"But we know it's David, how can that be," Marshall said grimly. He shook his head, something else unanswered.

"So," he returned to the problem of Ben Martin, "what might make him angry enough to thump someone?"

"The only thing that ever upset him really was drugs, even smokers annoyed him a bit. Possibly because of his wife. On the other hand, I've seen the sort of thing before. It's like there is a well of anger that people bury when they lose someone, and they build a shell to keep it in. I'd say he did it when his wife died and perhaps the blow to the head broke whatever was keeping the anger in check."

"Or," Marshall suggested, "if he is having feelings for Jenny's mother – he did seem to be 'noticing' her the other night – then that might have breached his shell too. If he's started feeling one thing then he might well feel everything, even those things he has been keeping buried."

Marshall sighed. "Though Alex Ranald seems to think it is more a medical problem caused by the blow to the head. I think we ought to bear it all in mind, he sounds like he could be in a fragile state physically, mentally and emotionally."

"What are we going to do when... if... he gets here?" Helen queried.

"He attacked a doctor so we're going to have to take him down to the station, probably for his own safety as much as anything else." Marshall paused and rubbed his eyes. "I think I must be tired; the library keeps flickering as if I'm seeing it through a heat haze."

"Really? I thought it was just me." Helen stepped back to look at the building properly. "It's just this one, the rest of the street isn't doing it."

Marshall stared hard at the doors in front of him. If anything, this aggravated the problem and the doors flickered rapidly, flashing in and out of existence.

"If you stare hard at it, it's like *Doctor Who*," Helen suggested. "When the TARDIS arrives somewhere and flashes on and off, only rather faster."

"Hmmm. Except this is an actual building, Helen, and – as far as I know – doesn't tend to disappear off to visit other planets."

They backed out into the road to watch the doors from a safer distance. There they were joined by a tall, ginger haired gentleman who was well-wrapped against the falling snow.

"Alex." John Marshall greeted him warmly. "No sign of your escaped patient yet."

"He's on his way."

"Sure?"

"Oh yes." Alex Ranald looked grim. "I passed his car coming down Northgate. Behaving really oddly, swerving all over the road. He's not going very fast but he's definitely heading this way."

"If it doesn't hit something first," Helen pointed out.

Alex shrugged. "Well, there is that, but having been on the wrong end of his fist once already tonight, I wasn't going to risk tackling him alone."

"No, no, wouldn't expect it," Marshall said and then stopped as something caught his eye. "That them?"

Two people had turned the corner into Museum Street.

CHAPTER 9

Annie was seriously frightened. She had finally abandoned the car at the end of Northgate when Ben, in one of his periods of invisibility, had clutched at her arm and the whole car had vanished around her.

"We're walking," she said, slamming on the brakes. "I find it hard enough to drive while you keep grabbing the wheel and I can't do it at all if the car disappears."

"Disappears?"

"You keep… I don't know… flickering on and off and it's scaring the hell out of me, Ben."

"Me too." Ben's face was a grim mask. "I'm trying to hold on but it's like I'm being pulled into this other place I can see."

"And you think it's because of what happened in the library?"

"Where else have we been recently where you can see places that don't exist?" Ben's hands were curled into fists, his whole body tensed. "It's taking all I've got, Annie, to hold on to reality. You'll have to lead me."

She took his arm gingerly and the two of them moved down Gallow Street and left into Museum Street. She had barely time to notice the group of three people in the road outside the library before there was a strange tug on her arm and she found herself staring at a cobbled street lined with thatched cottages. A white stag stood in the road in front of them. Annie blinked and – just for a moment – thought she saw Mike in all his St George's gear astride the antlered beast.

"Ben! What have you done? Where…" And Museum Street flickered back into existence.

"Maybe you ought to let go of me."

"No."

"But I pulled you in too that time."

"And if I let you go, I might lose you forever. I'm not going to let you go." Only with saying it did she realise that it was true, she needed him to hold to. She felt a twinge of guilt as she thought of Mike; was it really time she moved on? Was it what Mike would have wanted? For her to find someone else. Why had he been there, in this other place? Perhaps she was wrong to move on. Perhaps if she held to Ben she could get Mike back.

She could feel the street beginning to slip again. "Hold on, Ben, we're nearly there."

*

"They vanished." Helen Lovell stated the obvious just as the couple reappeared.

"We need to grab him before he does that again," Marshall ordered, doing his best to ignore all the implications of vanishing policemen.

"What if we all…" Alex began and then trailed off as he caught Marshall's eye. "Just a thought, John. We've no idea what's happening to him and it's not really possible. We could all start vanishing."

"I'll try," Helen offered. Before they could stop her, she strode towards the pair stumbling up the street. "Ben, good to see you." She took his hand and the three of them promptly vanished. After about ten seconds, they materialised again.

"Helen!" Marshall snapped.

She let Ben go and stepped back. "I saw a street. It was like stepping into the past but the library was still there. The other street sort of replaced this street for a moment and then we were back here."

"He needs to get in the library," Annie said loudly.

"There's no-one here, we've looked." Marshall yelled back. "What's happening to him?"

"I don't know." Annie sounded desperate. "He thinks it's to do with the bang on the head he got here. My daughter should be inside, she lives here now."

Marshall raised an eyebrow but turned and tried banging loudly on the door. Nothing happened.

"She's not in."

"She MUST be. She said she couldn't leave. I don't know what else to do." Ben and Annie faded out of existence again. This time it was half a minute before they returned.

"It's getting harder for him to come back," Alex noted.

"I'm open to ideas," Marshall said dryly.

"How about if we all grab him and one of us holds the building as well. Surely that would hold him here; he can't vanish an entire row of shops."

"All right, it's worth a shot. I can't think of anything better, I have to admit." Marshall turned to the, by now, tearful Annie. "Do you understand what we're trying?"

She nodded.

"Bring him closer and we'll form a chain. Let's see if we can anchor him here." Marshall gave one hand to Helen and watched her take Alex's hand with her other. "Right, Annie, give me your hand and, Alex, take hold of something solid."

Only as he took Annie's hand did he remember that they'd seen the library behaving just as peculiarly as Ben.

*

"What was that?" Lucy sat upright, her eyes wide.

"Sounded like someone else trying to get in." Eleanor leapt to her feet. Jenny's explanations were going to have to wait. She led the way as the three of them headed for the front door. "Do you suppose many people have been caught in whatever this is, like Lucy was?"

Jenny shrugged. "I've no idea. In a way it makes absolutely no sense that everybody wasn't caught, if you see what I mean."

Eleanor nodded and hesitated before the doors. The knocking hadn't been repeated. "Shall we?"

"Might as well." Jenny took the handle and pulled. The disconcerting cobbled street was still there but it was empty.

"No-one here." Jenny commented, rather pointlessly, and began to close the door.

"Wait!" Lucy leapt forward and then stopped. They all peered out. The road was still empty. "I'm sorry, I thought I saw someone out there briefly but it must have been a trick of the light or something."

Jenny swung the door all the way closed and they silently headed back to the office.

When they arrived, they stopped in surprise. A fourth chair now stood in front of the fireplace with a gentleman sprawled in it.

Eleanor couldn't take her eyes from him. He was slim and dark haired with the most amazing golden eyes that she had ever seen.

"What are you doing here?" Jenny asked taking the words from Eleanor's mouth and then, incongruously, added, "The mirror's closed."

"There are wilder and more dangerous than me out tonight, the mirror is breached." His words were soft yet held an underlying menace. Considering all he was doing was sitting in an armchair, he exuded an air of danger that was almost palpable. Eleanor couldn't imagine anything more dangerous; he must be lying.

"Breached? How?" Jenny sounded frightened.

"You need to find out and heal it."

"Who is this?" Eleanor looked from one to the other of them. "What is he talking about?"

Jenny sighed. "Hawkeye… err… Wayland… I…" She blushed.

"Hawkeye?" The man laughed merrily. "Well, why not, I have been Wayland for generations."

"What?" Eleanor was even more confused.

"His name's Wayland." Jenny threw herself into a chair, avoiding looking at the grinning man. "I didn't know that when I first met him, so I thought of him as Hawkeye for obvious reasons."

Eleanor suddenly found the golden eyes on her. He held her eye and smiled again. Her heart missed a beat and she took an involuntary step closer. She realised that this man was dangerous in more ways than one and she had a sudden sympathy for Jenny whose pink cheeks suggested a flood of emotion.

"So how did he get in?" Lucy asked.

Jenny looked even more uncomfortable. Hawkeye – Eleanor thought the name more appropriate than his given one – just smiled.

"Come on, Jenny." Eleanor sat opposite her. "You've been hiding something from me all evening. I'm not stupid and you are not a good liar. So how did he get in?"

"He came from the garden."

"What garden?"

The young girl sighed and got heavily to her feet. She walked over to the long mirror behind her desk and picked up a staff which stood beside it. Placing the top of the staff gently against the glass, she said something too quietly for them to hear. The mirror swirled and gradually cleared revealing a garden beyond it. "It's a doorway," she said.

"Right." Eleanor thought fast. "When you said the mirror was closed, you meant that he shouldn't have been able to get through."

"Yes."

"So, what does it mean that it's breached, and is it anything to do with what's happening outside?"

"Hang on." Lucy strode over to peer through the doorway. "This is impossible. There's a car park out there, or there should be."

"That's impossible? You just walked all the way from Five Oaks through a vanished town and you're worrying about a mirror that becomes a door?" Eleanor laughed.

"All right," Lucy bristled, "then it's doubly impossible because it's not snowing out there like it is everywhere else."

Eleanor went to join them in staring into the garden. "What is it?"

"Knowledge. Here it grows and lives." Jenny looked at her. "I think the answers to what is happening tonight may be out there but it is only really safe for me to go – as librarian."

"You said he came from there." Lucy jerked her head towards the indolent figure by the fire.

"He's a spirit, from the garden."

"He looks real."

Jenny shrugged. "It's complicated. Knowledge gains substance there and sometimes it gains so much power through belief that it has an independent presence within the garden and some spirits can even enter the library."

"So I can touch him?" Eleanor asked.

"By all means." The object of their discussion had left his seat and now stood close beside Eleanor. He lifted a hand and ran a finger gently down her cheek. Eleanor found herself drowning in golden eyes, her cheek on fire from where he'd touched her. Her breath quickened and her stomach tumbled and she leant towards him.

He stepped back. "It is not such a good idea." She was suddenly reminded of the danger in him. "I run too deep." He turned away. "Come on, Jenny, we need answers." He led the way into the garden.

Jenny hesitated and then gave a small apologetic shrug. "You better stay here and let anyone else in who's been trapped by whatever is happening. I'll be as quick as I can but he's right; we do need answers."

She followed Hawkeye into the garden.

*

Steve strode down what should have been a festive High Street but was little more than a dirt track. In his imagination he identified landmarks which were conspicuous by their absence; it went some way to quell the little voice in the back of his head which was desperately trying to scream at him that now would be a good time to panic.

"You all right?" Julian fell into step beside him.

"I'm glad I'm not alone."

"We've got through things before," Julian pointed out. "Not quite along the lines of losing an entire town, I admit, but we'll work it out." He paused and then lowered his voice. "I'm a bit worried about our bossy young friend, actually. I thought he was going to hit Tony back there."

"Yes, Tony says he thinks Rick went into the army after school."

"Ah, so he thinks he knows all about hostile territory." Julian shook his head. "Not sure how he thinks he is going to deal with an enemy he can't see but who's powerful enough to swipe the entire town. Maybe we ought to enlist Mark."

"Will any of us?"

"What?"

"Cope, Julian. Survive?"

Julian looked at him. "Of course."

Steve nodded, oddly reassured. If Julian was optimistic then it was bound to be all right. He remembered Julian delivering the eulogy at Mike's funeral, every word a positive one. He'd had them all laughing and smiling, remembering the good times. Steve had known then that the loss was bearable because Julian made it so. Funny how some people could do that.

"It's still there." The voice broke into Steve's reverie. He looked up. Tony was pointing away to the right where the large stone building of the library could be seen.

"Yes," Steve said doubtfully.

"I'd say those are electric lights around the door too." Julian smiled round at them. "That says 'modern' to me. Come on." He strode off forcing them all to hurry to keep up.

As they approached the front door a man and a woman flickered into sight in the road ahead and then almost immediately vanished again.

"What was that?" Steve paused.

"Looked like more people." Julian didn't slow.

They arrived at the library in time to see the people once more flicker in to view and away again. This time a man and two women.

"I'd say the real world is trying to come back," Matt said hopefully.

"Or more people are being sucked in," Mark said, "I think I recognised them."

For a third time the people arrived and disappeared.

"Slightly longer that time," Tony noted. "Maybe we're going to be okay."

"That was Helen-" Mark began then, with a suddenness that made them all jump, five people materialised in front of them. They stretched in a line across the street with the auburn-haired man at the end holding firmly to the library door handle.

#

"Not the library!" Helen yelled but it was too late. Alex had grabbed for the door. As Ben again flickered from view, the library also wavered and the chain of them found they were looking at the ancient street of thatched cottages which Helen had described earlier.

Staring back at them was a group of weirdly dressed men most of whom were carrying musical instruments. Marshall recognised the mummers from the pub, which meant Mark was here.

Before anyone could move or ask questions, Ben gave a tortured scream and clutched at his head.

"No! Not there!" He screamed, a tormented sound. "He can't... I won't... I can't go back there!" He attempted to pull from Annie's grasp.

"You said you had to come here." She held his arm.

"No!" He continued to scream and throw himself violently against her.

Marshall and Helen grabbed at Ben's flailing form leaving Alex holding the library door handle. Marshall was surprised but delighted to note that Mark had joined him in grasping the struggling constable. He spared him a tight smile before turning to the doctor.

"Alex, have you got anything to help?"

"Not on me. My bags in my car if we can get back to it but," the doctor looked about, "I do notice that we didn't go back yet. What was that you yelled about the library?" He seemed wary of letting the door go.

"We noticed earlier that it was fading and re-appearing too. I think you just forged some sort of link and dumped us here." Helen spoke loudly over the noise Ben was making.

"Can anyone help?" Marshall included the other group of men in his sweep round. "We think he's suffering some sort of problem due to a blow on the head."

"He didn't hallucinate this, John." Alex disagreed.

"Granted, but we need to calm him down."

"Oh, for Christ's sake." A young man who Marshall was fairly sure wasn't one of the mummers stepped forwards. With sudden but controlled violence, he punched Ben across the face. Ben's head snapped back, his eyes glazed and he collapsed. Only the arms holding him kept him upright.

"A little brutal, young man," Marshall said. "Effective, I grant you, but he is already suffering from one blow to the head."

"Rick Spiller. Corporal Rick Spiller. And that's the way you deal with hysterics."

Marshall raised an eyebrow but didn't argue the point. "What are you doing here, Mark?"

"We were walking home from The White Hart and realised we weren't in the town anymore, some of the men vanished and then Rick and Matt joined us, said their car vanished. Haven't seen anyone else until you appeared."

"Not exactly by choice. We were actually trying to stop him, not come with him. I think we just made things worse."

"There are lights on in the library," another one of the group interrupted. "I'm Steve, we were wondering about trying to get into the library; maybe that might be a way back home."

Marshall shrugged. "We did try getting in but weren't able to make contact."

"But, sir," Helen said, "if the library is here then maybe no-one heard us knock before."

"Makes some sort of sense. Alex, try again."

Alex nodded and knocked loudly on the door.

*

Eleanor turned from her scrutiny of the garden. "Was that the door?"

Lucy nodded from where she sat huddled by the fire.

"Stay here in case Jenny gets back, I'll go and see." Eleanor set off again for the front door reflecting that, at this rate, she was going to wear a groove in the floor before the night was out.

She pulled open the door, dragging a gentleman inside. He was rapidly followed by a whole group of others who stumbled in behind him. The last three carried in a fourth who seemed to be unconscious.

Eleanor shut the door behind them and then stood staring in bewilderment at a most oddly assorted crowd of people. There were two women and eight men not counting the one who now lay unconscious on the floor. Four of these were in their late forties, dressed in a variety of odd costumes and carrying instruments and swords.

"I take it," she said eventually, "that you got caught by the disappearing town too."

"Too?" One of the sword carriers asked. "We sort of hoped that the library might be a way home."

"Sorry." Eleanor wondered what on earth she was apologising for. "We're trapped here as well."

"We?"

"Where's my daughter?" The older of the two women looked up from where she'd been kneeling beside the unconscious man. "Where's Jenny?"

"Well..." And then Eleanor made various connections. "Is one of these Lucy's dad?"

"What?" The other woman blinked. "How... I mean... What do you know about Lucy?"

"She's here, arrived not long ago."

"Oh God. Yes, this is her dad." The woman indicated the man lying on the floor. "He's not very well." She glared up at a young man in the group. "Though I'm not sure knocking him out will have helped."

"There's a bed in the office. We could put him there."

Eleanor gradually got them all moving back through the library.

"Did you knock before?" She asked one of the men as they walked. "We thought we heard something but then there was nobody there."

The gentleman she had first pulled in answered. "We knocked from the 'proper' street, but no-one came."

Eleanor nodded; she supposed that made some sort of sense – as far as anything tonight was making sense.

CHAPTER 10

What should have been a cramped office seemed rather larger than Marshall remembered and the sofas and armchairs around the flaming hearth comfortably accommodated them all once they'd laid the unconscious Ben on the bed.

Lucy, after her initial exclamations, was persuaded to leave her father to rest and she sat stiffly side by side with Jenny's mother, Annie.

Marshall organised introductions all round and was working up to a summary of the situation when Annie interrupted. "So where is my daughter?"

Eleanor sighed and waved her hand towards where the garden still showed. "She went in there."

"With some man," Lucy added, "said he was a spirit of some sort."

"Oh no!" Annie put her head in her hands.

"A spirit?" Inspector Marshall moved to peer through the doorway into the garden. "I think I should possibly have taken up David's offer of looking through here a while ago. Speaking of which, where is David?"

"I don't know," Annie said in a muffled voice, "Jenny says she is librarian now."

"I've been trying to get a straight answer all evening," Eleanor said, "all I got was an admission that he's dead though god knows if that's true or not."

"Really?" Marshall raised one eyebrow but didn't question further. He was making a mental list of things he didn't have answers to. David and whether he was alive was outranked by a disappearing town just at present. If this was the problem David had seen then he had seriously misjudged Marshall's ability to solve it. "So why did Jenny go in there?" He asked instead. And with whom was another question he added to his list.

"She's looking for answers. About what happened to the town. She said they might be in there." Eleanor shrugged. "The man said something about the mirror being breached."

"Mirror?" Helen queried.

"That was a mirror before it was a doorway. I think it's supposed to keep things in the garden but this man, Hawkeye, got out and said it was breached."

"He said there was worse than him out as well," Lucy added in a small voice.

"Yes, he did. I'd forgotten."

They had gradually all moved and were now gathered round the mirror, peering out at the scene beyond.

"So should we…" one of the mummers began when the slamming of the office door made them all jump.

"What was that?" Rick whirled.

"Door slammed, that's all," Lucy said with a slight catch in her voice.

"How?" Marshall looked round, caught Rick's eye and the two of them headed for the door.

"What's the matter?" Eleanor demanded.

"We were all over there," Marshall clarified without turning.

"The constable's gone." Alex Ranald pointed towards the bed. He was right; there was no sign of the unconscious man.

"Get him back!" Annie yelled and headed for the door herself, closely followed by Lucy.

The crowd of them followed as Marshall led the way to the front door which now stood open. Ben Martin was striding away down the street.

"Dad!" Lucy pushed through them and headed off after him.

"No." Marshall caught Annie as she would also have gone. "We don't know what's out there and you're not equipped. "Helen, Mark, go and bring them back. Use force if necessary but don't overdo it."

The constable and sergeant stepped out into the snow and promptly vanished.

"What the hell?" Marshall's mouth fell open.

"Some of the others vanished on the way here," Steve said, "just disappeared like that into nothing."

"John," Alex grabbed on to Marshall's arm to keep him from going after his colleagues, "if you think about it, we only got here because we were holding on to Ben. The library is here – wherever here is – but out there, we don't… 'belong'. Does that make sense?"

Marshall snorted, "You're saying only certain people should be here, so we'll be kicked out, sent home if we're not wanted?"

"It would make sense."

"No, it wouldn't," Steve argued. "Why would this place want Julian, Tony and me but not Bob, Colin or Ian? What's so special about us?"

"Until we know what this place is, I doubt we shall be able to answer that," Marshall said.

"If someone's going after them, they had better go soon," Matt pointed out as Ben and Lucy disappeared amidst the falling snow.

"Are we saying, then, that only some of us are going to be able to go after them?" Steve asked.

"I'll go." Rick stepped out of the door. "I was 'invited' and I'm trained in enemy territory so if there's anything out there, I'm best equipped to handle it."

"Take this." Steve handed over his sword. "They're not really sharp because that would be dangerous, but I bet it could do a bit of damage."

"I'll come." Matt offered and he took Julian's proffered sword and joined Rick outside.

"All right, just get them back here but don't take too many risks." Marshall wasn't happy but he didn't have any better ideas. With reluctance he shut the door behind them.

*

"You think they go home then, the people who vanish?" Julian broke the silence.

"Well, where else would they go?" Alex said.

"After what I've seen tonight," Marshall sighed, "I'd say just about anything's possible." He looked round at the row of tired, shocked faces. "Go and sit down. We don't all need to wait by the door. I'll let them in when they get back." Most of them moved off, leaving Alex standing in front of him.

"Bit of a long way from London, hey John?"

"I think we're a long way from just about anywhere."

"Anything I can do?"

"You tell me." Marshall shrugged helplessly. "If you're right then we're no help at all going out there," he nodded towards the door, "and we're doing nothing stuck in here either."

"Can you get hold of your sergeant?"

Marshall got out his mobile and flipped it open. "No signal."

"Oh well, just a thought. I suppose he could knock to say he got back safely because they said they heard us earlier. Shame we've no way of asking him to."

"Hang on; you might be on to something." Marshall hunted through his pockets until he found his notebook and pen. "Let's try this." He scribbled a note down, ripped the sheet from the book and folded it. Then he opened the door and threw the piece of paper out on to the snow where it vanished.

"Interesting," Alex commented. He went to the nearest shelf, picked a book down which, by coincidence, was entitled *Streets Through the Ages* and threw it outside. It sat on the snow, going nowhere.

While the two of them stood there, there was a sudden knocking as if on the door, except that the door still stood wide open.

Alex jumped.

"I told Mark to knock if he got the note." Marshall smiled. "It's not much as communication goes but it seems to be all we've got."

"Morse code?" Alex suggested.

"If I knew anything past SOS that would be useful," Marshall admitted ruefully.

"This is a library. There must be a book on it somewhere."

"All right." Marshall started writing again, glad to be doing something. "I'll tell Mark to start learning Morse Code and he needs to track down next of kin. May be a good idea if he finds these other mummers who vanished as well." He passed Alex a piece of paper. "Go and get some details, Al. I'll let Mark know what's happening."

Marshall finished his note and threw it out. This was followed shortly by the list of contact details which Alex provided.

"Now, I suppose all we can do is wait. Do you want to see if you can find a book on Morse Code, Al?"

"Well…"

"What is it?"

"When I was back there, Annie was saying she is going to go after her daughter into that garden thing. I'm not sure she should go and definitely not by herself."

"No, you're right. We shouldn't split up any further and we shouldn't let anyone wander off alone." Marshall frowned. "Try and dissuade her but, if not, are you okay to go with her?"

"Yes, no problem. I'll get the mummers looking for books. One of them seems to be a historian, he's already talking about searching for books on what's happening here so they can look for Morse Code books at the same time."

"Good idea. That'll keep them busy at least and may stop them worrying."

"Or doing anything stupid?"

Marshall smiled. "That as well." He paused. "Glad you're here, Al. It's nice to have someone I can rely on."

Alex grinned. "Have to make me PCSO next. Better get back before she sets off on her own." He left Marshall standing before the library doors.

*

"Shit!" Mark Sherbourne glared at the glowing Christmas lights of Museum Street. "Shit! Shit! Shit!"

"Never thought of that," Helen said beside him.

"We should have." Mark growled in frustration.

"Oh, come on, Mark. It's not exactly an everyday situation."

Mark sighed. "No, I know, but I saw people vanishing all the way back from the White Hart. At least this answers where I suppose they went."

The two of them stared at the library.

"It's still flickering," Helen noted. She moved forwards and laid her hand on the building. Nothing happened.

"Last time you were holding on to Ben. I'd say that without Constable Martin, we're stuck here."

"Should we try and get into it?" Helen suggested. "Might that take us back?"

"I don't know. I don't even know if it's a good idea to want to go back. We should really be working on getting them here, not us there." Mark hit the side of the library. "Truth is, I don't know anything. I keep thinking I might wake up except I know I haven't even gone to bed yet."

"What's that?" Helen pointed at a piece of paper that had appeared on the ground in front of the library door. She stooped forwards and picked it up. "It's from Marshall."

Mark took the paper and read it. When he was done he passed it back to Helen and hammered loudly on the door three times.

"Not much use if we can't get a note back," She suggested.

"But at least they can keep us informed. It's better than nothing."

A second note materialised and Mark picked it up. "He wants us to try Morse Code to communicate with him." Mark rolled his eyes. "I'm going to have to learn Morse, John, if you want me to tell you anything," he commented and went back to reading. *There may be next of kin missing the people here and then there's the few who have been here and then vanished like you did. Track them down. List of contacts to follow. Keep people away from the library. John.*" Mark shook his head. "Next of kin? I know where they all are, they're all waiting at Steve's but what the hell am I supposed to tell them? Your husbands are missing but are perfectly safe in another reality? Thanks, John."

"I take it you'd like me to cordon off the library?"

Mark snorted. "Not sure how we're going to explain that one either."

"Well, anyone looking at it can see it's flickering. We can say it's an unknown phenomenon and, until it has been scientifically investigated, we have to keep people away for their own safety."

"All right, yes, that's worth a shot. You realise we're going to have the press crawling all over us by morning, but we'll have to go with it. I suppose you want me to do next of kin?"

"If we can get hold of these people who've been there and keep them from handing out scare stories, then we could tell relations that their loved ones are helping us with witness statements about some sort of incident. That might hold them for a while."

Another piece of paper appeared and Helen snatched it up. "Contact for three men walking from The White Stag through to Manor South. They vanished in Manor Park somewhere."

"I know all that," Mark said, "Bob, Colin and Ian. You take a car and go and see if you can find them near the manor and bring them in to stop them talking. Then we'll go to the relations and spin them a story. I'll also organise cordoning the library off and talking to the DCI and see if I can start learning Morse Code." Mark sighed. "I'd say it's going to be a very long night."

Helen nodded and set off at a fast walk towards the police station while Mark started making phone calls.

PART 3: THE HUNTER

CHAPTER 1

Bob Hall was six foot four, built like a rugby forward and not easily frightened. The fact that he was currently more shaken than ever before in his life would have been rather worrying to any companions had there been anyone to notice. The added circumstance that he was alone was one of the things he was currently finding most alarming. Up until an hour ago he had been surrounded by a group of friends. Admittedly, not in any place they had recognised, but a friendly group was preferable to the solitude he was now experiencing. The fact that he was now standing by the Park Road entrance to Manor Park was a definite improvement in scenery but it did little to explain where he'd been, why he could find no-one else he knew in the park and where all his friends still were. Nor, for that matter, did it explain how they'd made it as far as the park without passing through any of the housing estate.

"Bob!" He was disturbed from his morbid reverie by a familiar voice.

"Colin? Ian?" Bob hurried towards them. "What the hell happened? Where's everyone else?" he had been searching fruitlessly for what seemed like hours.

"Don't know – to any of that. Suddenly found myself back here and then Ian came and found me. We guessed you might be further back through the park."

"So, might the others be nearer the manor?" Bob suggested.

"Possibly, I'm sure they'll head this way if we wait." Colin said.

"Where were we?"

"God knows." Ian shrugged. "Any idea what time it is?"

"Gone midnight. Jill's going to be worried sick." Jill was Steve's wife and she always had the mulled wine ready on the hob when they got back from the mumming. "Particularly after last time." They had spent hours sitting in silence round Steve's kitchen table drinking endless coffees with Jill while they waited for Steve to phone from the hospital.

"Ring her," Colin said. "Tell her we got lost in the snow or something."

Bob nodded. He'd been trying to work up the courage to do this for the last twenty minutes. It seemed a bit easier now it wasn't just him reporting in. He pulled out his phone. "Jill, hi, it's Bob."

"Oh God, not again."

"No, no, nothing to worry about," Bob lied, hoping that saying it would make it true. "We got a bit turned round in the snow and we've ended up in the park and…"

"You mean Julian wanted to play in the snow." The voice on the other end of the phone laughed, sounding most relieved and Bob reflected that, for once, Julian's reputation for madcap ideas was going to come in handy. "Big kids the lot of you," Jill snorted.

"Well," Bob said, "something like that."

"Have fun." Jill laughed again. "I'll put some towels on the radiators to warm. You're likely to need drying off I take it."

"Thanks, be appreciated." Bob rang off, slightly dazed. "Amazing woman but thank god for Ju and his idiocies. Any sign of the others yet?"

"Nope." Ian looked round pointlessly.

"What do we do now?"

"Could carry on. If the others come back then they'll be near the manor."

"No, that's where I came back," Ian said.

"Where would they have gone next? On into town?" Bob looked round helplessly as if his friends might suddenly appear out of thin air.

"What town. It had all gone."

The three of them stood irresolute. "I suppose we could just go to Steve's and wait." Colin said eventually. "Jill's got to know sooner or later."

A car pulled up behind them in Park Road.

"Get in." The voice was young and female. The three men whirled. A police car had pulled up outside the Park Road entrance and a young woman hung out of the driver's window. "I take it that I am addressing Robert Hall, Colin Smart and Ian Ward?"

"Y…e…s," Bob hesitated his brain working furiously. "Have you found Steve and Ju?" He guessed. "Are they all right?"

"As far as we know." The young woman frowned.

"What's that supposed to mean?" Colin demanded.

"I believe you have had an… interesting experience in a… different… place?"

"You could say that." Bob exchanged glances with his friends. "How would you know?"

"I have been there briefly myself. I met your friends there. And I know Mark who, I think, was with you."

"Where are they now, then?" Bob peered past her but there was obviously nobody in the back of the car.

"They are still there, I believe."

"You believe? Don't you know?"

"This is beyond my experience," she admitted, sounding as if it pained her to do so.

"So, what do you want with us? We've no idea what the place is either or how we got there or how we got back. It all just happened."

"I realise that. I am attempting to stop panic spreading. We need to know the scale of the problem." She reached behind her and opened the car door. "Please get in."

"You mean you want to shut us up." Ian folded his arms and glared at the open door without moving.

The woman sighed. "For now, yes, until we have a clearer idea of what is going on. Surely you can see that that is a good idea?"

It hung between them and then Bob snorted. "Come on, she's right, it makes sense. Isn't it what I just did with Jill?" He strode over to the car and got in.

*

Steve wandered aimlessly along the library shelves not entirely sure what he was looking for. Tony had raved about the collections here and the possibilities but, unless a book leapt out at them called *Why the Town Vanished*, Steve thought the three of them were probably wasting their time.

The librarian might have been some help except that she was off wandering a garden that shouldn't exist. It also seemed that the librarian was Jenny Williams and Steve had known Mike's daughter since long before she had started school and he had trouble imagining her as the person in charge of the library and its impossible garden.

He sighed and stopped, slumping into one of the many armchairs that littered the corners of the labyrinthine place. The good feelings of earlier had well and truly gone now, replaced by a dull ache he recognised all too well.

Seeing Annie again, particularly an Annie half mad with worry and grief, was a much too vivid reminder of their last attempt at mumming. He hadn't seen her in almost a year, since they dropped the Christmas cards in last December, and they hadn't been welcome then. Annie had closed herself and her daughter away from the world to mourn, unwilling or unable to accept the help they offered.

They had tried, all visited in those first few months, but it was obvious that they weren't wanted; that she couldn't let them intrude on her grief. Steve had had one particularly upsetting row with her where she had specifically blamed them for Mike's death. If they hadn't done the mumming, if they hadn't done the folk sessions and the morris dancing, if Mike had never met Steve... She'd finished by handing over all his instruments and kit, saying she was well rid of such 'murderous' items.

It had been such a shame, Steve thought. The music, the dance, the companionship and love amongst the folk scene would have done her a power of good but she had walked away entirely; turned her back on them and the biggest part of what Mike had been. Steve still kept the row of guitars and mandolins in his spare room in case mother or daughter ever decided they would like them back. Jenny had been quite an accomplished player herself. He wondered if she bothered now.

"Not looking?" Julian appeared from amongst the books.

"I wish I knew what I was looking for."

"Well, we could find the policeman his book on Morse Code."

Julian crouched down in front of him. "Annie, yes?"

"Brought it all back, Ju, that look on her face like she's lost everything all over again and I didn't know what to say."

"I know. And Jenny here; she probably sees that as another desertion. I doubt if she's especially happy to see us either."

"I wish she'd let us help." A forlorn hope. She hadn't before and now she had gone on a wild goose chase after Jenny and declined all their offers of help.

"I know," Julian said again, patting his knee. "Don't feel much help at all tonight. Strange place, Ian and Colin and Bob gone, then Jenny gone and Mark. Annie and this policeman's daughter sitting there with identical looks of despair and absolutely nothing we can do about it."

It was the closest to giving up Steve had ever seen Julian get. Something else struck him too.

"That was it. I wondered why I thought I knew the girl but she had precisely the same look as Annie; sort of crushed and defeated and lost."

"I believe someone said that she lost her mother to cancer so she must be feeling all the old fears rising, just like Annie." Julian slid back so he was sitting against the stacked shelving across from Steve. "She and Jenny would have so much in common if their parents got together. If we ever get out of here. I suppose..." He stopped mid-sentence and leapt to his feet. "Bugger me."

He reached up to a shelf behind Steve and pulled two books down. "Look at this." He offered one of them. It was *A Beginners Guide to Morse Code*.

"Right above my head and I never even looked." Steve laughed.

"It was next to this." The second book was *Coping with grief and Loss*. Steve let his laughter die and stared at the book in silence for a long moment. "This is a very strange place," he said eventually.

"Obviously not well up on the Dewey System."

"No." Steve stood up. "I'm beginning to think it may not be a total waste of time to look for something on what to do if your town vanishes. Come on, let's take this to the inspector and see how the others are doing."

*

Tony was sitting at a table on which was set a magnificent pair of antlers surrounded by various books and papers. He was sorting through these, visibly enthralled.

"Wow, those are impressive." Julian leant in for a closer look. "Where are they from?"

"Don't know but someone has obviously been looking them up. This is wonderful, there's stuff here on the Abbots Bromley Horn Dance." Tony waved his hand at the paper. "Suggests it comes from an ancient rite where the god had to die as a stag in order for the summer to die, or something like that, I'm still reading."

"And there's this." Tony waved another piece of paper. "On mummer's plays. Says they're to do with the battle between the oak king of summer and the holly king of winter. Hence the death and resurrection; the seasons die so they can come round again."

"What about St George?" Julian sat down and pulled a couple of books towards him.

"Later addition according to this." Tony passed him the paper.

"Hang on," Steve said watching them in amazement, "this isn't what we're supposed to be doing."

Julian looked up at him. "Do we know what's happening out there, Steve?"

"No."

"Do you really think that finding a book on it will help? And even if there is one in this weird place, do you suppose we can do anything about it?"

"No." Steve sat down beside Tony as he noticed a book on symbolism in morris traditions.

"This stuff looks fascinating and is on something we're actually interested in." Julian paused, perhaps realising that he no longer needed to sell the idea. "Besides, if we're here then at least we're not rushing around getting in people's way. I'm sure the inspector will appreciate being left in control and if he wants something then he has only to ask. Look." He threw Steve a book entitled, *The History of the Mumming Play* and followed it with *Dance Down the Ages*.

"There's even an original of William Kemp's book about his dance to Norwich." Tony reached over and pulled something from a nearby shelf.

Soon all three were engrossed and the world outside was forgotten

The library, as Eleanor had noted earlier, had a way of providing what was necessary.

CHAPTER 2

Jenny looked round the familiar confines of the summerhouse. She felt more comfortable here than in the library office though she couldn't have said why. Perhaps because there were no demands on her here – she could shut out the real world. Today, oddly, there was a different guitar on a stand sitting in the corner when she entered. It looked rather like the one which stood in her bedroom at home. If it hadn't been for the lithe form of her companion, she would have abandoned any quest to find out what was going on and played instead. It was one of the things she had argued most with her mum about; the decision to get rid of all her dad's instruments. Every time she had played her own her mother complained about 'that bloody folk music' and 'look what it did for your dad'. She rarely had the heart to bother these days.

"There is trouble." David leapt to his feet from where he had been sitting behind the desk. Jenny started; she hadn't noticed his silent form. "I can feel it, something is wrong."

Jenny nodded. "Something has happened to the town, it's vanished."

"Something has happened to the library," Wayland corrected.

"Same difference."

"Not at all. The town is where it has always been, the library has moved."

"Moved where?"

Wayland shrugged. "Out of time, to an earlier time or the memory of an earlier time. I'm not sure that matters."

"We need to get it back." Jenny turned to David. "Has this happened before?"

"Not in my time…"

"You miss the point," Wayland interrupted him. "If we do not solve why it has moved then we cannot get it back."

"So why has it moved?"

"I told you, the mirror is breached."

"And it makes no more sense now than when you said it before." Jenny retorted. "How can it be breached? What does that mean?"

"It means the garden has a link to the world. The mirror no longer provides a boundary. Through such a link anything could get out." The golden eyes were serious.

"You think something has got out and dragged the library into some sort of past?"

"Possibly."

"Meaning no," Jenny snapped hearing the hesitation. "What do you think?"

"The library takes care of itself, Jenny, you know that." David spoke softly. She did know it, only too well.

"So?"

"I'd hazard that the breach in the mirror has led the library to take steps and that it has taken itself out of time in order to give the librarian - you - space to heal the breach. It has taken us somewhere where nobody else can be hurt by the spirits that might get out through such a breach."

"Nobody else? What about Eleanor and Lucy?"

"Eleanor?" David went white. "Why is she here?"

"I thought you were supposed to be telling me that." The two of them glared at each other and then Jenny rubbed her eyes. "I'm sorry, it's been a long day. I'm afraid I told Eleanor you were dead and then Lucy turned up as well."

"Lucy?"

"She seems to be Ben's daughter. You know, the policeman Mum has taken up with who came here on Friday when you …well, you know."

"Interesting." Wayland had sat himself in the vacated chair behind the desk. "That suggests further possibilities."

"Go on." Jenny's heart sank, she wasn't sure she liked his tone.

"It is possible that, in stepping out of time, you are being given the space to resolve all your… concerns with your new role."

"Concerns? You mean like how I didn't ask for the job and don't want to be stuck in here?" Jenny snapped, her patience giving out. "How about other 'concerns' like the fact that Eleanor wants to know about David… are you going to say that she is here so I can… What? Tell her, 'dreadfully sorry, your friend killed himself so I could have this job'? And Lucy because… her dad got hit on the head? Does that mean Mum and Ben are here somewhere too?"

"It is possible."

"I'm going to assume that's a 'yes'." Jenny had only known him two days, but she was already coming to recognise Wayland's evasiveness as long as he stayed far enough away to stop her knees going weak.

"Not to mention whatever breached the mirror is out there too." David failed miserably at a reassuring smile.

"And other spirits that have used the link and the power of the solstice to get out." Wayland's smile was positively predatory. "I may even wander abroad myself and see what may be seen. There is power in the darkest of days."

"What's out there?" Jenny demanded, seriously alarmed.

"All sorts of things walk the darkness."

"Who…" Jenny began but David broke in.

"Then we are in trouble, the Solstice holds a deep power and is not easily controlled."

Wayland stood up. "Sacrifice may be demanded."

"Whose sacrifice, David's?" Jenny asked remembering the morning when she had entered the dark grove to reclaim the sword. She had known, in touching it, that it would one day be her destiny to use it. It was not a good feeling.

"Ah no, the seasons are not so easily bought. David has paid already; he cannot give the price a second time."

"Then who?"

Wayland caressed her cheek sending familiar shivers down her spine. "You are guardian. To restore the sanctity of your charge, I would say the choice is yours. Who will you sacrifice to return the library to where it belongs?"

"Me?" But she was talking to empty air. Wayland had vanished. "He's not serious?"

"I fear so." David had come to stand beside her.

"I won't do it. What sort of person does he take me for?"

David simply looked at her and Jenny had a dreadful sinking feeling that choosing to not choose was something the librarian would not be allowed.

"So who might have got out?" She said after a moment but David held up his hand.

"There are others in the garden."

Jenny concentrated and realised he was right. As guardian she had discovered that she could feel the people around her in the library. It had told her of Eleanor's love for David, gave her an idea of why visitors had come. She enjoyed the empathy it gave her with those around her – something that she appreciated about this situation. If she had been focusing, she should have felt the interlopers in the garden before but concerns and arguments had taken her mind from her role.

"I told them to wait for me," She headed for the door. "Why can't people just do as they're told?"

"Worry, fear, not always disobedience, Jenny."

She nodded, pausing briefly. "I know that."

"I'll come."

"But… Eleanor?"

"If she has seen this much truth, Jenny, she can handle the rest."

"If you say so." Jenny wasn't at all sure, but she wasn't going to waste time arguing.

The two of them headed for the mirror.

*

They were most of the way back when Jenny had an epiphany. She stopped, let out a great sigh of relief and slapped herself on the forehead.

"Stupid!"

"What?"

"I'm stupid and I wish he'd stop talking riddles."

"I'm not sure I follow."

"Well, of course he's not expecting me to go round killing people. He means I've got to give up those I love, stop pretending that I'm not librarian and one day I'll go home. That's what he means by who

I'm going to sacrifice. Bloody obvious if you think about it, why would I be killing people? All right." She raised her voice. "I understand, I can't go back, I'm here and I'll let the past go. Now return the town, please."

"I think you probably have to do more than just say it."

Jenny nodded and set off again with renewed vigour. "I suppose." It would probably mean another confrontation with her mother. "You too actually. I'd say Eleanor needs to hear it from you and you need to give her up." She snuck a glance at him.

"You're probably right," he said without giving anything away.

"Good, let's go and tell people and get the library back where it belongs." She lengthened her stride; glad to have worked out what she needed to do and determined to prove to Wayland that she could do this for herself. If accepting this job was what it took to keep them in the present, then she supposed she'd have to do it.

*

Rounding the last corner of the maze she spotted three figures standing irresolute beside the entrance fifty yards away. They looked as if they were arguing about which way to go.

Jenny stopped. Eleanor was one of the three but it was not Lucy who stood with her.

"That's your mum," David said unnecessarily.

"I know, he did say she was probably here because of... well... resolving things." Jenny hadn't thought it would come so soon though or that her mother would have the courage to enter the garden after the things she had been saying about it for the past two days.

"So, who's the man?" David asked.

"I don't know."

"You don't?" David was taken aback. "But if this is to do with you becoming librarian..."

"It obviously isn't." Which put them right back at square one, and she had just decided they had solved it all. "If the people here are to do with my 'concerns' then you'd think I'd at least recognise them." Jenny could feel the usual futile anger rising at the sight of her mother's careworn face. Why did her dad have to die and why couldn't her mum leave her alone to escape from her grief? With her dad's stuff all gone, Jenny had nothing of him left to hold on to. Instead she had found herself almost a prisoner because Annie had clung tight to the only thing left and couldn't bear to be alone. And now there would be another argument about the library and Jenny's supposed desertion though this imprisonment was at least peaceful. Or it would be if her mum would leave it be. Jenny nearly turned back into the maze except that the argument was just likely to get worse the longer she left it.

She started off again, David trailing some distance behind her purposeful stride.

*

"But she isn't here." Eleanor had been as determined as Alex that Annie shouldn't go alone. Besides, she had reasons of her own for finding the librarian.

"This looks like a maze." Alex Ranald was doing his best to organise the expedition. "I'm not sure it's a good idea to get lost."

"I know that." They'd been talking it round in circles for several minutes and Eleanor could see that Alex knew that he was merely putting off the inevitable. Jenny wasn't amongst the lawns and flowerbeds of the garden they'd explored so far so it was into the maze or back to the library and she knew the latter wasn't an option as far as Annie was concerned.

Eleanor thought Annie was close to a total breakdown. She hovered on the brink of tears and alternated between pleading with them to move faster and castigating them for not doing so. Only Alex's restraining hand kept her from marching straight into the hedged maze.

"We don't solve anything if we get lost." He tried again, appealing to Eleanor. "You said yourself that she was with someone and seemed to know what she was doing."

"I must find my daughter. She needs to leave here and come home. Everything was fine until she came here."

"Nothing was fine, Mother, and you know it." Jenny appeared from the maze; her face stubbornly set. "Nothing has been right since Dad died."

"We'd have been all right together, but you went and left me too and . . ."

"I needed a life… a… a point; to be more than just the crutch you clung to. If it means being librarian then perhaps that's best. You seem to be getting on all right with Ben, you don't need me."

"Ben's gone." It came out as a wail and stopped Jenny's tirade in mid flow.

"Gone where?"

"Out into the snow, ran away, and it's all the fault of this bloody place and…"

"He was here?"

"Of course he was here. That thing knocked him out and now he's seeing impossible things and then we were here and he ran away." The words poured out in a barely coherent jumble. "He said he had to come here and then he didn't and now he's gone." Annie crumpled into racking sobs and Eleanor leapt forward to hold her when it became clear that Jenny was rooted to the spot.

"If I may, Miss Williams, Jenny?" Alex took a step forward.

"Who the hell are you?"

"Doctor Alex Ranald. I treated Ben Martin at the hospital earlier this evening and then followed him here when he started behaving oddly. He did, indeed, seem intent on getting here but then, once he was, he seemed just as intent on not being here."

"And how did you get here?"

"Inadvertently, I'm afraid. We tried to stop Ben from fading from the real world and all ended up here."

"All?"

"Inspector Marshall, a friend of mine, and a couple of his officers."

"So, you're not supposed to be here." She sounded relieved and Eleanor wasn't sure if it had been a statement or a question. Alex answered it anyway.

"I don't believe so and when two of the officers attempted to go after Constable Martin they simply vanished. We assume, well hope really, that they returned to the real world."

"Ben's out there alone with…"

"No, no," he hastened to reassure her. "It's all right. His daughter went after him and the two young men."

"What young men?" Her face regained its alarm.

"The two who arrived with the mummers…" Alex tailed off in the face of her incomprehension. "I'm sorry, there seems to have been rather a lot of us caught when the town did its vanishing thing and we've all sort of gate-crashed your library."

"The town didn't vanish; it's where it's always been." She said weakly and then, before they could question, "Hawkeye's wrong; all these people aren't to do with me."

A man appeared from behind her in the maze. His short, dark hair was going grey at the temples though his face was barely lined.

"I think we need to get back, Jenny," he suggested, "this sounds more serious than your problems."

Eleanor gaped at him. Jenny had said he was dead and now here he was, large as life, wandering around in this garden. She could feel her grasp on certainty slipping. Letting out a sigh of "David", she fainted.

CHAPTER 3

Rick moved as fast as possible which, given the terrain, was not very quick though at least it had stopped snowing. The trees had closed in within a short distance of the library and he and Matt were struggling through dense undergrowth. They kept going because all the signs were that Lucy had also come this way. They did their best to hack a clear route with the swords they'd borrowed but it was slow going.

"How can they be moving so fast?" Matt asked for the fourth time.

"I have no fucking idea." Rick scythed his sword through another patch of nettles and vines and curbed an irrational desire to decapitate his companion with the next swing. The closed in feeling was making him jumpy – much like the closed in alleys of Basra had after the open spaces of the desert. You couldn't see which way the enemy was attacking from or where the next threat would appear. Here the trees loomed over him and Matt's blundering incompetence was likely to get them both killed. Just how difficult could it be to chase down a man, twenty years his senior, with a five-hundred-yard head start? Except Rick knew from experience how easily the enemy could disappear into the shadows, blend in and never be found. He caught himself; this wasn't an enemy, just a mad old man who'd gone AWOL. Lucy's dad… and Lucy, he mustn't forget Lucy. She hadn't looked as good as he remembered though that was probably unfair considering what they'd all been through during the evening.

"How can…" Matt began again.

"Stop it! Just fucking stop it!" Rick swung round forcing Matt to take a step back.

"I only…"

"Five times. You have said that five times and if I couldn't answer it the first time then why the hell should it be any different now?"

"I'm just trying to make conversation." Matt bristled. "You're charging through here like its normal, but it isn't."

"Hostile territory's all the same; it doesn't matter where it is."

"It matters to me, Rick. I spend all day sitting in an office and I'm scared."

"Then why offer to come?"

"Because I thought I could help, that you might appreciate not being alone."

"Only way to be, that way you can't lose anyone you care about." Rick turned on the last word and began hacking at the undergrowth again to cover the brief flicker of emotion. For a long moment he thought Matt wouldn't follow and he'd have to force him to come because he couldn't leave him behind. Then Matt said softly, "I'm sorry, I didn't realise, I've no idea what your life is like. It just seems a shame to shut everybody out."

"Let them get too close and they'll hurt you one way or the other. Now, for God's sake, shut up, I'm trying to listen."

"Yes, do be quiet. It's amazing what sort of things you can attract out here." The voice was light, slightly mocking and came from just above their heads.

Rick raised the sword and wished heartily for the comfort of his rifle. "Who the…"

A figure leapt down beside them landing almost soundlessly. "You might find," it said, "that it's much easier going if you move half a dozen paces to your right on to the path. It might also answer your companion's oft-asked question." Rick got the distinct impression that he was being laughed at.

"You've been watching us?"

"Only briefly, I assure you. I was curious as to who you were blundering about in the moonlight."

"Same could be said of you."

"I don't blunder." It was a man, slim, half a head shorter than Rick and one who felt so full of danger that Rick didn't drop the sword tip an inch. "I do have manners, though," the man continued. "Friends, it seems, know me as Hawkeye." He seemed to find this amusing though Rick couldn't see why. "I believe the young lady you are following has given up and is on the path which, as I remarked, is to your right."

"Lucy?" Matt said unnecessarily.

"Lucy? Ah, then I have met her. I think I will accompany you and rush to her rescue." He waved a hand indicating that Rick should lead the way.

"After you." Rick said. "I like people where I can see them until I know that I can trust them."

*

Lucy was sitting sobbing in the snow on the path. She was shivering and bedraggled and didn't notice their approach.

"Lucy." Matt hurried to crouch beside her.

"I couldn't catch him."

"You need to go back; you're not dressed for this." Rick stood over the two of them. "You're going to develop hypothermia."

"I've got to find Dad."

"We'll find your dad," Matt insisted.

"She is more likely to be able to persuade him to come back, to get through to him." Hawkeye held slightly distant from them but he sounded serious.

"Are you trying to kill her?" Rick asked. "Look at her." He stopped as something about Hawkeye's appearance registered. "Aren't you cold?" The man wore a thin shirt and leather trousers. These looked black though the moonlight washed everything out to blacks and greys.

"No, I don't feel the cold."

"Well she does and…"

"Where's Jenny?" Lucy interrupted suddenly.

"What?" Rick frowned.

"Jenny, where's Jenny?"

"The librarian," Matt said, "Do you mean her?"

"Yes."

"She's in some garden or other with…"

"… him." Lucy pointed at Hawkeye.

"No, he just appeared in a tree over there." Matt waved a vague arm.

"But he also 'appeared' in the library and took Jenny into the garden. He said they had to find out what's going on."

"Are you sure?" Rick asked.

"Oh yes, that was me." Hawkeye smiled. "I have ways of… travelling." He stepped closer and Rick tightened his grip on the sword hilt and moved to stand between the advancing figure and where Matt and Lucy crouched in the snow.

"What's that supposed to mean?" Rick could feel the menace sparking in the air. "What have you done with the librarian?"

"She is still in the garden, I promise you."

"And what do you want with us?"

"I believed I was trying to help."

"Well, if you're so good at 'travelling', why don't you go and get her dad and save us all from catching cold."

Hawkeye snorted and said, coldly serious, "As I said, I think we need Lucy in order to get through to him. He will certainly pay no attention to me after our last meeting." Rick wondered what this man had done to Ben. He had no trouble believing that Hawkeye had probably annoyed the man immensely.

In the silence which followed this announcement, a harsh baying sound could be heard.

"What's that?" Lucy gasped, wide-eyed.

"We heard it before," Matt said, "up by the manor. It's just a noise."

"No," Hawkeye shook his head. "We're in trouble. If he is out already then this is bad."

The noise came again, strident in the crisp air. It sounded closer than before.

"Is that dogs?" Rick realised what the noise reminded him of.

"Like you've never seen," Hawkeye assured them. "These hounds are deadly."

"We should go back then." Matt got to his feet dragging Lucy up with him.

"But Dad…"

"I fear it is too late." As if to prove the truth of Hawkeye's words, the sound rang out again, louder and closer and from back the way they had come.

"We need fire," Hawkeye said. "That should hold them yet a while; the night is young."

"Fire?" Rick looked at the stark, snow-laden branches above him. "Then we're fucked."

"Have faith." Hawkeye started tearing at the bushes. "Find sticks and fast."

Rick never did work out how Hawkeye managed to get a damp bush blazing but, by the time he and Matt had pulled a quantity of branches together, the bush was aflame. Pushed on by the ever-closer yelps of what sounded like an enormous pack of hounds, they scrabbled for as many sticks and pieces of dead wood as they could find. Lucy attempted to help but Rick brusquely ordered her to try and get some warmth back in to her.

"This will keep the dogs away, will it?" Matt dumped another armful of hastily collected sticks.

"We may need to use it as a weapon." Hawkeye demonstrated by pulling a burning branch from the fire and whirling it in front of him. "But that should hold them off. Better than those swords will, at any rate." He held out a hand. "Give them here, they need an edge."

"You're fucking joking. I'm not handing over my only weapon." Rick gripped the hilt tighter.

"Hold it out then," Hawkeye instructed.

Warily, Rick did so; ready to pull away if he suspected the man of trying to take the weapon.

Hawkeye ran his hand up the blade, barely touching it. It glowed with a soft blue light where his fingers touched.

"That should help," he said after a moment. "Should be able to hold the hounds." He turned to Matt to repeat the process.

"For how long? Are these things easily discouraged?" Rick wished again that he was rather better armed though a test with his finger showed that the blade he held was now lethally sharp.

"I think they are not yet guided, and the night is still young. We should be all right."

"Not guided?"

"No horn," Hawkeye said cryptically and then, sharply, "there!"

Between the trees, a white shape fleetingly appeared.

"Shit!" Rick took his eyes from it to glare briefly at Hawkeye. "That's a dog?"

"As I said, the like of which you have never before seen."

That was, Rick thought, watching the gathering shapes, a total bloody understatement. They were about the size of Shetland ponies with sharp pointed ears and long white fur. They reminded Rick of setters, except these were over sized with mouths full of sharp teeth and their deep baying filled the wood. As they got closer, the firelight showed that they weren't all white. The tips of ear and tail were a deep russet and, when they caught the light, so were the eyes.

"How many?" Matt gasped as the shapes continued to gather through the trees.

"Enough," Hawkeye replied unhelpfully. He picked a branch from the fire and lunged at the closest creature which leapt backwards snarling angrily.

The night became a blizzard of whirling flame and leaping white. Yelping, growling bundles charged and retreated. Rick grabbed for branches and wove them with the sword in frantic patterns through the air aware that, beside him, Matt and Hawkeye did the same. Lucy began screaming.

"Shut up! Feed the fire!" He yelled, not daring to look.

And still the hounds came, filling the night with their baying, their baleful eyes and dripping teeth, rearing up and falling away. Now and again he struck lucky and the angry barking became a painful squeal, but most moved too fast.

His arms began to tire. The wood bearing its scarlet burden dragged at him. He felt as if he had become rooted to the one spot, forever fending off gaping jaws and blazing eyes. Time twisted and splintered. He wasn't sure when he first started seeing them but suddenly, he realised he was fending off armed men with their faces hidden behind masks to keep off the dust. Coloured faces with red eyes and harsh voices screaming at him to leave their home, that he was filth and ungodly and deserved to die. Anger surged through him and he struck out with flame and steel, battering at the jeering faces with vehement hatred as he hadn't been able to do in truth.

Then, strident and deafening above the din, a horn sounded. Musical, for all its volume, it rang out sharply and he was back amidst the snow and the leaping hounds. The desert had vanished.

The effect of the call was immediate. The hounds fell back and stood to attention in a circle around the fire. Heads up, ears pricked and tails out, they stood facing the gasping men.

Hawkeye leapt forward. "Find your quarry elsewhere, Hunter. I give the protection of Wayland and our souls are clear."

A deep voice boomed out. "Not all."

"I say so." Hawkeye insisted and there was a deepening to his voice also. "For this moment, you have no claim."

After a long pause, the voice returned. "For this moment but the night is young and a worthy quarry will be found."

"You have that right," Hawkeye agreed.

The horn sounded again, a different tune, and the hounds turned, giving voice once more, and flowed away.

"I am not sure I can hold him again." Hawkeye turned urgently. "We must find your father and return to the library as fast as we are able." His earlier mocking tone was absent.

Rick dropped the branch he was holding and realised that, at some point, he had burnt his hand. It stung now with a bright pain. "Who the hell are you?" He stared at the slim figure.

"And who the hell was that?" Matt sounded shaken and scared.

"That was The Hunter. The Horned One. Tonight is the solstice and he has right to a quarry." Hawkeye raised his hand as Matt opened his mouth to ask further. "There will be time for this later if our luck holds but we cannot bide longer. Come with me, speed is of the essence." He grabbed a flaming brand and set off further into the wood.

Slowly, the three of them did the same.

CHAPTER 4

Mark had just spent a rather uncomfortable half hour explaining to Detective Chief Inspector Edwards why it was necessary to cordon off the library. This was complicated further by doing so while obliquely suggesting that his superior was currently at the library organising events. Technically, this was accurate, and Mark felt that he'd been inventive enough with language to stretch the truth to breaking point but with no outright lies. He had also managed to avoid any mention of alternative realities.

Now he faced his second awkward meeting. Helen had escorted the three men she had picked up into an interview room and he had to explain to them that, for the time being, that was where they were staying.

Avoiding this sort of responsibility was one of the main reasons why he preferred to remain a sergeant.

Taking a deep breath, he pushed open the door.

Helen had provided the men with coffee and biscuits and they sprawled comfortably round the table in the centre of the room. They looked round at him curiously and without animosity. Helen smiled encouragingly at him.

These three were typical of the world's vision of 'folkies'; greying, bearded men who had divested themselves of their coats to reveal an odd assortment of costumes. The pile of strangely shaped cases at the side of the room held instruments; a pipe and tabor, a concertina and an accordion.

"Good evening, gentlemen." He went through introductions for Helen's benefit. Bob was the tall bearded one, built like a brick outhouse with hair pulled back in a pony tail. The other two he had got confused when he first joined the team as they both had neatly trimmed grey hair and beards. They weren't obviously alike but nothing stood out in order to help memory until Colin spoke. Mark had filed him under 'Welsh' originally though he now knew him as a postman and gifted musician with Ian being an IT specialist.

Mark sat down opposite them and loosened the tie he'd donned for the meeting with DCI Edwards. "I hope you have everything you need."

"Explanation might be nice," Ian said but then continued before Mark could reply, "except I doubt you have any more idea of what's going on than we do. Do you know if the rest of them are ok?"

"Last we heard." Mark explained briefly and pulled out the notes Marshall had sent. The constables he'd left on duty at the library had strict instructions to phone him immediately if any more such letters were found. How Mark assumed letters from the Inspector were going to suddenly arrive — or why — he just hadn't discussed. Sometimes rank could be useful if you wanted uniform to obey orders without question.

He spread the list of names out. "These are all the people currently believed to be in this other place."

"Library World?" Helen suggested.

"What?"

"I thought a name might help."

Mark shrugged. "All right, library world it is. These are the people we know are there. What I wondered was whether the three of you had any ideas to help us as to why these people in particular. Do you know them? Is there something you all have in common that might explain what happened to us and them? If we can work out a link, we might be able to get them back."

They all leant over the list. "Well," Bob said slowly, "Steve, Julian and Tony are obviously the other three of us."

"I realise that." Mark nodded. "How about the other two young men who joined us?"

"They were in the White Hart, watched us and then turned up on the walk home," Colin explained to Helen, "they said their car vanished."

"Tony said he used to teach them," Ian supplied. He pointed to the list. "Those two, Rick and Matt."

Mark nodded, it looked like they were getting somewhere. "So, a link there then. You knew them."

"Well, not really." Bob disagreed puncturing Mark's optimism. "Tony taught them years ago and the rest of us didn't know them at all."

"But it's a start." Mark pointed out another name. "How about this pair, Annie Williams and her daughter? Ring any bells?"

"Annie?" The three mummers exchanged glances. "Shoulder length blonde hair? Daughter is Jenny?" Colin asked.

"That's right, do you know her?" In the silence, Mark almost felt the history in the room.

Eventually, Colin sighed. "I'm surprised you don't." He pointed at Helen, "I'm sure it was you who took my statement two years ago and I know we've mentioned Mike to you," he added to Mark.

"Though possibly not his surname," Bob admitted.

"Mummers!" Helen slapped her head, "I never thought, it's been so strange this evening." She turned to Mark, "The hit and run, that killed the bloke you've replaced. Couple of Christmases ago, like I said on Friday. And I did take a number of statements though not sure I ever really took much notice of the details and what he was called. It wasn't my case."

Mark could have kicked himself. In the general weirdness of the evening, he'd never given the previous incident a thought though he had had the history explained to him when he took on the mumming. Thinking back, he didn't think he'd ever known what Mike's surname was. So, another case involving the mummers and their walk home. Things were falling into a pattern except he wasn't sure what it showed.

"Two years ago, to the day." Colin said. "We only do the mumming on the solstice. Mike was Annie's husband who was killed. He used to do Saint George for us."

"Get the file," Mark told Helen. "It may be of use."

While she was away, Mark turned his attention back to the list. "How about Ben Martin and his daughter Lucy?" Three blank looks met his gaze.

"No, sorry." Ian shook his head.

"He is one of our constables. I believe Annie is going out with him?" Mark pushed; though the relationship was a very recent and slightly sudden one and they possibly wouldn't have any reason to know about it.

"Possibly." Bob sat back in his chair. "I'm sorry, Mark, Sergeant, but Annie shut us out when Mike died. Shut the whole bloody world out. It's just her and Jenny now. I think Steve still makes the effort occasionally but I haven't seen her since the funeral." He sighed, "We did try and encourage her to join the ladies tonight but she was quite rude about it."

Mark rubbed at his eyes, he was sure there was a pattern here somewhere but he couldn't make the pieces fit. "How about Eleanor Jenkins?" This also met with shrugs and incomprehension.

He pushed the sheet aside. "I don't think we're getting anywhere. I thought for a minute there might be something linked to the hit and run but I can't see any coherent reason for all of us ending up there, or any reason why some of us came back and the others didn't."

Helen returned clutching a large red file which she placed on the table in front of her and began to flick through.

She gave them a running commentary as she skimmed the pages in front of her. "Hit and run by a suspected drunk driver who was never identified. No identification of car. Michael Williams died at The Nightingale following major head trauma. I have six witness statements." She checked the list of names. "Steve, Julian, Bob, Colin, Ian, Tony, matches up with this list of those affected tonight," she tapped a sheet on the table.

She scanned through the statements while they watched in silence.

"Let me check this," she said eventually. "Three of you stepped into the hedge to relieve yourselves and the others paused on the road with Mr Williams at the back. The car ploughed into him coming from the direction you were walking from and just drove on."

"That's right," Colin agreed. "Night drinking beer so Ian, Bob and I were answering the call of nature therefore we didn't see anything, we just heard the car and Mike scream."

Mark tried to visualise the scene; a dark lane in winter, no streetlights and a group of morris men standing making ribald comments about those who were watering the hedge. Suddenly, lights, a car and a man down. No identification of the car so… "The others saw the driver," he hazarded. "Not the car because we obviously had no number plate to trace."

"You're right," Helen said. "I have three descriptions of a white, staring face seen as it passed but they were too busy worrying about Mr Williams to notice the number plate. As this one," she checked the name, "Julian puts it: 'when your best mate is lying bleeding to death in the road, you don't stand around thinking '*Oh I wonder if I can get a number plate*', you just dial 999 as fast as possible'."

Mark nodded, seeing the beginning of a pattern emerging. "That's understandable, but that means the three people in – what did you call it?"

"Library world."

"The three in library world are the ones who saw the driver of the car. Do they say they'd know the face again?"

"Two years ago they were definite about it but a lot can happen in that time."

Mark stood up so he could pace while he talked. "This is thinking aloud, so bear with me. In this 'library world' we have the three people who saw Mr Williams' killer. We also have what could be classed as the four people most likely to be affected by having the killer known — the victim's wife and daughter and the wife's new boyfriend and his daughter. That leaves us with three others."

"Four," Helen interrupted.

"Four?"

These three – Richard, Matthew and Eleanor – and a strange fourth person who took the librarian into the garden. We don't have a name for him except Hawkeye… or something… and we don't know anything about him but he's there too."

"All right, four." Mark stopped pacing and looked at them. "That makes a pattern. Witnesses, let's call them victims and – and this is a leap of faith – possible killers."

"There was only one person in the car," Helen noted.

"I said possible killers."

Helen frowned. "You're not wrong, that's a hell of a leap, Mark. And actually, we forgot the Inspector and his doctor friend."

"Ah, but like us, they probably shouldn't be there. I imagine they would arrive back here if they left the library, just like we did."

"It's still a huge jump to assume that because we can embroider this case around some of them, that one of the other four has to be a killer. And why do that, why not just 'gather' the one person who was the killer? What are the others for?"

"Maybe they are just the four people who drove down that road at about the right time that night." Bob suggested.

"Were there only four?" Helen asked.

"No, lot more than that." Ian said. "Neat idea, but there were loads of cars out that time of year going to Christmas parties and things."

"It was just an example," Bob said. "I mean, perhaps whoever is gathering people doesn't know who was definitely driving but these are – for some reason – the most likely suspects."

"It's a distinctly dodgy theory," Colin said. "I don't mean to be rude but, even supposing there is any truth at all in this, what the hell can we do about it? The only way of finding out what those people were doing that night would be to ask them and we can't do that, can we?"

"Inspector Marshall could." Mark said.

"And how do you propose to tell him?"

"He suggested Morse Code…" Mark hesitated. He could just imagine trying to tap out all these questions and vague theories on the library door. "I realise that's not very practical."

"Not practical? *'Inspector, we think one of the following people might be a murderer because we've come up with a vague connection between the others.'* What if, by some remote chance you happen to be right and they are sitting listening to you tapping away at the door. They're hardly likely to tell the truth after that, once you've announced it to the whole library. And if you're wrong, that'll do wonders for morale and harmony won't it?" Bob shook his head. "I think you're clutching at straws, Mark."

Mark slumped back into his chair. Bob was right and he was now totally stumped.

"Actually, maybe not." Helen was still flicking through the file and something had fallen out onto the floor from the back. "Take a look at this." She put a drawing on the table.

"What is it?" Mark tried to see round the others who had all leant over the picture.

"An artist's impression of the driver using Steve's description and help less than twenty-four hours after the incident." She smoothed out the drawing. "Recognise it?"

Mark did. He'd looked into the same features barely an hour ago. "Oh shit." He stared round the group of anxious faces. "Now what do we do?"

CHAPTER 5

Marshall was worried. After the initial knocking, there had been no further contact from his team. He was beginning to be less sure of his conviction that they had returned to the real world. He was also rather alarmed by the amount of time it was taking to track down Ben Martin. He repeatedly checked and the street remained resolutely empty.

"Come on," he muttered, "what's happened to everyone?"

"First sign of madness, you know." Alex peered out over his shoulder.

"What?"

"Talking to yourself."

"Sometimes I find it's the only way to get a sensible answer." Marshall pushed the door to. "No sign of Ben or the young men who went after him and they've been gone nearly an hour. He was only at the end of the street."

"Do you suppose they vanished too?"

"Alex, I wish I knew. They could be home, they could be lost, they could be dead for all I know. I feel so bloody useless stuck here but there seems no point in risking going God knows where if I step outside. At least you made it back from the strange garden."

"Yes and I have some good news."

"I could do with some."

"We found the librarian." Alex paused as if weighing his next words. "In fact, we found two of them."

"Two librarians?"

"Yes, Annie's daughter and a bloke called David who, according to Eleanor Jenkins, is dead."

"David? Dead?"

"Yes, seems our current librarian told her he was dead. Eleanor fainted clean away at the sight of him."

"I'm not surprised. Why would Jenny make up something like that?"

After a moment, when the lack of answer hung too heavy in the air, Marshall continued, "What haven't you told me?"

"This David character also seems fairly convinced that he's dead."

"Please tell me you're joking."

"No and neither is he. He claims to have committed suicide so that Jenny could be librarian."

Marshall hesitated, torn between a need to stay by the door and a desire to talk to David about the latest strangeness. "They'll knock, won't they?" He didn't wait for an answer but headed for the office; he just had to know what was going on.

*

The three women were sitting in silence around the fire in front of which stood a very alive looking David. The room seemed smaller than earlier; Marshall was surprised they'd all managed to fit in so comfortably.

Experience suggested to Marshall that all four of the room's occupants were in the middle of an argument. The stiff set of shoulders and faces spoke volumes even though no-one currently spoke.

"Can someone tell me what is going on?"

The rapid flood of voices soon convinced him that there were not one, but two, arguments in full swing. While mother and daughter were violently disagreeing about Jenny's role as librarian, Eleanor and David were engaged in a rather pointless 'I'm dead', 'you're not' quarrel. Occasionally Annie would break into this cycle by launching a tirade of abuse at David.

After trying, futilely, to listen to four people at once, Marshall waved his hands. "Stop! Everyone stop!"

Four indignant faces glared at him, halted mid-sentence.

"John…" began David.

"David, I'm trying to understand what is happening tonight in order to try and return things to normal. Now can you, please, talk one at a time?"

"I don't think it's your job to return things to normal, John," David said. "This isn't a police matter."

"That's a bit of a volte face from Friday," Marshall said, "I thought you wanted my help."

"I thought you could," David said, "I was wrong, this is Jenny's problem."

Marshall shook his head. He had been wondering what David had expected him to do all weekend but now, perversely, he was convinced he wasn't going to give up just because David had decided he wasn't needed. "I think I'll make that decision if you don't mind. Now, Miss Williams, I assume David is the gentleman that you left with earlier?"

"No." Jenny and Eleanor both shook their heads.

"All right, so what happened to the man you left with?"

"Vanished." Jenny waved her hand at the garden he'd seen briefly earlier. "In there and then, just like that, gone. He said he was going to see outside."

"Vanished? There seems to be rather a lot of that going on tonight." Marshall turned his attention to David "What happened to you?"

"I *used* to be the librarian here."

"And now?" He had to ask though the answer promised to be more unbelievable than anything else David had ever said.

"I'm dead, Inspector."

"Of course he's not dead…" Eleanor began.

"Madam, allow me to ask the questions, please. I'm not sure arguing is going to solve the question." Marshall looked to Alex who shrugged and mouthed 'I told you so'.

"Are you telling me that you are now a ghost?"

"Sort of… think of me that way if it helps."

"Can you prove it?" Evidence he understood.

David shrugged and then faded out of existence. Eleanor went as white as a sheet and Alex moved forwards hurriedly as David re-appeared.

"Will that do, John?"

"It will have to, yes."

"We should have got to know each other better this last year; you are admirably open-minded."

"I'm standing in an office whose size and contents seem to be variable, staring into a garden I know can't exist while outside the entire town seems to have vanished, why the hell shouldn't I believe in ghosts as well?" Marshall took a deep breath, determined to try and remain professional despite the situation. He turned his attention to Jenny. "I was led to believe that you had gone into this garden of yours in order to work out where the town had gone. Did you find any answers or just a dead librarian?"

"John?" Alex interrupted, his tone warning.

"I know, long night, Al. We desperately need some answers, Miss Williams."

"I wonder," Alex continued, "whether we should get the mummers. If we're discussing what's happening, then I would say they have a right to know too."

"You're right, go on." It gave them all a moment to regain some composure. Alex hurried out.

"He said mummers before," Jenny said warily. "Does he mean who I think he means?" She looked to her mother who sighed heavily.

"Yes, Steve, Ju and co. Not all of them but yes, they're here. Inevitable really, they ruin everything."

"You can't seriously think that all this is their fault," Jenny said.

"Why not, everything they touch…"

"For fuck's sake, mum, don't be so bloody paranoid."

"Paranoid? If your dad hadn't…"

"Ladies, please." Marshall had the feeling he was listening to an argument that had been going on for some time. "We need to remain calm. How about we wait quietly for everyone."

Though there was history here and perhaps it was having an impact tonight.

*

Alex and the mummers arrived back shortly after and joined the group around the fire. Steve and Julian hugged Jenny in passing.

"Hello lass, good to see you." Julian said.

"You too." She gave a fleeting smile.

Annie pointedly ignored all the mummers.

"So," Marshall tried again, "what answers did you find, Miss

Williams?"

"Not many. We," she indicated David, "think the library has shifted in time somehow. The town is safe where it should be and just the library has moved."

"That's not right." Steve interrupted. "We came all the way in from The White Hart with no sign of town. It can't be just the library that's moved."

"I think – for now – we need to accept that, in some way, the library has become divorced from the town and placed in a different time zone of some sort." Marshall said. "For some reason, at the point the library moved, I would say that all those present were also swept into this place. Now, I think 'how' is a question that may be unanswerable, so I think we have to find out why in order to try and reverse the process."

"We have a couple of theories though I'm not sure how much water they hold." Jenny paused. "I think I probably need to explain about how I came to be librarian." Aided by David she gave a brief summary of the events of Friday. Marshall mentally filled in the gaps in the story as he had seen it.

Noting the look in several faces, he forestalled all questions. "I'm sorry, I realise that ordinarily that would be a totally incomprehensible story but I have reasons to know that there is no point in disbelieving it and with everything we've already seen I'm going to have to accept the truth of the statement we have just heard. Please save any questions for later and let us move on and consider how it might help us." He waved for Jenny to continue, his mind turning the story over as she did, looking for the holes and facets of it as he would with any witness.

"Well, Hawkeye suggested the mirror is breached in some way allowing spirits out as they choose. We think maybe the library moved in order to contain anything that got out in this gap of time and allow me – us – space to deal with the problem."

"And any others you may be having with your role," David added for her.

"Other problems?" Marshall prompted.

"Hawkeye says I need to sacrifice the life I had and accept what I am." She paused and then finished in a rush. "So you're here so David and I can explain and… and… sort of… let go… sort of… and… well… then the library will take us home."

Marshall, who'd interviewed a lot of suspect people in his time, could tell a fabrication when he heard one even when, as in this case, he was fairly sure that the witness was lying to themselves as well. He attacked; it was the only way. "So, having explained, you're telling me I can open the door on to Museum Street as normal? That's good to know, shall we go?"

"Well…"

"You see, I don't think telling us about your wonderful new role did anything for our current problem. There's this 'breach' with the mirror, for example." He smiled without humour. "Miss Williams, I listened very carefully to what you said, it's what I do. In fact, rather a lot of what you said seems to be a repeat of what this Hawkeye character said or thought or did. However, leaving that aside, if we take the story in its entirety, I would say that the fault is rather more serious than you telling us you've decided to be librarian here. You tell us that the mirror is a boundary you can open or close to keep spirits in and yet, I know that, on the first occasion you closed the mirror, there was a spirit in this room attempting to burn the library down. There, immediately, as far as I can see is your problem. You tried to close all the spirits in when, in fact, one was out. I'd say that was a fairly comprehensive breach."

"No," David said. "Shutting the mirror with a spirit this side simply kills the spirit. They cannot survive without the link."

"You know that, absolutely certainly?"

"Well, I have found it to be the case on the couple of occasions I have accidentally stranded a spirit here."

"And one that was purposefully here? One that was trying to burn the place down?"

David looked worried. "You are correct, that would explain the breach if Laodhan had found a way to survive outside the garden. I don't know how such a thing would be possible."

"I would have to say," Marshall said, "that we have to assume that such a thing is possible. What we need is to find out where he is now. I am assuming further that getting this spirit back into the garden will cure the breach and, therefore, our problems - though that might be jumping the gun a little. Because I also note," he had watched Annie carefully when the mummers arrived, "that you all know each other but your mum is unhappy about the fact. There are other issues than your role that might need resolving tonight."

"Murdering..." Annie began and Marshall saw the mummers bristle before Jenny interrupted.

"No, Mum, they didn't kill Dad. It was the driver did that."

"But if he hadn't been on the road, if he hadn't-"

"I see," Marshall interrupted, his puzzle-solving instincts filling the gaps, "your dad was the mummer who was killed two years ago?"

"On our walk home from doing the mumming, Inspector," Steve said.

"So," Julian said, "you might be right, there are other issues here, memories and patterns."

Marshall nodded, so he might have a role here tonight as a policeman; perhaps David was right. Perhaps his job was to find a killer, which might lead to the conclusion that it was someone trapped here with them. He paused but decided to explore a different tack instead rather than drop that particular speculative bombshell. "So, do we know what else has escaped through this breach?"

"Hawkeye said all sorts of things might because of the Solstice." Jenny replied.

Making a mental note to wring a lot of answers out of 'Hawkeye' if he ever got hold of him, Marshall probed further. "The Solstice? What sorts of things?"

"It's the darkest night of the year when people used to stay in and keep a fire lit to keep the dark away," Eleanor said. "All sorts of spirits were believed to walk abroad."

"And the play is believed by some to be an answer to that or a representation of it," Steve said softly.

"Like?" Marshall prompted. "What spirits?"

The answer came from an unexpected source.

"Herne. The Horned One. The Hunter." Tony smiled at the ring of startled faces. "We've just been reading about him."

CHAPTER 6

Laodhan exulted in his new-found freedom. The body he inhabited allowed him to experience so much more beyond the confines of the garden he had existed in. Now the consciousness he shared the form with was asleep he was able to escape. Moving deeper into the wood he looked for somewhere to hide. His memories stretched back beyond these medieval forests and he knew what spirits hunted the solstice. He had no wish to be caught by the pack. The snow was beginning to fall again but he had no faith that the covering of his path would fool The Hunter's hounds even if it might foil his human followers.

He doubted that climbing a tree would hide him sufficiently, but the landscape offered no alternative and he could hear the creatures closing in.

Pulling himself into the branches, he watched the hounds gather below. This could be an ignominious end and perhaps he should have stayed in the library. He had forgotten how dangerous the Hunter could be in the sudden realisation that he had control of this body.

Behind the milling animals below, four figures appeared. Laodhan recognised one of the youths from earlier: the man who had knocked out his host so releasing him. Without Ben's memories to search through, he couldn't be sure of the two he didn't recognise, though a vague unease suggested he should know the girl. He drew a sharp breath; the fourth character was all too familiar and, given his predicament, a welcome enemy.

"I'm up here!" He shouted. "Can you help?"

"Dad!" Laodhan cursed. Of course she was familiar; the policeman's thoughts were full of her. He thought hard. There seemed little chance of Wayland countenancing a rescue if he revealed his true self. "Lucy?" He tried, trying to remember all he'd learnt. It was no good; he hadn't paid enough attention to his host. With a mental finger he prodded at the consciousness trapped with him.

"Wake up. I need you if we're both to get out of here alive."

*

Someone was calling his name. Ben struggled to open his eyes only to discover that they were already open. It was the oddest feeling he'd ever experienced. He could see but as if through a gauze and something was sharing his view of the world.

Ben opened his mouth but found that he had no control of his voice.

"Be still and listen to me." The voice was harsh and right inside his head. *"Look down."*

Ben felt the presence in his head move backwards slightly allowing him to peer below. The shock of confronting the leaping, snarling dogs and of seeing Lucy beyond them in this winter madness nearly made him fall. The other consciousness leapt forward and took control, grabbing at the tree. Ben watched in bemusement as his hands moved of their own accord.

"Who are you?"

"I am Laodhan."

"What are you doing in my head?"

As he asked, Ben wondered if this was the psychosis the doctor had been talking of. Perhaps he was imagining all this. Except it felt like he really was in this tree and someone really was in his head with him.

"When the librarian shut the mirror, I needed to borrow your body to avoid death."

"What?" Ben dazedly tried to work things through. *"What do you mean borrow?"*

"You were unconscious. It allowed me to slip in. Such would not normally be possible."

"So where ..."

"Let me share."

A flow of pictures ran through Ben's mind showing him the events of the past couple of hours while he'd been unconscious. It frightened him how his body could be made use of in such a way.

"Why..." Ben began before he felt his companions scorching anger.

"We have no time for pointless questions. You need to convince your daughter and her friends to rescue us. I shall allow you to take over, but I will be watching. Do not give me away to Wayland." The presence retired and Ben had to make a sudden grasp as his hands slid on the tree trunk.

"Dad, are you alright?" Ben realised, from the frantic nature of the questions, that she must have been yelling at him for a while. He bit back the first retort that came to mind, recognising it as the product of Laodhan's tenancy rather than his own feelings.

"Lucy, can you help me. They'll tear me to pieces if I let go."

"Do something!" She turned to a slim dark man who, Ben realised, was Wayland. One of the two weird individuals he had met in the library. With renewed shock, he realised that the second of the pair was now living in his head – or claimed to be. Perhaps he really was going mad.

Wayland raised his voice. "Hunter, this man also has my protection."

"The moment has passed, Smith." The disembodied voice was colder and deeper than any Ben had ever heard.

"There is night left, no need to end the chase yet," Wayland said.

There was a pause and then the unseen person laughed – it was not a pleasant sound. "Chase, Smith? You are right. I have had little sport so far. You may have him and… a small head start." At a short horn blow, the hounds pulled back and stood in silence watching Ben where he hung precariously in the tree.

"Get down!" Ben nearly fell at the sharp order. "Jump! Fast!"

The urgency got through. Not to Ben but to the other who shared his body. Ben found himself falling and fought the drop. He twisted and landed awkwardly, his leg buckling under him as he fell. His ankle wrenched horribly and Ben would have screamed had he any control over his voice.

"Fool, you will kill us."

"How was I to know you were going to jump?" Ben snapped.

"Dad!" Lucy bent over him to help him up.

He staggered as he tried to put his weight on his foot. "I've done for my ankle," he managed to get out.

"That is unfortunate," Wayland said crisply. "We need to run."

"Run?" One of the young men asked.

"What else do you suppose he meant by a 'head start'?"

"I can't run," Ben protested.

"Matt? Rick?" Lucy looked round wildly.

"I'll carry him." Rick threw the sword he carried to his friend, pushed Lucy aside and swept Ben up over his shoulder.

"Now run, follow me." Wayland snapped and set off back the way they'd come.

They had gone barely five hundred yards when the baying began again behind them.

"Faster," Wayland ordered. "He will not hold for me a third time."

*

Rick settled the policeman firmly on his shoulder and ran through the dragging snow. Like the sand of the desert this pulled at his feet making each step difficult and his burden didn't help. The body snagged on branches as he passed, pulling him backwards and depositing further snow falls on his back and shoulders.

The noise of the hounds behind pushed him to move faster. "It's a training run with a backpack," he told himself, "I can do this. No bloody dog is going to get me. No hunter is going to track me down." His breath came in short, hard gasps as he forced his legs on following the lithe form of Hawkeye in front. The smaller man seemed to be moving with effortless ease through the fallen snow. In the lead, Matt towed Lucy onwards, ignoring her pleas to halt.

"Move, woman," Rick ordered. "They'll tear you apart if they catch us."

"I can't…" she gasped.

"You fucking can and you fucking will. I'm not leaving you out here. You'll come even if Matt has to drag you. Now shut up and move." Rick had no sympathy with weakness – never had. It had taken months for the army to knock the concept of teamwork into him. Now he understood but, in the dark with dogs baying at his heels and the world he knew vanished, he could feel such certainties deserting him. He wasn't going to be ripped apart and if that meant he had to sacrifice someone else then so be it.

In war, if all else failed, you sacrificed the weak to allow the strong to fight another day.

Shifting his grip on the man he carried, Rick picked up his pace. "Move! They're gaining. Last one to the library's dinner!"

It didn't improve his mood to watch Hawkeye easily remain with him.

CHAPTER 7

"We found these, you see." Tony picked up the magnificent antlers. They had all followed the mummers out into the library.

"They're mine," Eleanor said. "Well, not mine exactly. They were sent to the museum and I brought them here to find out about them."

"Sent?" Marshall couldn't imagine who would want to do such a thing.

"Yes, the accompanying letter said they'd been found in a Stone Age grave."

"People normally just 'send' you such things?"

"It's unusual but yes, Inspector, it does happen." Eleanor took the antlers from Tony. "Jenny and I were investigating before Lucy arrived."

"Well, as I said, we found them." Tony indicated the other mummers. "We got to reading some of this stuff. Absolutely fascinating some of it. We found a load on the history of mumming and related tradition and…"

"The Hunter, Mr Hood?"

"If you'll let me finish, Inspector."

Marshall waved his hand. "Sorry, carry on."

"The Hunter is part of the old traditions. It's all a bit confused but then that's always the way with tradition."

Marshall recognised the signs of a teacher about to launch into a lesson. "Mr Hood, I appreciate your knowledge, but time may be short. Can you summarise briefly?"

"The story of the Hunter is long and varied. There's the character of Herne that stems from a royal forester who sacrificed himself to save the king from being gored by a stag. The tale is more complicated than that, but it will do. It is said that he now looks for other sacrifices." Tony took a deep breath and rushed on, obviously determined to get some of his 'lesson' across. "The tale is complicated by additions, but it refers back to even older traditions of Woden and the Wild Hunt that collects souls. Then there's Cernunnos…"

"Are you saying that what is out there is some sort of hunter who's after our souls?" Alex Ranald butted in.

"I have no idea what is outside. I am merely telling you the legends of the hunter as I was asked to. As I was saying…"

"Thank you, Mr Hood, I think we get the picture." Marshall let them wait while he thought. "If this hunt is as deadly as you suggest and if this Hawkeye is accurate about it being out there then I don't really hold out much hope for Constable Martin and his pursuers."

"We heard it," Steve said softly. "Right before Bob disappeared or just after. It didn't sound good."

"No," agreed Julian. "I hope it didn't get Bob."

"What can we do?" Annie sounded rather fraught and she stood stiffly apart from her daughter looking pale and fragile. "Can we do anything to help?"

"The tarot," David suggested. "I always find that useful when I need guidance. How about a reading, Jenny?"

"What?" Annie turned on him getting in slightly ahead of Marshall who had to agree with her. "That's supposed to help is it?"

"There are ways of finding help without stepping outside."

"Well, you carry on," Marshall said. The man was totally mad; first convinced he was dead and now this, and he had seemed remarkably sane during the past year. Marshall felt it was probably safer to leave him reading tarot cards while he went and did something practical without interference. Currently the group of them seemed to hover between panic and lunacy. "I'm going to try and contact my sergeant, see if he has found any way to get us back."

"And if he hasn't?"

"Let's worry about that later, Mr Hood." Marshall strode back towards the door with Alex in his wake.

*

Those left gathered around the table. Steve and Julian pushed the antlers and papers out of the way so David could spread out the cards he produced from his pocket.

"You shuffle," David handed the cards to Jenny.

"Me? They're yours."

"Not any more. Besides, I think you stand at the heart of this. Let the cards read you."

Jenny frowned and took the cards. She looked round as she shuffled. Her mum sat at one end of the table, her face white and her eyes red-rimmed. Eleanor sat beside her, grimly staring at David. He sat across the table from Jenny and gave her a small smile as her gaze passed. The mummers, men she had known all her life, sat at the far end. They looked strangely 'at home'. But then, Jenny thought, they always looked at ease, part of the furniture of a place. Whether it was morris dancing outside Woolworths in winter, on West Cross Village Green on May Day or in the front room of the White Stag with a pint each, they inhabited the moment and belonged there. They represented her childhood; the comfort of growing up surrounded by love – a feeling which had been ripped away when her dad died. Now she was stranded here, shut away from the world. It seemed odd to have her old friends sitting here looking as they ever did.

More so, tonight of all nights.

In a way it wasn't fair when she hadn't felt right since she had noticed Eleanor today and her mother's appearance had forced her back into the shell she had begun to leave.

"I think that will do." David reached for the cards she was absently shuffling.

He placed them on the table in front of him and carefully turned over the top card. Jenny recognised the King of Wands, crowned and seated amongst the greensward. Then the picture shimmered and changed and she was looking at herself, sitting at a table surrounded by people.

"Shit! How did you do that?" Julian leant forward. "That's Jen."

"The King of Wands is the librarian's card. It will sit at the heart of the spread." David looked up. "Do you know the tarot?"

"I've heard of it," Julian said. "These look like unusual cards."

"They read true. I shall explain as we progress."

David turned over a second card and laid it beside the first. "Here we have the issue at hand." The card showed a wheel of trees. "This is the wheel of fortune. It represents change and the opportunity to progress. It is apt if we consider this to be Jenny's reading."

He then laid out ten cards in quick succession, face down. One on top of each of the two cards already laid, one above and one below and one to either side — right then left. Then he placed four in a row up the right-hand side of the cross, starting at the bottom.

"This is a Celtic cross, a fairly comprehensive reading. We start with these two." He touched the first two he had lain down across the original cards at the heart of the cross. "First we have the prevailing influence." He turned over the card. It showed another king, crowned and sitting before the trunk of a huge oak tree."

"What's that?" Julian asked.

"This is the King of Swords." David ran a finger lightly across the card and it changed. A man now stood, staring proudly out at them from fierce green-gold eyes. His head bore a magnificent set of antlers and a large ivory horn hung from his belt.

"The Hunter," David said softly.

Jenny peered closely. There was a cold, hard power to this one. She resisted the urge to reach out and touch, fearful of what she saw in him.

"Looks a bit like the inspector," Eleanor said softly.

David continued. "An impartial but cold judgment on all he comes across. Expect no mercy." He turned over the card beside it. Again, it showed a king. "The opposing force."

Jenny drew in a sharp breath as the card flickered to show a face she knew. "Laodhan."

"Who?" Julian seemed fascinated.

"The spirit that was caught outside the library," David explained. "This is him." They looked at the tall, graceful figure with grey eyes and long blonde hair.

"Looks like Marshall was right then," Steve observed. "This thing found a way to survive."

"Hmmm," David frowned.

"So," Tony sounded puzzled, "I thought you said this Laodhan tried to destroy the library, so surely he's not on our side but here you're saying he's opposing Herne, so…" He tailed off.

"A reading is not always as simple as taking sides for good and evil." David leant back to look at Tony. "How can I put this? A tarot can tell you all the influences and potential outcomes but it cannot make your decisions for you. It will not lie but neither will it give you a 'good' outcome and a 'bad' outcome. It simply shows you things as they are." He paused and then said. "Not clear? All right, try this. These two influences could show you your house burning down on one side and the temperature outside as minus thirty on the other side. Neither option is good as such but they are two equally valid and opposing influences on the decision to be made. So here," he indicated the two cards, "we have The Hunter and we have Laodhan. Neither is necessarily beneficial but they are the opposing influences Jenny has to cope with. Is that clear?"

Various people nodded and Steve reached over and squeezed Jenny's hand. "Clear, but don't lay it all on Jen. We'll get through this together."

David nodded but didn't comment. "Shall we continue?"

"Go on," Julian said. "It can't get worse, can it?" Jenny thought he didn't sound sure and nobody attempted an answer.

"Card three shows us an ideal solution." David turned over the card at the top of his cross. A woman stood holding a pair of scales.

"Even I recognise that one," Julian noted. "That's justice. You get her on court houses."

"Justice for who?" Steve asked.

"Not just justice. It may also be the reestablishment of balance, a correction to the world." As David spoke the picture faded to be replaced by a scene showing the front doors of the library set in the middle of Museum Street. Christmas shoppers hurried past below the gleaming lights strung above.

"I see." Julian nodded. "I'll grant you that. It would be the ideal solution. Go on, what's next?"

David placed his hand on the bottom card of the cross. "The heart of this matter." He turned it over. Jenny gasped. A man hung from an oak tree, his lifeless body twisting gently.

"That's not nice," Eleanor said.

"I can't see the face properly," Steve said. "Is that intentional?"

"The hanged man represents sacrifice, that's all."

"Fairly graphic way of doing so," Julian said, "particularly when there are ladies present."

"Back to this." Jenny sighed. "I know this. I know I'm supposed to be giving up the past and moving on. I understand but I don't know how. What next, David?"

David touched the next card, the right arm of the cross. "This may help. It shows influences of the past which may be affecting the current situation." He turned the card. It showed a single sword, hung upside down, its point dripping blood. "The Ace of Swords," he said unnecessarily.

"Meaning?" Ian asked.

"Old wounds, unhealed." David waved his hand over the card lightly. "A downward spiral of self-destruction."

Jenny opened her mouth to ask what he could possibly mean when the card flickered and she found her father staring back at her. Not her father as she had last seen him, cold and grey in the hospital, but smiling at her, his eyes alive and full of love.

"Mike?" Julian said and then, always quick to see the heart of things. "Oh Jen, I'm sorry, seeing us tonight – of all nights – must have been so hard. These wounds are our fault, aren't they? The Inspector is right, this is something else that needs sorting."

"Not necessarily." David raised his hand. "Do not leap to conclusions. Be open to the whole reading." He lifted and flipped the card on the far left of the layout. "To balance the past we have future influences."

The card showed a man with a long grey beard wearing a pointed hat and a dark robe covered in stars.

"A wizard?" Julian asked, incredulous. "What, we need David Blaine or Harry Potter or something?"

"The magician." David smiled slightly watching as the picture dissolved.

Eleanor pushed to her feet. "Him, I might have known he had something to do with it, the way he waltzed in here earlier and then disappeared again. Hawkeye, didn't you say?"

"Wayland… Hawkeye," Jenny shrugged. The gold eyes were serious in the card, staring intently out at her. "He's on my side… our side."

"Are you sure?" Steve squeezed the hand he was holding. "What does the card mean, David?"

"The magician is an adviser, someone who may test or push you in order to guarantee the integrity of the soul." David frowned slightly. "I would say that the magician represents someone who works for the greater good rather than the good of any particular individual."

"I'm not sure that's very optimistic," Tony said. "I can think of rather too many historical examples where a lot of people suffered and died for the greater good."

"Next card," Steve said pointedly.

David nodded. "These cards show personal influences on the subject of the reading – in this case, Jenny." He pointed to the four cards he had lain in a row up the right-hand side. "From bottom to top they show her attitude, domestic influences, her fears and her hopes." He turned the first one. It showed six ornate golden cups stacked in an upside-down pyramid. The structure balanced on a single cup, teetering on the point of falling.

"Don't tell me," Julian said, "it means Jenny feels like she's got the weight of the world on her shoulders and is balancing too much."

"She is burdened, yes, by the past. A new cycle is possible but old memories weigh her down."

Jenny wished they'd stop talking about her like she wasn't there or like there was some point to this reading that would help her. So far it seemed to be telling her nothing she didn't already know.

"And the next?" Steve pointed. "You said 'domestic influences'."

David turned the card. A leering devil capered madly, its face set in a nasty grin. As they watched it gradually took on Annie's features though, unlike the others, the rest of the picture remained the same.

"Oh, come on now. That's unfair." Eleanor snapped as the woman beside her paled even further.

"Hold." David waved a hand at her. "Read carefully. The devil is not evil. The card shows a fear of the unknown. People fear death, fear to let go because of the possibility of hell. So the card shows deep seated fears, chains which bind and a fear of letting go and moving on to another place in case it is a dreadful place." He moderated his voice as he continued. "Tarot cards take a lot of care and practice to read accurately. Let me guide you, please."

"All right, sorry." Eleanor paused. "I suppose it makes sense if you explain it that way."

"Carry on, David," Jenny said coldly, thrown by the evil picture of her mother nastily laughing at her and worried by how often in the last two years she had seen her mother as a jailor, chaining her to a home she no longer felt she belonged in.

"Fear then next." David flipped the card. The cowled and robed figure of death stared up at them. It didn't change or shift; it merely was. They all looked at it in silence. When it did nothing, Jenny reached out to touch it and then stopped. David could tell her that it was endings she feared and she couldn't argue but, just as surely, she knew there was death in the air tonight. She pulled her hand back lacking the courage to read deeper.

"And hopes?" She whispered.

David turned the final card.

The King of Wands.

"That's not possible," Steve protested, "you put that one down first." He moved the picture of The Hunter from where it had been placed across the initial card. They all looked in amazement at the picture of the fool.

After a while's silent contemplation, Eleanor said, "Forgive me, but this reading seems to say that Jenny needs to move on, get over her father's death and make a new beginning. Any good counsellor could have told her the same. Just how does it solve our predicament?"

Before anyone could answer, a shout came from the front of the building. "Help! Everyone! Office, quickly!"

"It's the doctor fellow," Steve noted.

They leapt to their feet and headed for the office leaving the cards abandoned across the table.

CHAPTER 8

"Take it easy, John." Alex called as he followed Marshall towards the front door.

"Come on, Alex, Tarot readings? Herne the Bloody Hunter? Is that really supposed to be of use?"

"Who's to say they won't be?"

Marshall paused and let out a sigh that felt like it had been pulled up from his toes. "I know, and that's what's so bloody terrifying. I want to be doing something I recognise. I want hard facts and evidence and…"

"… a criminal?"

"Yes, maybe that as well. I want to be in control, Al, not feel like I'm being led round by the nose." They'd made it as far as the door and Marshall had a quick glance outside. Nothing had changed. "You know, Alex, my grandad spent the last part of the war in a Japanese Prisoner of War camp. He would never speak of it but Mum told me once it was because he lost control of who he was. They could make him do anything and he had to do it to survive. I'm thinking I might have some idea of how he felt if I end up stuck in this goddam library much longer. I think someone is playing games with us and I don't like it."

"Maybe."

"And what if our history teacher is right about some creature out there hunting our souls?"

"Facts?" Alex smiled.

"Yeah, just ignore me. Doing nothing except speculating is pointless. Had enough of this last Christmas when I first came across this place and David makes complementary noises about how well I coped but a year's distance means I probably assumed it was less weird than I remembered. Anyway, I'm going to give Mark an update such as we have and see if he's got anything for us." He scribbled for a few minutes on a piece of paper and threw it on to the snow. As he did so, Alex let out a shout. "John, look."

At the far end of the street several running figures had appeared. Behind them came a pack of the largest, ugliest hounds imaginable and behind them…

"Shit!" Marshall hissed. "I hoped he was wrong."

"Fire!" The bellow came from one of the racing party. "We need fire. It will hold them."

"Where do we get fire?" Marshall asked but Alex was already heading for the office, calling for help as he went. Marshall dashed after him, remembering Friday evening and where there was fire. In the office, the huge fire blazed merrily in the hearth.

*

Rick panted on, the weight he carried dragging him back. He could almost feel the hot breath of the pursuing dogs on him.

As if in answer to the thought, Hawkeye paused. "Too close, we have to fight."

Rick dropped the constable unceremoniously in the snow. Ahead he could see the library; people peering from the open doorway.

"Fire," Hawkeye yelled, "we need fire." The heads vanished and Rick grabbed at the sword Lucy still held. Whirling hard he slammed the blade into the first of the advancing creatures, hearing the crunch of bone as it sliced down. "Get going, Lucy!"

Beside him Matt waved his sword threateningly in a visibly shaking hand. "I don't want to die," he muttered, his face pale and sweating.

"Then fight," Rick snapped, lunging into his next blow as a dog leapt at him.

His blow never landed.

*

Alex skidded to a halt.

"How can we get it out?"

"Here!" Marshall dragged the sheets from the bed, working frantically. He ripped them and wrapped them round sticks from the stock beside the hearth. Others joined him as Alex breathlessly explained and then they put the cloth to the flame. With burning brands they hurtled back to the front door.

The small party in the street had turned at bay fifty paces from the door. Matt and Rick were frantically waving the borrowed swords while Lucy helped her hobbling father on.

"John!" Alex yelled as Marshall reached the door. "You can't go out there." Alex stumbled to a halt beside him, pulled his arm back and launched the burning brand overarm. It sailed into the middle of the approaching pack of hounds.

"Run!" Marshall called as he also threw.

Lucy pulled her father on while Steve and Julian leapt out waving their torches and yelling loudly. Alex and Marshall grabbed further flames and hurled them at the circling animals. Their barks turned to yelps as the flames caught and they rolled in the snow to extinguish them.

Rick pushed his sword at Lucy as he passed and then swung Ben up, aided by Matt, and hurtled for the door. Within seconds they were all inside and Marshall slammed the door closed.

"Will that hold them?" Alex asked.

"We're about to find out."

Marshall turned to the gathered crowd. "Stand ready..." he stopped. Steve was staring wildly at the group who'd just barrelled in.

"You," he gasped, "it was you!"

*

He had hurried to the door, clutching the flaming stick thinking of no more than to help others trapped in the same madness as he was. Now Steve was caught by a double nightmare. He had been frozen briefly by the sight of the huge hounds and the towering horned figure astride its horse. The policeman's thrown fire, arching through the night, broke the spell and he followed Julian, leaping into the snow-spangled dark to launch his own flame in a graceful curve.

Only then, as he looked to those they were rescuing, did his heart stop a second time. The young men had thrust their swords into the girl's hands so they could swing her father up between them. She rushed at him, white knuckles gripping a hilt each side, eyes staring fixedly ahead and her mouth set in a grim line. This was why he recognised her, not for her grief so like Annie's but for this; a pale staring face rushing towards him through the dark.

Then she was past and he was swept back into the library and Marshall slammed the door behind them.

"You," Steve glared at her. "It was you. You were driving."

"Steve?" Julian took his arm.

"Look at her, Ju."

"Well, yes, I suppose it's possible."

Standing there in the harsh electric light of the library entrance,

Steve felt his confidence ebbing away. If she'd laughed it off, then asked them what they were on about, he would have assumed he'd been mistaken in the whirling dark. Lucy did neither. Dropping the swords with a clatter and covering her face she let out a sob.

"I didn't mean to kill him. I never meant it."

"What?" Marshall said, "Kill who?"

"She was driving," Steve said, "I saw it just now when she rushed out of the dark like that, Just the same as when she hit Mike."

Before Marshall could react, Annie leapt forward.

"Bitch. You killed him; you killed my husband."

"Annie!" Steve and Julian grabbed at her, pulling her backwards.

"I'll kill her and…"

"Mrs Williams, you will stand back." Marshall stepped between the two women. He looked round and stared at the dark man who had arrived with the party despite not setting out. "I'm going to assume that you're the Hawkeye I've been hearing about."

"Yes, that's him," Eleanor said.

"In which case, as you seem to know a lot about it, can you tell me if that door will keep those things out?"

"Yes, for now," Hawkeye said, "but it is a problem that will not go away."

"Understood, but I think I need to deal with one problem at a time." Steve, still holding Annie's struggling form, was impressed with the policeman's command. He took control effortlessly and even Annie quietened a little.

"Lucy Martin, are you confessing to the manslaughter of this woman's husband?"

Lucy nodded; her body still shaken by sobs. No-one moved to comfort her and Steve wondered why her father hadn't done so but Ben just stood behind the other policeman doing nothing.

"You knocked him down."

"Yes." It was barely a whisper.

"Were you, as the police at the time assumed, drunk?"

"No... well... no... I'd been on... on orange juice and... and... well... you can ask Matt." She pointed at the startled young man.

"Mr Cork, you were also in the car?"

"I'm sorry," Matt shook his head, "I have no idea what we're talking about. When did this happen?" Steve thought his puzzlement was genuine.

Julian stepped in. "Two years ago, to the day. We were walking back from the Red Lion when Mike was run down."

"Two years? Red Lion?" Matt mouthed and then flushed bright red. "Oh shit!"

"What?" Steve demanded. "What do you know?" The lad hadn't known about Mike but he obviously knew something.

"Matt was at the Red Lion," Lucy said having regained some composure. "We had a couple of drinks; he can tell you I wasn't drinking. I knew I was driving home."

"Well," Matt cleared his throat a couple of times. "Well, the truth is, I was out with the lads from the Rugby club and we saw your play thing and then decided to go on to a club and Lu wouldn't come with us. She got all prissy about going home to daddy so I may have spiked the odd drink."

Marshall didn't seem surprised. "Spiked with what, Mr Cork?"

"Double Vodka. You can't taste it in orange juice."

"How many drinks would you say, Mr Cork?"

"Well, it's hard to say exactly."

"How many drinks, Mr Cork?"

Matt stared at the floor and muttered something none of them caught.

"I don't intend to ask again," Marshall snapped.

"The barman was a mate of mine, Okay? I left him the money to add a double vodka to everything she drank all night." Matt glared at them all, his face bright red. "She was waiting for her dad but he was working, as usual, and hadn't turned up so I thought she could do with cheering up. It was just a bit of a joke. I thought the stupid cow had enough sense to realise she was pissed before she drove."

Marshall nodded but passed no judgment. "How many drinks, Miss Martin?"

"Five."

"That's an amazing memory if I may say so considering it was two years ago. It suggests to me that you might have had occasion to work the number out. Would I be right?"

"Yes." Lucy stared round at them like some cornered beast might. "I just thought he'd done one at first when I went out. But then I couldn't see right and… and… and then I hit something and…" She tailed off.

"So you continued home and never thought to come forward?"

"I was scared to."

*

Marshall turned away from Lucy. He'd solved one crime, not that it currently did him a lot of good. Next question was Ben's involvement. "Constable Martin, did you know about this?"

They all looked away from Lucy to find that Ben Martin had bent and retrieved the swords his daughter had dropped and was now waving them menacingly.

"Oh, you can ask," the voice was harsh and cold coming from Ben's lips, "but he can't answer you right now, I'm afraid." The figure laughed though there was little humour in the sound. "I could check for you. Let me see. Yes, the brave constable knew his little angel was a drunken killer but he couldn't bear to lose her, so he said nothing. Does that help?"

"What the hell?" Marshall took a step forward and found a sharp sword barring his way.

"I do admire you, Inspector, for trying so hard to be a good policeman but now I have a few words so you will listen. Oh, and before you think of heroics, ask the Smith about his way with weapons would you?"

"The Smith?" Marshall asked, confused.

"He means me," Hawkeye said. "I sharpened the swords; they were of little use as they were."

"So," Ben – except it wasn't Ben – continued, "amusing as this little discussion is, I happen to know a thing or two about our friend outside. He won't go away, I promise you. In fact, I suspect he probably can't go away. We seem to be outside of time with nowhere to go and that makes your situation rather tricky. Now I, like you, would like to get back to somewhere where I can step outside without being devoured. I've grown rather fond of this body and I think I'd like to own it a while longer. The only way I know to achieve that, ladies and gentlemen, is to give the Hunter what he seeks."

"And what would that be?" Marshall kept a very tight rein on his temper. For a brief moment there he had been in charge, had interviewed suspects, had been a policeman. Now he was losing control of the situation again but he was going to keep as calm as possible.

"A sacrifice. The Hunter collects souls." Ben's face twisted into a smile. "Now I could choose one of you nice people and, believe me, if my patience runs out then I will throw whoever I like out of that door but I will offer you the opportunity to find a noble hero prepared to save us all. Shall we say an hour for a decision? After all, we don't want to wait all night. The inspector has people to arrest." He grinned and turned to hobble away. "You have an hour."

CHAPTER 9

Rick had leant his weight against the stout library doors. He'd only caught a brief glimpse of the mounted figure that led the hounds, but he knew death when he saw it. This was something other than he was used to. Fiery hate beneath the burning sun he could understand, even evil that crept with stealth through the stifling dark, but this was different. Cold as the snow which fell around him, the horned figure had watched his hounds attack with implacable calm. No hate, no anger, no tension to the head which bore the huge antlers so easily. Rick shuddered at the memory. Like a force of nature, this was not something he could reason with or win over.

Steve's anger and Marshall relentless questioning gradually penetrated. It seemed that Lucy wasn't quite the 'goody-two-shoes' she'd always made out. Rick almost laughed except he was too good at reading faces – had to be to survive in a place where anyone could be the next enemy. Annie, the widow, meant murder. The two men held her for now, but Rick could already see the mind closing and hiding behind the glaring eyes. The daughter's face was already shuttered, quicker to dissemble and more practised at keeping her emotions hidden but her hands were balled in tight fists, the teeth clenched against the words inside. Rick summed up the others; he could see no sympathy for Lucy and she had no escape here with the monstrosity outside. They were caged. Rick closed his eyes briefly. He'd come home with relief, finally able to escape the heavy tension of hatred in the air and now here it was again.

His eyes flew open at the strange voice and he realised it came from the policeman he'd spent half the night chasing. Rick tensed. The man was a copper so wouldn't be unfit but he had twenty years extra age and several pounds round his middle put there by soft living. Rick waited his chance, barely listening to the corrosive flood of words. Here was an excuse to release some of the anger and fear he'd accumulated tonight. Just in front, he was aware that the Inspector had also tensed, watching for an opening, but Rick knew he was faster.

As the creature which controlled Ben turned away, Rick took his chance.

With all the deadly speed and grace at his command, Rick leapt at the retreating form and found himself nearly impaled on a sharply raised sword.

The blade sliced across his arm leaving a thin trail of blood. He twisted, seeing the flash of steel as he moved. The pain was sharp, and the red stain spread immediately as he landed. Rick swore violently, clutching at his arm; all that time in the desert without a scratch and now this. What did he know about bloody swords; he needed his gun.

"Unsurprising," Ben commented. "You have an hour." He headed off between the shelves.

"Bastard." Rick glanced at the cut. "It'll do. I'm going after him."

"Is that sensible?" Marshall asked, his brows drawn.

"What else do you suggest? We sit around and decide who he can bloody kill? I'll take my chance; he won't get me again. There's no way he should be so fucking fast, but this place is a godsend. All these shelves." It would be interesting to be the one doing the creeping round and hiding for a change.

"What happened to my dad?" Lucy looked distinctly wild eyed.

"I'd say," Marshall replied, "that we now know how this spirit survived outside of the garden."

"An interesting thought," Hawkeye agreed. "I believe the police officer was unconscious so that may be possible. Awake, a person would never allow their body to be invaded in such a way."

"Right, so simply knocking him out isn't an option." Rick avoided Lucy's gaze. "It didn't work last time; it just lets this creature take control. Sorry, Lucy, but I've got to deal with him." He turned away from them.

"Take this," Marshall handed over his baton and demonstrated how to flick it open into a long stick. "Not sure it'll do much against the swords but at least you'll have some defence."

"Thanks," Rick set off between the shelves, following the path of his prey.

*

"It's easy," Annie stated suddenly. Marshall realised that she had been paying no real attention to the conversation after the revelation of who was driving the car which killed Mike.

"What is?" Steve was still holding her arm but less firmly.

"We'll send her out," Annie continued. "She deserves to die."

Lucy gasped and swayed slightly. Marshall thought she had run out of all resources of strength.

"I have no intention of sending anyone out to die," Marshall said. "I think we could all do with a drink and a sit down. I'm sure our soldier friend knows what he's doing."

"I'll take a look," Hawkeye offered. "I have ways of moving unobserved."

Marshall wasn't at all sure he was happy about that. He would have liked the time to get some answers out of this strange man and to be the one making the decisions but before he could object Hawkeye had strode off into the library.

Marshall shepherded the rest of them towards the office moving slowly and carefully, peering round shelving at every corner. There was no sign anywhere of either Ben or Rick. He breathed a sigh of relief when he sighted the office door ahead, aware that he'd barely dared to hope they'd get this far without something else going horribly wrong.

At which point Annie lunged past him into the office and headed for the fireplace. A sword hung above the ornate mantelpiece.

"No, mum, don't." Jenny yelled also passing him. "You mustn't handle that."

"You'd even protect the bitch who killed your dad?" Annie paused, swung round and slapped her daughter. The sound was loud in the sudden silence. "Ben has the right idea. Once I've got a sword, I'll make sure she goes out."

"Mrs Williams, I forbid…" Marshall began.

"Bollocks. You don't tell me what to do. She killed Mike and now Ben's gone…"

"That's not her fault, mum."

"How dare you," Annie screamed at her daughter from two inches away. "How dare you defend her?"

"Jenny's right," Steve tried to pull Annie away towards the seating. "Killing Lucy won't bring Mike back. The Inspector can deal with it."

"Don't any of you care? I knew you didn't. You and your fucking mumming…"

"… of course we care, but there are ways of doing this, Annie." Julian said.

"Here? In this bloody library? I don't think so." Sudden cunning lit the snarling face. "What was all that in those cards about Jenny moving on, dealing with her father's death? Well this is the way she does it, isn't it?"

Jenny looked suddenly confused. "I don't… do you think… but…"

"Of course, that's what this place wants. Then we can all go home." Annie pressed her advantage, her eyes glittering triumphantly at Marshall who was wishing he could take Rick's advice from earlier about how to deal with hysterics. "The Inspector's rules don't work in here. It has to be like this, Jen, you see that don't you. To get us all home."

Annie reached out her hand to take her daughter's. "I'm sorry I snapped, Okay, but this is the way."

Marshall could see Jenny faltering before her mother's cunning reasoning. Why couldn't the blasted woman have stayed acting like a maniac; she was making too much sense now and he could just see them all deciding to launch Lucy out into the snow.

"Look…" he tried and then was interrupted by a scream of pain unlike anything he'd ever heard before.

*

Rick peered round yet another shelf. There seemed to be no purpose behind Ben's meanderings – they were nearly back to the main doors. He was probably just killing time. That was an advantage; he seemed to have no idea that Rick was following. On the other hand, all Rick was doing was pursuing. He wished he had a better idea of the layout of the place. Then he'd be able to get ahead, to set a trap. If he could do that, he might be able to use the fact that the guy was still limping against him.

Out of the corner of his eye he noticed Hawkeye disappear, creeping silently, along a parallel row. One golden eye winked at him.

Rick grinned. Two against one was better odds and this strange man did seem to know what he was doing.

He looked ahead. Ben had slowed to take a book from the shelves. "Interesting," he said aloud, "'Arts of Tracking'"

Rick cursed briefly. He was really starting to hate this library. Then a sound ahead distracted Ben. Hawkeye stepped into the aisle.

"Hello Laodhan, or are you Ben?"

Rick began his silent move forward, clutching the stick Marshall had given him, hoping Hawkeye would keep the policeman's attention forward for just half a minute.

"Wayland," The man spat the word. "No way you can stop me now."

Hawkeye's gaze slid up briefly to where Rick crept down the aisle. Rick swore as he saw Ben start to turn, slightly off balance on his twisted ankle. Rick launched himself in a dive, hoping he could catch the man before he was steady again.

He saw the swords coming round as he leapt. One neatly sliced the baton in two. Bright pain flowered along his side as the other sword hit home and he crashed to the floor, a scream forced from between his lips. The pain was excruciating, red streaming from the jagged cut across his middle.

Running feet sounded and Ben turned and was gone. Rick thought he was laughing.

Hawkeye simply stood, looking the length of the aisle, his expression unreadable as Ben limped away.

*

Alex fell to his knees beside Rick and with swift, efficient movements pulled the young man's coat from him and wadded it against the wound. The rest of them gathered round, shock in most faces.

"I need water, heat, alcohol, and needle and cotton if you can provide," he snapped at Jenny. When she didn't move he continued, "Don't just stand there. John, any way we can get him out of here?"

"He'd be ripped to pieces out there," Matt said.

"I meant home."

"Hawkeye?" Marshall asked. "Or whatever your name is. Can we get him home?"

"I doubt it," Hawkeye said unhelpfully.

*

"John, get me thread and water, please." Alex interrupted. "His insides are falling out and he is going to bleed to death if I don't make some effort to sew this cut."

"We'll send her out," Annie continued her previous argument as if oblivious to the doctor's dilemma. "She deserves to die. The library will take us home and Rick will be saved."

"John, help me!"

Marshall hesitated only briefly. If he left, he had visions of Annie throwing Lucy to the wolves, almost literally, aided by these friends of her husband. On the other hand, there were ways round that and more pressing concerns. He rubbed a hand across his eyes and then took control.

"Julian, Tony, I want you to go with Jenny and bring back what Doctor Ranald needs as fast as you can." He put all his authority into the tone. He could make hardened criminals sit and shake in an interview room so snapping these people out of their inertia should be possible. "Steve, take Mrs Williams away. I think she needs to sit down. She's had a shock."

"What I need is…"

"Mrs Williams, we will deal with your problems shortly but for now we need to save this young man's life."

He thought for a moment that she wouldn't go but then she pulled herself apart from the men holding her and turned stiffly away. "This isn't finished," she said coldly as she left.

"She'll kill her." The harsh voice came from the prone figure on the floor.

Marshall crouched. "What?"

"I've seen that look before," Rick said between gritted teeth. "Eyes full of hate looking out between scarves as they watch you go past. She hurts and she'll make Lucy pay."

Feeling rather melodramatic but also seriously worried Marshall nodded and turned to where Lucy still stood above him. "Miss Martin, this may sound rather over the top but I wish you to remain with me or Dr Ranald at all times. You should consider yourself under arrest but I also recommend it for your own protection. A large number of people here tonight loved the man you killed and… well… tonight is strange and people may do things out of the ordinary." He looked to Matt. "I'd say that probably applies to you too. Is that clear?"

They both nodded, wide-eyed.

"How is he, Alex?"

"Not good. This is quite a cut and things are going to slip out. He's losing a lot of blood. I need to sew it and that won't be fun, particularly without anaesthetic and even then, I can't guarantee anything."

"I'll cope," Rick said fiercely. He was taking quick, shallow breaths and his hands clutched the wad of cloth Alex had created tight against the wound. It was almost soaked through. "You need to think about his deadline."

"We've got time to come up with something." Marshall didn't like to think of the row which would ensue if he raised the subject. Just briefly, he wished he hadn't answered the phone to Alex tonight; it had been such a good evening up to that point. He suddenly became aware that the stranger, Hawkeye, was standing quietly watching him.

"I thought you were supposed to know things, but you haven't been a lot of help so far," Marshall snapped.

"Unfortunately, my friend, Laodhan is right. The only way to appease The Hunter is to give him what he wants."

"I can't believe that."

Hawkeye shrugged. "That is your choice."

"You can't seriously expect me to countenance sending someone out to die?"

"Not you, no."

"Not...?" Marshall frowned, unsure what was meant.

Hawkeye saved him the trouble of working it through. "This is Jenny's library; the choice is hers. She will choose someone fitting."

"No, she won't. Weren't you listening? She'll do what her mum wants and send Lucy out in revenge."

"Is that not fitting?"

Marshall closed his mouth sharply on a retort as he realised that the man was testing him. Matt had no such forbearance. "Of course it's not bloody right. A death for a death, what dark ages are you from. That just isn't right."

"Really, ask your soldier friend."

Matt glanced down. "What does he mean, Rick?"

"He means," Rick hissed, "that war is built on the idea of an eye for an eye."

"Hush," Alex insisted, "save your strength."

"You think Lucy should die?" Matt demanded.

"I didn't say that, Matt, but I do understand it."

"We could draw lots," Lucy suggested in a small voice.

"We could stop," Marshall said firmly, "even considering the idea and come up with a way of stopping the creature that is currently inhabiting one of my constables." Even if the man was guilty of harbouring a criminal and perverting the course of justice.

Any further speech was interrupted by the return of Jenny clutching various objects. "Steve had a first aid kit in his 'doctor's bag', a real one," she said, "and Julian had some sewing things because the Turkish Knight's hat keeps coming adrift. And I had whisky if that will do for sterilising."

Pointedly ignoring Lucy, she handed over the bundle of items to Alex and then turned on her heel. That wasn't good, Marshall thought, it suggested she was being swayed by her mother's opinion.

"We could do with a hand, Miss Williams."

"I'm sure Miss Martin will manage if you feel you can trust her with someone's life."

"That's unfair …" Lucy began but she was talking to Jenny's retreating form.

Marshall watched her go as Alex started rinsing objects in the whisky Jenny had provided. The inspector had a dreadful feeling of sides being taken and battle lines drawn. In the office would be Jenny and her mother and friends and he could just imagine them plotting Lucy's death. On the other side, he stood as protector and, yet, did he have any right to inflict his laws on this place? That was a worrying thought and one which Marshall quickly dismissed; whatever this place was, he was still a police officer and would abide by the laws he was employed to uphold.

"John, stop worrying at it and give me a hand," Alex ordered. "Though God knows what I'm doing here. There's no proper sutures, or needle or…"

"It will do," Rick hissed, "seen it done, mate out in the sands."

"In theory, yes, it should do until we can get you to an operating theatre," Alex snorted, "Doesn't make me happy about it. Hold him still, John, this won't be pleasant."

As Marshall knelt down, the strange golden-eyed man joined him and laid his hands on Rick's head. "Look into my eyes," he instructed. The young man glanced up and then held, his eyes widening as they were caught by the glowing orbs staring into his.

"Work fast, doctor. I am already fighting to keep his attention away from the pain."

*

Ben struggled to hold on to any form of consciousness, the horror of what Laodhan was doing with his body threatening to overwhelm him.

On the other hand, a small voice in the back of his head was telling him that there might be a chance. He was fairly sure that, at least for the present, he'd just kept the soldier alive.

He'd seen Hawkeye's glance past them and felt Laodhan's understanding that someone approached from behind. In that instance he'd also realised what the spirit intended, the swords swinging up to meet Rick's leap.

Ben had fought it with all his strength, concentrating every bit of will on the hands holding the swinging metal. He'd had no real hope that it would work. All his attempts to take control of his body so far had failed pitifully.

But with Laodhan preoccupied and Ben's will focused so narrowly, he'd suddenly felt the give in one arm. It hadn't been enough to stop the sword hitting Rick, but it hadn't been the killing blow intended. Perhaps if he had had a purpose behind his movement rather than simply reacting to try and stop the blow, he would have had more success.

Ben felt the spirit's amusement.

"He will die anyway, policeman."

Ben felt this was probably right unless something drastic happened shortly but his main intent now was on gaining more control and finding some way to make that work for him so he kept quiet, refusing to rise to the bait.

He was a policeman; he seemed to have forgotten it this weekend, got swept away by emotion and events beyond his control. Now the spirit was separated within his head, he had more time to think things through and he silently vowed he would be a policeman. This thing in his head was a criminal – had attacked a man – and he had the most perfect way to tail him. If he could control him then he might make a difference.

Ignoring where Laodhan was going and his intermittent taunts, Ben resolutely began pushing, seeing what he could achieve by focusing on one area.

He had less than an hour to make a difference.

*

Feeling superfluous, Marshall watched as Alex sewed together the edges of the wound as well as he could; stitching with a set face but steady hands.

"This is crap, John. It won't hold long and it's done nothing for any internal damage which I can't see."

"What can I do, Al? Send a girl out to die? We only have the word of... of God knows what... that that would help."

"I've just sewn a man together with something I wouldn't trust to hold a button on and that thing he was stabbed with has spent half the night being dragged round a forest and skewering wolves. The risk of infection is an almost dead cert, I'd say and the likelihood of me finding anything to cure it in here is non-existent. Not to mention the pints of blood he will shortly need."

"Alex…"

"If we don't get him to hospital fast, John, we might as well throw him outside and be done with it." Alex Ranald ran a bloody hand through his hair. "Sorry, John, I realise it isn't your fault and, God knows, I've lost patients before, but I always felt that I'd tried everything I could."

"I know." Marshall looked at the slim, dark-haired figure holding the patient's head and found he was being watched.

"Is Rick all right?" Which was a stupid thing to say under the circumstances, but he was understood.

"Rick passed out. Too much pain even for a stubborn soldier." Hawkeye smiled slightly.

"Have you any ideas?"

"About?"

"Getting him to hospital. Getting him out of here."

"There are other problems which need addressing before you can return home."

Which, Marshall thought, was amazingly unhelpful.

"And if we can't solve all these other problems?"

"As I said before; *you* can't do anything."

"Then what is the point of me being here?"

"I believe that if you were to step outside and were lucky enough to avoid the hunter the two of you may return home as your colleagues did."

Marshall opened his mouth and shut it again having no answer; his stubbornness kept him here but the thought of what might happen to the people in this library – to Lucy in particular – if he abandoned them was too awful to contemplate. He might have very little control, but he wasn't about to give up and walk away.

"Are you thinking what I'm thinking?" Alex asked.

Marshall doubted it; his thoughts were distinctly bleak. "What?"

"We came here because of Ben. Might we be able to get Rick back by the same method?"

"What? You mean take him out with us and hope he comes home because we've got hold of him?" Marshall thought about it. "We'd have to try and take Lucy too…"

"And leave me? Thanks very much." Marshall sighed; he'd forgotten Matt's part in this.

"It won't work will it?" Alex said sadly.

"No, one man who had to be here dragged several of us here against our will. I don't think our… 'pull' home will be strong enough to take Rick or Lucy anywhere." Marshall slammed his hand against the floor; frustration finally getting the better of him. "I hate this. I hate being so bloody impotent. We're going round in circles, getting nowhere. I can't stand and watch a man bleed to death and do nothing any more than you can but…" he turned on Hawkeye. "Don't you understand that?"

"For the third time, my friend, it is not I or you who are in control here. You need to convince Jenny of her way forward." He sounded genuinely concerned though Marshall wasn't going to be fooled by anyone who so obviously was washing his hands of the whole thing.

"Right," he said having decided he was going to get no help here, "Lucy, Matt, stay with Alex. Al, I'm going to go and see about knocking some sense into our young librarian."

"Be careful. Watch out for your constable or whatever he is now."

"Will do." He looked at Hawkeye. "Are you going to come and sit on the fence some more?" He set off without waiting for an answer.

CHAPTER 10

"So you're saying that's Lucy Martin, your partner's daughter?" Ian demanded of Helen Lovell. "And you didn't notice that two years ago?"

"Not to mention him noticing," Bob put in.

Helen had paled but replied calmly. "As I said, Ben and I didn't work this case and we don't all look at the information on everyone else's cases, not unless they're big enough."

"You're saying Mike's death wasn't 'big'?"

"No, I didn't mean it like that. We were up to our ears in the present burglaries. Every spare man was helping us and we had no time to help out on another case." Helen sighed. "Look, even if I'd seen that I might have said, jokingly, 'looks a bit like your Lucy' and he might have said, 'yeah, does a bit' and we'd have moved on. However hard it is to accept, there are some things you just don't – can't – suspect. I'm only thinking it now because it's being rather blatantly thrown at me."

"So, are you saying," Colin asked, "that her dad might not know?"

Mark, listening to the exchange, let out a rather bitter bark of laughter. "Have you ever seen the damage done to a car by hitting a person at speed? If he saw the car there's no way he can't have put two and two together. We might not look into all the details of each other's cases, but you have a general feel for what's going on." Mark admitted his fears. "I don't think there's any way Ben can't have known; she will have been at home with him with a wrecked car all over Christmas."

"So," Colin said slowly, "all this time Mike's killer has been wandering around, quite possibly regularly drink-driving and risking other lives and a policeman knew and did nothing?"

"If we're right," Mark conceded, "then, yes, that's possible."

"Then," Colin was working through this and looked no happier than Mark felt. "If we tell your Inspector Marshall that Lucy is a killer then the one person he might rely on to help him uphold the law is the one person who has been helping her avoid it."

"Rely on?" Lovell laughed. "The reason Mark and I are back here is because Ben went AWOL and we tried to chase him. He's the reason we got involved at all. The doctor suggested there's something wrong with his head."

"Which," Mark pointed out, "may not be a good state of mind to be in with the inspector trying to arrest his daughter."

The five of them stared at each other in contemplative silence for a while.

"If I can backtrack a bit," Bob said eventually, "our original thought was that there were witnesses, people most affected by the death and possible suspects. If we assume that Lucy is the killer then who are the others and why are they there?"

"God knows," Mark shrugged. "May be no reason at all. Let's face it, we're making this up as we go along."

A brief, sharp knock on the door halted the discussion. Helen let in a fresh-faced constable who grinned round at them before addressing Mark. "Sergeant, you said to bring you any notes that might appear." He removed a slip of paper from his pocket and handed it over. "Don't know where it came from, but this was outside the library doors." He waited expectantly for an explanation that wasn't forthcoming. When this became apparent, he continued, "Will there be anything else, sergeant?"

"No, thank you. Go back out there in case anything else turns up."

Mark opened out the paper once the constable had left. "This is from Inspector Marshall, listen."

"Should we..." Bob began.

"Yes, you're part of this now. You might as well." Mark began reading. "Mark, an update. Ben and his daughter are still missing. So are the men who went after them. We've found Jenny Williams and David who claims to be dead. Rest are fine. Dead librarian now reading tarot cards to everyone. Trust me, this gets weirder by the minute. Can you get us out?!" Mark raised an eyebrow and put the letter on the table so they could all see. "He's got to be worried, a question mark and an exclamation mark. He'd crucify me if I misused punctuation like that in a report."

"We can't get him out," Helen said, "but if Ben and Lucy are still missing then now could be the perfect time to tell him what we worked out."

Mark paused for barely a second. "Might as well."

*

It took a while to find a computer and work out the Morse code for the message they eventually agreed upon. Then Mark had to help deal with a violent drunk that uniform had brought in from the clubs and who had decided to wreck his cell. While they waited, Bob got a phone call from Jill.

She sounded more worried than last time which he supposed was to be expected. "Bob, what's going on? Where are you?"

"We sort of got sidetracked. We're down at the police station."

"Oh my god."

"Oh no, nothing to worry about." Bob crossed his fingers. "We just saw something odd in the park and thought we ought to report it." Which was cutting the truth as fine as he dared.

"Odd? In what way?"

"Err, I'm not sure I should discuss it. I'll check with the police and we'll tell you about it when we get home."

"Can I speak to Steve?"

"Err . . . he's busy at the moment." Bob rushed on knowing she wasn't believing a word of it. "We'll be a while yet because the sergeant keeps having to go and deal with people who had too much to drink at their work Christmas…"

"What's really happening, Bob? I can't get an answer on Steve's phone and he would never not talk to me, particularly if he had to tell me he was 'helping' the police. Was the bit about snow and being in the park true earlier?"

Bob covered the mouth piece. "She doesn't believe it. What do I tell her?"

"This is Jill," Colin said, "tell her the truth."

Bob took a deep breath. "All right, sweetheart, I'm sorry I lied. God knows I didn't think you'd believe the truth but here goes." As succinctly as possible he outlined their evening's oddities. "So," he concluded, "we think the others are all right but we have no way of contacting them and no real idea of why it's all happening. I'll keep you informed as soon as I know anything." When there was only silence at the other end of the line, he carried on. "Jill, are you still there?"

"Yes, I'm here. Thank you, Bob. Keep in touch."

"Are you all right?"

"I suppose so. I'd better talk to the other ladies." She ended the call leaving Bob staring in concern at his phone and wishing he had somehow handled it better.

*

Jill was a strong woman, always had been. She was also a realist and very few people had ever managed to pull the wool over her eyes. It was how she had known Bob hadn't told her the whole truth at first and why she was rather afraid that he now had.

"That was Bob," she told the other women sitting in her kitchen.

Julian's wife was tall, slim and strong willed. She had to be in order to curb the enthusiasm of her husband which occasionally ran a little out of control. Diane also had a silly streak of her own; she wouldn't have survived twenty-five years of marriage without it.

"They're not still in the park?"

"No, this time he told me the truth."

"That sounds ominous."

"It sounds downright weird. Suspend your disbelief, ladies, pour us another large mug of mulled wine each and listen to this."

*

A while later, Jill refilled their mugs again.

"Somehow I always knew the business of Mike's death wasn't over," Diane said, "Just a feeling but… disappearing towns? Stags? Odd libraries? It just all seems so far-fetched."

"Doesn't it though?"

"Bob didn't sound drunk?"

"No, stone cold sober. They wouldn't wind us up, not after two years ago." Steve had phoned that time to let her know he was going in the ambulance with Mike. Firm – as she knew she was expected to be – she had insisted the rest of the mummers come to her as planned. They would want to be together to wait so what was the point of waking other wives who weren't anticipating their husbands home just so they could watch them lie sleeplessly waiting for a phone call? Better to use the mulled wine and sleeping bags she already had prepared.

There'd even been a few songs and tunes, gentle and yearning, while they waited. Jill would forever remember sitting on the sofa holding Steve when he eventually made it home while Julian sang, *"What is the life of a man any more than a leaf. A man has his season so why should we grieve."*

He'd sung it again by the graveside but the words had held more power for her in those twilight moments of dawn surrounded by the men she'd watched the night through with; not then marred by Annie's hysterical grief or the sounds of the traffic hurrying uncaringly past the cemetery wall.

This time they had decided all the wives would spend the evening together, supporting each other as their men were.

Diane touched her hand bringing her back to the present. "You're right, they wouldn't joke, so it must be true."

"I hope they're all right." Jill took a steadying breath. "I'm not sure I can stand another all-night vigil."

"We'll make it." Diane smiled. "But how about some of us go down to town?"

"To the police station?" Jill could understand that; their wives could be with Bob and Ian and Colin. She wasn't sure whether Lily would be welcome; it sounded like Mark was having to be a policeman rather than a mummer.

"I was thinking *we* might go to the library," Diane said. "We might come up with something the police have missed. I doubt they have much more experience with disappearing people than us."

Jill barely hesitated. "Why not?" She grinned at Diane. "If the rest of you are all right waiting here." The rest of them did at least know where their husbands were. "I do hope the police really are too busy, though. We've had three glasses of mulled wine so we probably shouldn't be driving."

Diane laughed. "Well, that'll serve them right for the worry we've gone through if they get out of this library thing to discover we've been arrested for drunk driving."

The two women shared a laugh, a hug and then set off.

*

As earlier, when Marshall reached the office at the rear of the library an angry and noisy debate was taking place.

Marshall listened. It seemed the lines of battle might not be as clear cut as he feared.

"You can't do this, Annie," Steve insisted.

"How dare you tell me what I can or can't do? She killed Mike. Don't you care?"

"Of course I care and I'm quite prepared to stand up in a court of law and say so but that doesn't mean I want her dead. We don't do that sort of thing."

"But here, perhaps we should," Jenny put in softly.

"What's that supposed to mean?" Julian stood side by side with Steve in front of the fire facing Annie and Jenny who were ranged behind the oak desk.

"I'm librarian here because David chose to die. Death is part of what this place is."

"You're saying it's more primitive?" Julian sounded sceptical.

"It's built on different rules." Jenny sounded less fierce than Annie as if trying to justify her desires from a reasonable standpoint; trying to make an urge to kill rational. "So maybe we have to obey those rules and, yes, death seems to be a part of it. Hawkeye said I had to sacrifice someone. I thought he was talking metaphorically but he wasn't. And I don't want to lose my friends but this…" She stopped and took a deep breath. "… she killed Dad so surely she deserves it if anyone does?"

"You can't say that." Steve joined in. "What right have you or any of us to say someone should die?"

"But someone has to…"

"You don't know that. I'd much prefer to sit it out and see what happens if no-one goes out there because this Hunter doesn't actually seem able to get in."

"But then we're stuck here," Annie snapped, "and she gets away with…"

"That inspector won't let anyone 'get away with' anything, Annie."

Marshall nodded, his respect for the mummers increasing.

"Maybe not if we could get home but while we're here she's just laughing at us…" Annie seemed to have lost all grip on reality.

"Be sensible, Annie, she wasn't…"

But Annie continued, regardless, over Julian's protest.

"… and unless we kick her out we'll be stuck here forever with a murderer who…"

"And if we send her out there then we're murderers and no better than she is. Do talk sense Annie." Steve finally lost patience. Marshall was impressed he'd managed to stay so calm for so long. "We're going round in circles here and it's all academic. The Inspector isn't going to let you send anyone to their deaths."

"You're right," Marshall entered the office, "I'm not."

"This is my daughter's library, Inspector. She shall do as she chooses." Marshall thought that was quite a turn around in attitude since he'd first met Annie.

"No, Mrs Williams, she will not."

"Actually," Tony was sitting quietly by the fire and surprised them all with his sudden interjection, "Jenny is the librarian; it's not her library."

There was a half second pause and then Annie continued, unabashed. "That's irrelevant, Tony. I don't see the owner about, do you? Jenny is their representative and what she says goes. If she says Lucy…"

"Mrs Williams, I cannot allow your daughter or even the owner of this library were they here to break the law." Marshall, watching Tony, had a feeling that the historian was one step ahead of him and had a handle on something he was missing.

"There are no laws here," Annie retorted. "Haven't you seen that? There's no town, no Christmas, no… nothing." She smiled and Marshall thought it was the most dangerous and unstable thing he'd seen all night. "Tell me, Inspector, how do you think you're going to convince anyone about the manner of Lucy's death if I throw her out of here?"

Marshall was rather pleased at that point that he was blocking the doorway. "I have placed Miss Martin under arrest and under my protection." This didn't have quite the effect he desired.

Annie laughed wildly. "Am I supposed to be impressed? In case you didn't see, Inspector, there's a man out there with two swords who wants to throw someone out of this library. A man who is technically my boyfriend." Marshall wondered if she had any idea what was happening to Ben, whether that had penetrated her self-centred world or the fact that he was the father to the girl she was so keen to throw to the wolves. "If I tell him Lucy is the one to die, then he will make it happen."

"If necessary, Mrs Williams, I will insist that you and your daughter remain in this office for the duration of our stay and have no contact with anyone."

"I can't let you do that." The golden-eyed spirit leant nonchalantly against the door frame. "Jenny is librarian of more than just this office." Marshall sighed, here it was again, the 'Jenny has to do it all' argument. Why couldn't the man see that it really wasn't such a good idea while her mother was in control of her thinking?

"Hawkeye!" Jenny took a half step towards him, away from her mother's side.

"Wayland," Tony said softly.

All three of them – Jenny, Marshall and the man so named – looked at Tony.

"You called him Wayland earlier when we were doing the tarot."

Marshall frowned. "What am I missing?"

"A knowledge of folk lore, Inspector. Let's say that I'm not sure the owner is as absent as Annie believes. I might even go so far as to say that I fear we might be caught up in a rather elaborate form of staff appraisal." Tony was looking at Hawkeye rather than Marshall.

The spirit gave a brief, respectful inclination of the head which Marshall only just caught out of the corner of his eye. "The threat is real, as is the librarian's freedom to act," Hawkeye said and then added, "the librarian's suitability for continuance in her post may well be judged by the appropriateness of her actions in dealing with a crisis."

Tony frowned and leant forward, suddenly serious. "If I have understood correctly, there is only one way for the librarian to be replaced."

"You have understood perfectly," Hawkeye smiled, "and rather more than intended but during the current... unanticipated developments that might be... useful."

"Would one of you care to tell me what on earth you're talking about?" Marshall looked to Tony; experience suggested the mummer was the more likely source of information.

"In a nutshell," Tony replied, "if Jenny makes the wrong decisions tonight then she'll be sacked."

"But David said…" Jenny began.

"I use the term in its most fatal sense," Tony said bluntly. "They'll want a new librarian if you can't get the job right. This is more than just stamping books, Jenny, and I get the feeling that the survival of the library is more important than anyone else's survival."

"And is murdering Lucy right, according to these laws?" Steve asked.

"Obviously…" Annie began but a new voice spoke behind Marshall.

"No," said Eleanor, "it's not."

CHAPTER 11

She'd spent the past half hour with David watching his nervous fingers shuffle tarot cards over and over while Jenny's spread lay abandoned on the table between them. They'd come here to avoid the argument brewing over Lucy and because they needed to talk. Eleanor still wasn't totally sure she could accept the fact of his death when he was sitting talking to her as large as life, but she had come to realise that whatever she thought they had had was over.

On the other hand – and this was most strange – they were closer now than they had ever been before. Thinking about it, Eleanor decided it was because they no longer had any secrets. The way she had been able to come here and talk to David about anything was now reciprocated. The slight evasiveness whenever she'd suggested meeting outside the library was explained not as any lack of feeling on David's part but as a side effect of his job.

The feelings were there and could be openly discussed at the same time as they had to be put aside as no longer actionable.

"So, Jenny is stuck inside here like you were?"

"Except the garden allows the librarian access to past, present, imagined future, legend, belief, even fiction if it is substantial enough." David grinned at her. "I met Frodo Baggins once, just to see if I could. The difficulty – and what takes the learning – is knowing where in the garden each piece of knowledge and belief is to be found."

"So you never missed just walking into town?"

David stopped shuffling cards and looked into her eyes. "Unfair, Eleanor. Which answer would you like me to give?" He ploughed on before she could answer. "The truth is that I can get into the town through the garden if I choose the right place to look. But such is not fully me because part of me remains here. But," he reached to touch her hand and his own seemed solid enough, "such a truth is not one I could ever share with you before tonight. I decided that if I could not give you all of me then I would not burden you with only a part." David squeezed the hand he held. "I never missed walking into town, Eleanor, but I did miss getting to know you better and for that, I'm sorry."

"Better late than never," she smiled slightly. "I've learnt a lot tonight."

"But this is all there is. I cannot give you…"

"… You've given me more tonight than ever before," Eleanor disagreed.

David looked thoughtful. "I'm beginning to think I should have trusted you, told you all this a long while ago."

"Perhaps," Eleanor said slowly. In her mind's eye she saw again Annie meeting her daughter in the garden. "I… I'm not sure."

"What is it?"

"Well, Annie knows it all and you've seen the way she is with Jenny. She hates this place, wants everything to be back the way it was. Maybe I'd have been the same; hated the fact of you being stuck here."

"I don't think you're quite like Jenny's mum."

Eleanor had a sudden insight. "That's what this really means, isn't it?" she indicated the cards on the table. "Not that Jenny has to move on and accept who she is but that she has to get Annie to…" she looked across the cards, "… in fact, it doesn't mean that she needs – what's the term, 'closure' – on things with her mum and dad and so on but that she needs to let it all go."

"What do you mean?"

"Like you said. You couldn't give me everything, so you gave me nothing."

"Yes… so?"

"So she shouldn't be trying to care for her mum or mourning her dad or even caring about who killed him. She's got to say, 'that life is over and done with, I don't care, it's nothing to do with me'."

"I think she may find that difficult," David frowned, "but, yes, you're right. It's been too long since I was new here; I'd forgotten how hard it was to break the connections after so long never forging them."

"We need to tell her."

"She won't listen."

"Pessimist," Eleanor retorted though she wholeheartedly agreed with the assessment. "We've got to try."

*

It was not, she decided looking at Jenny's set face, going to be easy at all. She really was wasting her breath. Eleanor ploughed on anyway. "Murdering Lucy is wrong, not only from a legal point of view but in your role as librarian."

"Why?" Jenny asked coldly.

"Because if you do this then you're taking part in something which is outside of the library and you have to let all of that go. It isn't your concern any more. You don't just have to be physically here but mentally too." Eleanor paused; she didn't think she was doing justice to the explanation. If anything, she was probably making things worse. "David couldn't be with me because he can't have that sort of link. The library had to be the most important thing in his life."

"You're saying I ought to ignore the fact that my dad is dead and that the person who killed him is here?"

"Yes."

"And what do I say to my mum? Tough, not my problem any more?"

"Well..." Eleanor floundered. Sound as the theory might be, in practice it just didn't come across well.

"You really expect me to do that?"

Eleanor sighed; at least here she was on firmer ground. "Not me, Jenny. I think it is what the library expects of its librarian. You belong to this place now; you aren't supposed to have any other concerns."

"So, are you saying," Inspector Marshall interrupted, "that the right choice for Jenny is no choice; that she ought to refuse to sacrifice anyone?"

"I suppose so," Eleanor said. She hadn't thought that far.

"No," David said bluntly, "the right choice has to be the one which benefits the library. That has to be Jenny's only priority as it was mine."

"So sacrificing nobody..." Marshall prompted.

"I have no idea. It might keep the Hunter out, the library here and break the link which allows the garden to flourish," David said, "or it might return the library and the hunter to the real world and increase the chance of mayhem within the world as the library unravels."

Eleanor opened her mouth to spell it out but the inspector was just as quick. "Neither of those options benefits this place."

David said nothing, simply waited.

"So, you're saying someone has to die for the good of the library," Marshall turned to Tony, "and you, if you're right, then the wrong choice means Jenny gets to die for the good of the library instead, or possibly as well."

Eleanor wasn't sure what had prompted that insight but it had the ring of truth to it. David had died for the good of the library when it was the only thing left, it seemed to be expected of its librarians.

"Meanwhile," Marshall continued, "I have a man out there who is going to die if I don't get him to a hospital soon and one of my constables seems to be suffering some form of possession."

Eleanor thought the Inspector was beginning to lose his temper about his inability to control events. It was an admirable and concise summing up but it held an undercurrent of despair he could no longer hide.

"Where is the constable?" Ian asked which was a question no-one could answer.

"In the library somewhere," was the most helpful Marshall could provide.

"Jenny, can't you find him?" David said.

"Oh yes," Annie launched into a fresh tirade, "you'd like to send her out to confront a madman with a sword. Not content with locking her up in this bloody place and telling her to forget me and…"

"Madam, your daughter, as librarian, has certain powers here including the ability to sense the presence of people and spirits within her domain. I am suggesting she use such detachment if she is still able to."

*

Jenny found herself surrounded by a ring of expectant faces. David looked hopeful and yet, if she closed her eyes and stretched out her senses, she could feel his disappointment. He'd been so supportive, so sure he'd been right to give her the wand, and she was letting him down. Which, naturally, led her to thoughts of her mother who was also convinced she was being let down. Tonight, their shared fury when they realised what Lucy had done, was the closest they had been in months. If she refused her mum now it would be the ultimate betrayal but…

Jenny realised that she wasn't searching for Ben and Laodhan. Giving herself a mental shake, she stretched her awareness out. The humans were in two groups, gathered round her here or clustered round Rick's weakening form near the library entrance.

She paused in her search. Marshall was right; Rick was dying for all Alex's frantic ministrations. If she didn't do something fast then his death would be her fault.

Except, why should it?

Why should it all be laid at her door?

She shook her head and continued the search. The constable was prowling the library and getting ever closer to them. She could read both the spirit and the man. Each seemed full of set, deadly purpose which surprised her. She'd expected Ben to be lost or confused but his aura was as calm and stubbornly defined as the spirit linked within him.

"I don't want to worry you," Jenny opened her eyes to look at the silent group, "but I'd say Ben has come to some sort of accommodation with Laodhan."

"What do you mean?" It was Marshall, ever ready to accumulate and dissect information.

"They read the same."

"In what way?"

"Determined, deadly, grim."

"Anything else?" David asked.

"He's heading this way. I'd say our time is up."

"What do we do?" Steve asked. "He's going to want a decision. Is there any way to stop him?"

"If we could get him into the garden," David said, "and seal the mirror behind him then that should heal the breach."

"And trap Ben in there with that thing inside him?" Marshall asked. "Not to mention what happens next time you open the mirror."

"And the Hunter," Tony pointed out.

"Let's make it a family get together," Annie insisted. "Send his daughter out as well."

Showing abysmal timing, Lucy chose that moment to appear at the door. "Inspector, your friend says he's losing his patient. He doesn't think he made any impact on any internal damage. Can you do whatever you're doing, faster?"

"Look," Julian said, "I realise this isn't… well… very PC and all that but you're saying we need someone to die and someone is dying…" he left it hanging, leaving them to complete the thought.

There was silence while the office occupants digested this idea.

"I don't think," Steve said, "that I would feel totally comfortable sending a mortally wounded man out to face those hounds."

"But a sacrifice doesn't need to fight," David argued.

"All the same."

"… not the hounds," Julian butted in, "but we're going to strand him out there with this thing that has taken over the policeman. He won't need to wait for any Hunter to die."

"I'd say," Eleanor said, "that it's all fairly academic unless we're sure we can get Ben through the mirror. The state Rick is in is the result of the last attempt to overpower this spirit, so anyone got any other ideas?"

"Laodhan is armed and deadly and older than you could possibly imagine," David told them rather unhelpfully. "He is also no fool. You're right, he won't go near the mirror."

CHAPTER 12

When they got to the library, they discovered that they had a problem. All five of them had trooped down in varying stages of expectation that, when they arrived there, their friends would be waiting for them. This was a forlorn hope.

What halted them was the group of people with cameras and notebooks gathered by the police tape.

"Bugger," Helen said. "Press is so bloody quick these days." She reversed the car round the corner. "Now what?"

"Can't we just..." Ian began.

"We've put up a cordon to warn people off because that flickering might be dangerous. How's it going to look if we simply march up to the place and begin hammering on the door?"

"Ah, right, yes, good point. Can't you just tell them to go away?"

Mark laughed. "Never dealt with the media, have you? You don't just tell them to go away. As soon as we go up there looking as if we're heading for the doors, they'll be demanding interviews, filming our every move, taking pictures. Then someone will be off trying to work out who you are and why you're involved. Before you know it, there'll be press on your doorsteps asking questions there too." Mark sighed. "I never thought. I should have asked if the vultures had descended. I suppose a flickering building is pretty big news."

"Our wives are sleeping at Steve's. Unless anyone tells the press otherwise then they'll probably all be safe," Colin pointed out.

"In which case you need to go back to the station and I need to drag a SOCO team out here to put up a tent round the door and things to disguise what we're doing. I don't really want the town's press listening in while I tell Marshall that Lucy killed Mike."

"That's going to take a while," Bob said.

"I shall hurry it along, but it can't be helped."

*

In the end it didn't take as long as Mark feared. Flickering buildings were, in fact, big news and everyone in the station was avid for a chance to go and have a look. The press had so much police activity to watch that Mark was fairly certain that his hammered message behind a protective tent was missed while so many other officers were out taking spurious measures and – in some cases – photographs of their own.

In the way of things this excitement eventually communicated itself to Chief Inspector Edwards who went himself to talk to Mark just as the sergeant arrived back to discuss next moves with Bob, Ian and Colin. They had moved to Inspector Marshall's office and had just sent Helen for more coffee when the Chief Inspector strode in, unannounced.

He stopped in surprise at the sight of them all relaxing in the office.

"Sergeant, I've just had a call from the government about this building."

"Yes, sir?"

"I was wondering what I ought to be telling them."

"Well, I…"

The chief inspector steamrollered on. "You see, I've just been down for a look for myself. Most impressive phenomenon but what impressed me most was a total lack of Detective Inspector Marshall."

"Sir?" Mark could feel the explosion coming. So much for being economical with the truth.

"Now, I'm not stupid and I do appreciate your loyalty and obedience to a senior officer but now you're going to tell me just what has happened to Inspector Marshall."

"He's in the library."

"I see and just how did he manage that? I've been down there, Sergeant. No-one can get into that library."

Seeing his career crumbling before him, Mark told the truth. It sounded like some sort of fairy story but round him he could see the mummers nodding.

"It's true, sir," Helen reappeared in the doorway with a tray full of coffees. "I've been there too."

"And Marshall told you to 'forget' to mention all this to me. Something in my town is vanishing people and buildings and he thought I didn't need to know."

"He left it to my discretion sir." Whether or not the chief inspector knew had been the last thing on anyone's mind, but he felt it might be more tactful if he didn't mention that.

"And your discretion told you what exactly, sergeant?"

"That you could see and would believe a flickering building, sir, but might not believe a tale of Inspector Marshall being stuck in the past or maybe another dimension which is where we believe the library currently is. Helen and I were hoping we might find some way to get him back."

Chief Inspector Edwards was not an unintelligent man and he

could see how serious his sergeant was. "All right, sergeant," he said, moderating his voice, "I can see why you might have hesitated to bring me such a tale. The fact that you are quite happy to discuss it in front of these three gentlemen suggests they have encountered similar experiences."

"Yes sir. They were thrown out too but they also have friends in there."

"There are more than DI Marshall trapped?"

"Yes sir."

"Do we know how many, sergeant?"

"Fourteen we believe."

"Fourteen? Fuck!" The chief inspector grabbed a chair and pulled it up to the desk. "Full details please, sergeant. Everything you can tell me. I want to know every last thing." He included them all in his glance. "I need to know who to call in. I think you would agree that this is well beyond our experience."

"Yes sir."

"Then talk. I need facts."

Mark sighed. "I'm not sure I've got a lot of those, sir, but I can give you what we know and what we've assumed and see if you can make a better picture out of it.

*

A sudden deafening noise had the whole office jumping in surprise. This settled into a series of loud and soft bangs which echoed round the library.

"What the fuck is that?" Julian said

Almost simultaneously Steve asked, "Has the Hunter got in?"

Marshall almost laughed. "No, I think my sergeant is attempting to communicate except I haven't the faintest what he is trying to say. I don't even know what I did with the bloody book you found."

"Hush, I know." Eleanor waved them all to be quiet frowning hard.

"You do?" Marshall said in surprise.

"Girl guide. Hush." After several more bangs and crashes Eleanor laughed, hysteria tingeing the sound.

"What is it?" Marshall demanded.

"My Morse is a little rusty but I'm fairly sure your sergeant says, 'Be careful, we think Lucy Martin killed Mike Williams, could be dangerous'."

"That's it?"

"Yes."

"Oh, for fuck's sake," Marshall snapped, "tell me something I don't know. You're supposed to be getting us out of here, Mark." Marshall realised as he said it that moaning at his sergeant who probably had no better idea of how to solve the problems and, moreover, couldn't hear him was utterly pointless. He sighed.

Annie snorted bitterly. "Ever useless police force. If you're so determined to get us all home, Inspector, why don't you make sure Ben and the thing in him get into the garden and take his murdering daughter with him."

"You said I'd be okay if I stayed with you." Lucy moved closer.

"Get it into your thick heads," Annie shouted at them, "he can't make any promises here. His rules don't apply. This isn't normality. And I promise you that I will make you pay for killing my Mike." She punctuated her words by slamming her fist against the desk she stood behind.

*

Ben had had a victory of sorts. Lying on the floor, feeling the pain in his elbow where he had slammed it against the shelf as his body fell, he wondered how he could put the knowledge he had just gained to use.

"Enjoy that, did you?" Laodhan re-asserted his control. *"The only one*

you'll hurt is yourself." This seemed to be true, but Ben felt the knowledge was worth the pain.

Having struggled impotently to regain control of where he was going and what he was saying, it had been surprisingly easy once he wasn't attempting to own all of himself to take control of one small part. Concentrating hard on the twisted ankle he had mis-stepped, tripping over the shelf corner.

Ben had visions of his body falling, banging his head, knocking Laodhan unconscious and leaving him back in possession. Unfortunately, Laodhan was much too quick. As they fell, Ben felt the spirit retreat leaving him in control of the descent. He jerked his head aside and crashed into the shelf with only his elbow. It wasn't quite the result he'd intended but as he lay looking at the one sword he still held and had narrowly avoided falling upon it raised interesting possibilities. He had, at least, halved the number of weapons.

Laodhan obviously intended to avoid suffering, retreating away from the surface and giving Ben momentary use of his own form. Now, how could he make that work to his advantage?

Laodhan regained control and set off again and Ben realised he could hear a lot of people with raised voices. He listened with a sinking heart. He had thought there was a little spark between Annie and he – something he'd missed for years – but here she was loudly declaiming that he could be thrown out to get rid of Laodhan and she wanted Lucy dead too.

Part of him understood. He could remember, in the months after Sarah's death, desperately looking for someone to blame. Maybe if she'd had more tests, more operations, more chemotherapy then she would have lived. It had been futile and, in the long run, hadn't made him feel better. Not that he could currently explain any of that to Annie.

Laodhan suddenly stopped, brought to a stop by a banging that echoed hollowly about them. *'The Hunter,'* Ben thought, *'he's trying to get in.'*

"*Don't be stupid.*" Laodhan laughed at his helpless ignorance. "*The Hunter can come in the way he left, through the garden. He has no need of hammering on doors.*"

'He can get into the garden? And then into here through that mirror thing?' He wondered if Annie knew that. She didn't even have to throw Lucy outside.

"*That's right.*" Ben could have strangled the smug voice in his head filled with its corrosive amusement. "*As long as I'm out here and that mirror can't be properly shut,*" Laodhan said, "*The Hunter can go wherever he's called.*"

Ben had a sudden horrific understanding of Laodhan's intent. Trapped as he was, unable to use his body, Ben would have to stand uselessly by while Laodhan called The Hunter in. He couldn't even warn the others that they weren't safe; that the library was not the haven they believed.

Clear and strident, Ben then heard Annie telling Lucy she would pay and realised that they had arrived at the office door.

Looking round from behind Laodhan's awareness at the circle of angry and despairing faces Ben knew that he had to act immediately before the spirit had any inkling of what he planned.

Laodhan's arrogance worked in Ben's favour as he strode past where Annie and Jenny stood behind the desk to approach the mirror so that he could call the Hunter.

Using every ounce of mental strength he possessed, Ben raised the sword he held towards his own neck. "*I will kill you,*" he spared a thought to tell the spirit, "*rather than let you and Annie kill my daughter.*"

Laodhan had no respect for his intelligence; didn't look behind the stated intent or action. He merely laughed. *"You don't learn, do you?"* As the advancing blade touched his neck, Ben felt the spirit relinquish his control. *"Only you will die."*

Knowing he had no time, Ben dropped the sword, grabbed Annie's hand and leapt for the mirror. Something pushed Annie hard from behind giving them added momentum and the two of them almost fell through the shimmering doorway. "Shut the mirror!" He remembered to yell as Annie collapsed on top of him knocking the wind from a body he no longer controlled. Laodhan's efforts to get up were hampered by the woman sprawled across him but it wouldn't be long before he was up and the mirror still stood open, Jenny hesitating before it.

*

Jenny watched the creature that was Ben, and yet not Ben, arrive with her mind more than her sight. Since she had stretched her senses out to locate the spirit, she had felt detached. She realised she could see more clearly if she looked with these new, deeper senses.

In fact, this wasn't new and she had noticed it on Friday and had enjoyed experimenting on Saturday, attempting to work out what visitors wanted from the library before they spoke. She had been startled and enlightened in reading those she met.

Tonight, she had forgotten, caught up in her mother's pain and arguments again. She realised that she had deliberately avoided reading her mother or Ben in this way, shying away from eavesdropping on their budding romance or their thoughts about her.

Perhaps if she'd looked earlier, she might have discovered Laodhan.

Listening now she could feel the madness hovering beneath her mother's determination. Deprived of her husband and betrayed by her new 'love', the only thing shoring up the grief that threatened to tear her apart was the desire for revenge.

Jenny considered Lucy while they all stood listening to the frantic banging from outside. The girl was scared but underneath Jenny saw the same grim determination holding back grief. Here was someone who had dedicated her life to finding a cure for the disease which had claimed her mother. No-one else would lose someone as she had. Except that coupled to this, and almost crippling her, was the knowledge that she had deprived Jenny and Annie in exactly the same way. Having vowed to save others the loss she had suffered, Lucy had inflicted it. Jenny saw that Lucy was as close to the edge as her mother was.

Too many wounds had been opened tonight. Sympathy washed over Jenny. Lucy had suffered enough, what use would her death serve?

Marshall's swearing drew her attention. Here was another nearing loss of control. Determined to maintain law and order, he couldn't cope with a situation which didn't obey any rules he knew, no matter how he attempted to force it into a shape he recognised.

Jenny pulled her sight in, battered by too many frantic thoughts and felt, as she did, an island of calm. She turned towards the fireplace. Tony, Steve and Julian stood before it, concentrating hard on events but they spared her a smile as she glanced their way and they exuded palpable belief that she would do the right thing. She saw – through them – the little girl they'd known since birth and the faith they had in her bolstered by love.

As Ben arrived in the office, Hawkeye uncurled himself from the chair beside the fire and Jenny was startled to realise that he also showed the same calm belief in her. She supposed it shouldn't really surprise her; he had chosen her two days ago in this very office.

Now he took her arm and turned her towards where Ben had

moved towards the garden entrance.

Something odd was happening. Despite David's belief, the spirit showed no concern about going towards the mirror. She could see his arrogant belief that they were beaten and a certain deadly purpose in his move forward. What could the breach give him? Why was Ben with him?

She paused in her scrutiny, suddenly realising that she had been mistaken. The purpose she'd felt in Ben held a different objective to that of the spirit which inhabited him. Obviously fighting hard, Ben was forcing the sword he held towards his own throat.

Lucy gasped, "Dad, no!" while Jenny grasped a possibility that had not occurred to any of them; that Ben might attempt to destroy the spirit inside him. Hawkeye's firm grip on her wrist stopped her from leaping forwards. "Watch with more than your eyes," he ordered.

"I am doing." All Ben's efforts were concentrated on raising the sword but his thoughts were in no way suicidal. With Laodhan controlling the rest of the body, he obviously hoped to hurt the spirit with his move. As she willed Ben on Jenny felt — at the last moment — Laodhan slip away out of danger. She sighed; a good attempt but doomed to failure.

Then, as Hawkeye left her side, Ben leapt for the mirror and Jenny re-thought. This wasn't an attempt to kill Laodhan, merely a ruse to allow Ben the time to make it to the garden.

By the time Ben yelled to shut the mirror she was already moving. Hawkeye was there before her, holding out the staff. Jenny reached for it and froze as she finally registered who else had joined Ben in the garden.

Her mother stared back at her from beyond.

A sense of time repeating took hold of her. She stood before the mirror watching her mother on the other side. Her choice governed her mother's fate. Last time, her acceptance had saved her mother. This time, she would doom her. The spirit within Ben already struggled to move Annie with no regard for if he hurt her.

Jenny looked back at Hawkeye and discovered that he now held two objects. In one hand he held the staff. In the other – and she had no idea how – the golden-eyed spirit grasped the sword from above the fireplace.

He said nothing. Her choice was clear. She wondered if he would strike her if she did nothing.

In the garden, Laodhan struggled violently to push her mother from him while Annie stared back at her daughter.

In the frozen moment while everyone waited for her decision Jenny caught a movement in the garden beyond the struggling forms. She blinked and the figure was gone but for a split-second Jenny was ever afterwards sure that she'd seen her father astride a white stag raising a hand in farewell.

She took a half step forward and then grabbed the proffered staff and placed it firmly in the doorway. Silver spread and flowed outwards and with it came the same sense of changing and belonging she remembered. This was right and who she was now. Her dad would, if necessary, take care of her mother. In Hawkeye's smile she saw a reflection of her father's gentle pride.

With no surprise at all she noted that his hands were empty. She knew that, if she looked, the sword would be in its accustomed place. She didn't look; she had no need of confirmation.

Instead, she smiled round at the office full of people, ignoring Lucy's agonised stare at where her father had disappeared. "The breach in the mirror is sealed. Now what shall we do about The Hunter."

"Not Lucy," Marshall said still trying to impose order.

"Not your decision," she replied as swiftly and with as much authority. This was who she was now; this was what she had accepted. Before he could respond she held up a conciliatory hand. "For the reasons my mother gave, I would now agree, Inspector, not Lucy. But Eleanor is right – the librarian is here to protect the library. If that dictates Lucy's sacrifice, then I will order it."

"You will condemn someone to death for the good of the library?"

"For the good of us all, Inspector. That is my role. Surely that is better than condemning someone to death out of a misplaced desire for revenge."

"I think it is merely a question of semantics and it would be rather better to kill nobody at all."

"If that was an option, Inspector, I would agree." But now her senses were open she could feel the Hunter and his need to harvest. What Laodhan had released could not be so easily returned.

"And we're supposed to just stand here and let you choose?"

She frowned slightly, not really listening but thinking and it was David who replied. "The library provides."

David? There was something wrong with that, but she had grasped his meaning and had no time to work out what was out of place. "You know, you're right. I really haven't been thinking tonight. You said earlier that everyone was here to help sort the problems I was having and I got so caught up in whether I knew everyone that I didn't actually listen properly."

"You mean," Tony said, "that one of us was specifically brought here to solve the 'problem' of you needing a sacrifice?"

Jenny nodded, finally clear about the path forwards. "Of course. And Julian was right if we'd bothered to take any notice earlier."

"I was?"

"You were. We need a man to die and a man is dying. Come on."

She led the way from the office.

*

Marshall, left alone to bring up the rear, wondered what Alex would have to say about this intended use of his patient. Actually, he knew full well what his friend's opinion would be, hence his hesitation. As he paused, he became aware that he wasn't alone. Hawkeye stood as if listening beside the mirror.

"Sometimes," the golden-eyed man said enigmatically, "in providing for the future we forget how powerful the past can be."

CHAPTER 13

"You are a fool," Laodhan's sarcasm was corrosive. *"Did you think you would cure all problems by walking out here?"*

"It seals the breach in the mirror you mentioned." Ben ignored Annie's glare as he communed with this inner demon.

"And as soon as it is opened again, as it must be, then I shall walk this body back out."

Ben sighed. He'd known that it would probably come to this. The idea of what to do forming in a heartbeat as he'd leapt for the mirror. "Do you suppose the Hunter and his hounds will leave anything for you to walk anywhere? I sort of imagined that they would have no qualms about claiming both the souls I currently possess." Ben smiled slightly. "I did tell you. I will kill you — and myself — rather than see my daughter dead."

Laodhan suddenly laughed. *"Clever. I underestimated you, but I will not fall for this ruse a second time. You aim to make me leave by this threat. I will call your bluff, my friend, and stay. Call the Hunter if such is really your intent."*

Ben hesitated and then said softly, "It would be nice to actually talk face to face. I feel like I'm going mad, talking to myself."

"Now that we're here, that is a problem I can solve while going nowhere." Laodhan sounded fairly smug about this.

There was a sudden wrench and, just as earlier, Ben found he was looking at two places at once. He could see both Annie in front of the garden entrance and the grey-haired Laodhan standing in a small clearing before a giant, ancient tree.

"This is the symbol of my growth." Laodhan caressed the massive trunk. "This is 'home' if you like."

"But you're still in my head?" Ben wanted to be clear; was this a possibility to escape? He was pleased to note that here in the reflection of the soul he was in uniform, a policeman to the core.

"Oh yes, I am just sharing a piece of myself with you. Don't worry, I have not 'stepped out'." The spirit grinned.

"Well then," Ben hoped this would work, hoped he'd understood enough of the way they were now linked. Feeling a little self-conscious, he held out his hand. "Err, well, nice to meet you."

Laodhan laughed and took the proffered hand in a firm grip. Without stopping to think, Ben flicked his handcuffs out of his belt, over the linked wrists and locked them together.

"What have you done?"

"Caught a criminal the only way I know how."

Laodhan's eyes burned, but deep within them Ben thought he saw terror begin to flicker. "And now I'm going to sentence you." Ben took a deep breath and both in the clearing they inhabited and out into the garden he yelled. "Hunter! Come to me. I offer myself to you."

As the echoes of his great shout faded, the sound of yelping could be heard drawing closer.

Ben looked back at his captive. "Not a bluff. Not this time."

*

Rick shuddered. He was so cold.

The doctor had done his best and his concerned face hung over Rick, obsessively checking and re-checking the stitching.

It was all pointless.

Rick had seen people die. He knew it was only a matter of time.

Which meant – if he was true to the soldier's creed – that there was only one thing left for him to do. He'd thought it earlier; you sacrificed the weak to allow the strong to fight another day.

And now he was the weak link and the Hunter needed a soul.

He marshalled his strength to tell the doctor what he should do and saw the man's head go up. People approached and Rick realised he wouldn't have to do this alone.

*

"Why?" Laodhan hissed.

"I told you; for Lucy."

"If I promised…"

Ben could feel the desperation. "You might but she wouldn't."

"She?"

Ben focused his gaze on the other vision. Annie stood over his still figure anger in every line of her. "She wants Lucy dead."

"Then talk to her. You need to explain. Please, you do not have to do this. Use whatever you need to convince her. Save us both." Ben felt Laodhan fade back into his consciousness though this time his awareness of the spirit ran two ways. There remained the link that he had imposed, and he could still vaguely see the glade.

Ben shook his head, amused by Laodhan's incomprehension. He was pleased to find that his head moved as he expected it to. "I would like to talk to her, though," he agreed.

*

Rick was dying. That was obvious to everybody. Alex had stopped doing anything and now sat on his heels beside the body, his head in his hands.

"How long?" Jenny crouched down opposite the weary doctor.

Alex shrugged. "Some men wouldn't have lasted this long. He's tough. Could be a while yet."

"Can he hear me?"

"I can hear you." It was barely a breath of sound between clenched teeth, but it was clear.

"I have something to ask." Jenny looked into his eyes and knew that she didn't need to explain. This was a soldier. He understood that sometimes death was all you had left to offer to the fight.

"You want me to die for you?"

"I want your death…" Jenny paused, searching for words that weren't such a hopeless cliché.

Rick took a pain-wracked breath. "If I bleed to death here it's pointless, it achieves nothing. If I die for the Hunter then you go home."

"Yes," Jenny nodded, relief flooding her. She knew this was right, hadn't expected it to be so easy.

"Open the door."

"You can't do that," Alex said. "He's dying."

"And he's choosing to make his death count. I'm sorry, doctor, but nothing can save him. On the other hand, he can save us."

"Open the door," Rick insisted trying to push himself up.

Alex glared at Jenny for a half second longer and then nodded, unable to argue with his patient. "Open the door."

Jenny leapt to her feet and grasped the door handle. As she did, her senses told her that something was wrong; there was no longer a presence waiting outside. She threw the massive doors wide with a resounding crash. The hounds were gone. The lone, towering figure dipped its antlers respectfully and faded from view.

"No!" Jenny stared open mouthed and then realisation dawned as she understood where the spirit headed. "Mum!" She turned and sprinted for the mirror.

Halfway there she skidded to a halt as the pieces fell into place. "No," she said, "not mum." She turned to those who had followed and, with a heart full of pity, held out her hands. "I'm sorry," she told Lucy, "but this is your dad's doing. Either because of Laodhan or to spite him, he has called the Hunter. Truly, this is not the way it should be."

"He did it for me," Lucy whispered. "He always protected me."

"Perhaps."

"Will it save Rick?"

Suddenly thrown, Jenny looked up and met Hawkeye's golden gaze where he was coming from the library with the inspector. "I don't know. It isn't the way... I really don't know."

"If it's possible," Hawkeye said, "I will make it so. The Hunter only needs one." He turned back towards where Rick still lay. "As soon as time runs again, I will go."

"Should think so too," Marshall muttered.

"What?" Jenny asked startled.

"Something he said back there. Your all-knowing spirit friend got it wrong. Oh, I'm sure he had great faith in you to leave the past behind when it came down to it and he lined up a heroic soldier to die for us but he didn't bargain with the other mad spirit getting out or the fact that other people might not get over the past so well. Saving Rick's life can only be just in this mess he created."

"You may be right," Jenny said thoughtfully.

*

"Going to pay attention to me now are you, or just lie there ignoring me all night?" Annie sounded more desperate than angry. "What did you just do? Are you going to talk to me?"

"Annie, hush. I had to deal with this thing in my head."

"Don't you dare hush me. Dragging me out here like that and then just lying there and I don't know what the hell's going on except now your murdering daughter is in there and I…"

"Annie!" Ben resisted the urge to slap her but if the hysterics continued, he didn't see much option. As he was about to do his best to patch up what was left of their relationship before he died, he wasn't sure that slapping her would help. "I had to bring you with me. I had to make you see that killing Lucy was wrong. It isn't who you are."

"How would you know who the fuck I am? I sure as hell don't know who you are. I thought you were an upstanding policeman, an honourable man but no, you protect killers and…"

"I am also a widower who saw himself losing his only daughter because of an accident. I didn't even truly know that it was her who…"

"Don't give me that. The police looked into Mike's death for months. You must have known all the details."

"All right, perhaps so but I could tell myself I didn't know because I never asked. In my eyes a man or woman is innocent until proven guilty. If I never asked, then I never had proof and I could tell myself that I had it all wrong."

"Is that supposed to make me feel better?"

"I was hoping that, as a parent, you might understand. We try not to believe the worst."

"We? Don't you make out that I'm like you."

"But aren't you? Don't you keep telling me and Jenny and yourself that this library thing is a phase and she'll be home soon?" With Laodhan retired, Ben could contemplate Jenny without anger. "You say how wonderful everything was with Jenny at home, but I could see from the moment I met you how claustrophobic it must have been for her."

Taking a deep breath and deciding it really didn't matter what he said, there was too little in common between them, Ben continued. "I adored being with you this weekend, it made me feel young again but even so I can see that you were simply grasping after something to hold to. Tonight, at the hospital it was like you were losing a husband all over again and yet I've known you barely forty-eight hours."

He thought, briefly, in the silence that followed that perhaps he had got through to her.

Then she said, "Like losing the husband your daughter killed."

"Annie, you've got to let it go. John Marshall is a good man who will see Lucy faces the due process of the law. You can do nothing further."

As he spoke, Ben realised that the constant yelping was now within the garden itself. He didn't turn. The sudden terror in Annie's eyes was enough to let him know they had arrived.

"You called them?" She stared at him. "Why?" She took a step away from him, tripping and falling back. "No, you mean to kill me to save your precious daughter."

"What? Haven't you been listening?"

"You tell me I mustn't kill and all the while you're planning…"

Ben slapped her. While she glared at him, her mouth open, he said clearly, "I have called them for me. I will die so that the Hunt finishes and you can all go home. My life for Lucy's." He turned away from her. "I don't expect you to understand." Ignoring his own words, he tried one last explanation. "I love her, I would do anything for her. I gave up my honour and sullied my reputation for her. I walked outside the law for Lucy. Death is such a little thing, really, to add to that." He could remember the horror when he had realised what she'd done and the understanding that – no matter what – he couldn't lose Lucy like he'd lost Sarah. Which, he supposed, meant that he could identify with Annie's desperate desire to believe that Jenny would come home.

Inside, Ben could feel Laodhan desperately attempting to regain control but Ben's strength and determination when it came to Lucy had always been more powerful than any other consideration. He spared a glance for the other vision. The hounds were there too, milling around the base of Laodhan's tree.

A figure appeared from the maze. A tall man, clean shaven and bare-chested with a pair of magnificent antlers sprouting impossibly from his brow.

"Who called me?"

"I called." Ben felt his voice tremble slightly before the power and majesty of the creature that came. "I offer my life to the hunt."

"And the life within you?"

"His will is linked to mine." Which was true in one sense and a policeman – particularly this policeman —knew how to bend words his way.

"And the woman?"

"No…" Ben began sparing Annie a glance to find her staring raptly at the Hunter.

"Mike," she whispered.

"No," Ben's flesh ran cold. "Annie, this isn't…" His voice dried as she pushed herself to her feet and headed past him through the milling hounds.

"Annie, come back."

She ignored him or didn't hear.

"Do you come to me willingly?" The Hunter asked and Ben thought he heard thunder in the sound.

"Of course, my love. I miss you so."

The Hunter took her hands and looked up to meet Ben's gaze. "I accept three souls for the Hunt. It is bounty unlooked for."

Ben nodded unable to speak and then a memory caught him. "I stabbed a man. I didn't mean to. Can you leave him?"

The antlers dipped briefly. "All will live. Now come to me."

Ignoring Laodhan's impotent screaming, Ben walked forwards to take the Hunter's hand.

PART 4: THE SMITH

CHAPTER 1

They were too late to stop what was happening and Jenny thought that they would have had no success even if they had arrived earlier. She cleared the mirror and stood side by side with Lucy to watch as their parents took the Hunter's offered hands.

"Your mum too?" Lucy said in surprise.

Jenny didn't answer, she was watching the spirit standing slightly apart. Her mum had gone to be with the man she loved. Jenny felt the tears welling up inside, but they were for two years lost to a pointless clutching after shadows.

"I'll move on, Dad," she whispered. Or move back. Seeing Steve and Julian tonight had reminded her of all she had missed; the friends, the music, the love. Her mum could have used their strength and support but instead she had held brittle and aloof and gradually frozen to the point where tonight had simply broken her.

"Your dad's there?"

"Maybe," Jenny smiled, "I think Mum believes he is and that's all that matters."

"You want her to die?"

"No." Jenny wasn't sure she could explain so Lucy would understand but she tried; "Mum stopped living, stopped doing anything when Dad died. She's not been 'Mum' for two years now. I thought meeting your dad was a turning point; she was actually going out and doing things. Then tonight happened and I can't see any way back for her…" She shrugged. "Her only reason now for walking out of there would be to see you dead."

"And you?"

"I'll miss her… no; I'll miss the woman she used to be but…"

"No, I meant, do you want to see me dead?"

Jenny turned from the mirror to look Lucy in the eyes. Reflected there she saw the same loss she suffered and the same shuttered heart her mother had had.

"Forgive me the words, but I feel you gave up on living anyway. All you do is exist, working to find a cure for your mother's death. No friends, no lovers, just you and your dad and your research."

"How can you know that?"

"Partly, I see my mum in you. Partly because of who I am, here in this library." She reached out and took Lucy's unresponsive hand. "I'm sorry for anything I said earlier but this may be harder to hear. If I look properly, now that I remember I can, then I cannot hate you. But I do fear that you are shutting yourself away as Mum did. One day you will break. You must face your loss, face your guilt and then move on."

"It's not so easy."

"Of course it isn't. Nothing worth doing is ever going to be easy."

The two women looked at each other while the Hunter vanished from the garden taking with him Annie and Ben; together as they had never been meant to be.

*

"It's back!"

Eleanor arrived in the office at full tilt. "The town's back and there's all sorts of police and press outside and Rick vanished and David says it will be okay and…"

"David?" Jenny interrupted.

"Yes."

"I shut the mirror with David outside and he survived?" Jenny wondered what on earth she'd been thinking of to miss something so important. "How did that happen? And Hawkeye?"

"I don't think," Eleanor said, "that Hawkeye is all he seems. He's not a spirit like the other one was."

"Maybe not, but David…"

"You'll have to ask him."

"I intend to." Jenny strode to the door only to meet David coming in. "You've been lying to me," she snapped.

"Not totally."

"You said spirits trapped in here would die without the link."

"Yes."

"But you…"

"I do not think I am a spirit of knowledge or belief."

"So what are you?"

"He's a ghost, I told you that earlier," Marshall said also arriving in the doorway, "which probably isn't far off being the same thing but it's a question of semantics. The spirit of a remembered person or the knowledge people have of them; same difference in my book. But," Marshall smiled slightly, "and this is an insight of Mr Hood rather than myself – we have spent the past few hours in a ghost of a place or the spirit of a remembered time. Perhaps, David fitted the library's remembrance of that time."

"I'll admit that the street was very similar when I became librarian," David agreed. "That makes for an interesting theory."

"Where is Tony?" Jenny asked missing friends she was just beginning to feel she might need.

"Meeting others outside. Don't worry, they'll be back in shortly. David mentioned your limitations, so I thought we'd hold the debrief here." He looked round. "I believe your office is big enough." She didn't miss the gentle sarcasm.

"Did Tony have a theory about Hawkeye… Wayland?" Eleanor asked.

"He said that he thought its founder took a lively interest in the running of the Smith Foundation."

"Ah," Eleanor nodded, "I see."

"I wish I did," Marshall replied and then immediately continued, "I'm going to get everyone in. I'm afraid we've attracted the interest of the press, the government and my boss so we've got some explaining to do. I think the explanation better be good and consistent."

"Believable, you mean," Lucy said.

"That as well. I'll be back shortly and then we need to be inventive."

*

Jill watched the flickering building from a safe distance. What she wanted to do was press her hands to the wall as if by some means she could touch Steve, wherever he was.

It simply wasn't possible. Even had the police not been there keeping everyone away, the press made it impossible to get close.

She and Diane had stood well back, doing their best to avoid bored journalists and their microphones.

"Not amazingly exciting, is it?" Diane said. "The media are

fascinating. The building is a bit of a let down."

Jill gave her a small smile, appreciating her friends attempt at humour. Then she straightened, something was different.

"It stopped."

"Bugger me, so it has." Diane grabbed her hand. "Come on, we're going to have to run to get there before the press."

"Shouldn't we wait for the police to let people in?"

"You want to?"

Jill shook her head. No, she wanted to see Steve, to know he was all right.

"Come on then, run."

The two of them set off through the mass of cameras and journalists, angling straight for the doors as fast as they could.

*

Nurse Hartwell hated Christmas.

Not the actual day; that tended to be very quiet. What she absolutely loathed was the month beforehand and the week after. How so many people could get so drunk and do so many stupid things every damn year was beyond her. And then there were the idiots with the lights who electrocuted themselves, fell off roofs and ladders and pulled trees over on top of themselves. To top it all, suicide seemed to be the favourite pastime of all lonely, desperate individuals at this time of year.

And then there were the number who managed near death experiences through taking up a new year's resolution in the most extreme way possible.

All in all, Rosie Hartwell felt it was a poor time of year to be an A&E nurse.

Tonight was no exception. The latest drunk to have fallen through a plate glass window was singing off-key, at the top of his voice and she had just finished disposing of the results of the severe vomiting of a suicidal sixteen-year-old whose boyfriend had dumped her at the Christmas ball.

Rosie checked her watch for the umpteenth time; only ten minutes to go and then it was home for a long soak in the bath and breakfast before bed.

When she looked up again, she found herself staring into a pair of golden eyes. Rosie jumped violently. The man was barely two feet away and definitely hadn't been there when she looked down at her watch.

She opened her mouth to yell and then her instinct took over. She didn't know how the stranger had arrived in A&E but the man he was carrying obviously needed urgent attention.

"Dr Ranald says he needs opening up again, there's probably internal bleeding," the man said, offering his burden forward slightly.

"Alex?" She looked round reflexively but there was no sign of the doctor. "He…"

"He had limited resources. Trust me; we don't have time to talk."

"No, follow me." She set off for the emergency operating room, yelling for help as she half ran whilst trying not to get too far ahead of the dark-haired man and his burden.

He followed her into the room at the end of the corridor and laid the unconscious man on the bed she indicated.

"What's his name?"

"Rick… Richard."

"And you are?"

"A friend."

She raised an eyebrow but began to remove the injured man's clothing and stopped in surprise. "He's icy."

"It is snowing."

"He's been outside like this?"

Golden eyes held hers for a moment and his lips twitched slightly. "No, but it's a good story."

"What?"

"Sorry, yes, I thought the cold might slow the blood flow and keep him alive."

"That was well done," Doctor Murphy had arrived while they worked. "Now if you'd like to tell me the cause of the wound and then go and wait outside, I'll take it from here."

"It was a sword stroke. A clean stroke but the blade was dirty."

"A sword? Have the police…"

"The police are involved."

Dr Murphy nodded and the man turned to go. Rosie watched him leave the room with half an eye before turning her attention back to the patient. She wasn't surprised the injured man was cold; there was no sign of a coat at all. Mind you, the other man hadn't had one either.

She glanced up. He was standing in the doorway watching them. As he caught her gaze he waved a hand and vanished; simply disappeared as if he had never been.

"Do you know," she told an unconscious Rick later, "I think he must have been your guardian angel. Eyes like I've never seen and Doctor Murphy doesn't even remember him properly. I think it was a reminder to me, to not be so cross about Christmas here."

She patted his hand, checked his charts and nodded happily to herself. It might be overtime but she'd seen a miracle and they didn't happen every day.

For a man so recently close to death, Richard Spiller was an amazingly healthy man.

*

Maggie Arkwright never regretted moving from the celebrity gossip column of the Fenwick Advertiser to the more serious business of news reporting. She'd never met an 'A' list star and she had become sick to the back teeth of interviewing 'Z' list wannabes about the times they almost slept with the girlfriend of the husband of the hairdresser of some pop star's roadie.

Real news was something different.

And this one could get her noticed if she just sold copy to some of the nationals.

When Geoff – her boss – first told her that the police had cordoned off a building in the town centre she had leapt to the more obvious conclusions. "Pub? Nightclub?"

"No, a library, I think. On Museum Street."

"They've cordoned off a library in the middle of the night?" Her mind raced; there was no way this was a 'usual' story. "Why would they do that?"

"Initial suggestions are… get this… that the building is behaving oddly."

He hadn't been joking either. Maggie had been watching the place for several hours. It flickered rapidly like a bad film and staring at it for too long made her slightly queasy.

There was plenty of police activity to watch though none of it seemed very productive. There were also plenty of theories. Maggie amused herself by wandering amongst her fellow journalists and collecting a list.

It was the darkest part of the night – though you had to look fairly closely to notice amid the swirling snow and the blazing Christmas lights and television spotlights – when the building stopped. As mysteriously as the strobing had started, it ceased.

The door opened and then slammed again and police activity increased.

Sending her photographer in to take pictures of what he could, Maggie hung back. There would be time enough to interview policemen later. She wanted to be the first to speak to the people who had opened the door and so must have been trapped inside. She wondered if she could actually get in.

Maggie edged away. There must be a way over the police rope somewhere away from the chaos where no-one was looking. Checking that nobody was interested in where she was going, Maggie wandered nonchalantly over to the police boundary.

"Nice night."

She jumped almost out of her skin and whirled round. There was a man behind her with what had to be contacts in. She'd seen enough of the coloured ones on the celebrity circuit; normally on people whose only claim to fame was weird contact lenses. She racked her brains but couldn't recall this particular face. Which was odd, she thought she'd remember him; there was a certain magnetism.

She realised she was not only staring but had also forgotten what he'd said.

"Pardon?"

"Nice night," he smiled, "for enjoying the snow and looking at the lights and getting home to a nice warm bed." His voice had a soft, hypnotic quality to it. She could almost smell the coffee brewing while she ran a hot bath and…"

Maggie shook her head. "I've got a story here. If you'll excuse me." She made to move off.

"Story of what?"

"About the building flickering." Hadn't he seen it?

"Looks fine to me."

"Well it was flickering. We've got pictures."

"Have you?"

Something in his voice gained her full attention. "What do you mean?"

"I wondered how a camera which took stills could record a 'flicker'?"

Maggie nodded; she'd already thought that one through, thank you, Mr Clever Clogs. "There are such things as video cameras," she pointed out. "I've even taken it on my mobile."

She waved her state-of-the-art digital phone with camera for him to see.

"You have video on that?"

"Yes, care to see?"

"Indeed."

She showed him. Unfortunately, it looked like a shaky, badly shot picture of an uninteresting building. The flicker was barely noticeable.

"Unpredictable things, video," he commented.

"The bigger ones will have better pictures," she said though he was beginning to worry her.

"You may be right." He smiled and wandered away taking an interestingly circuitous route that took him past several camera crews.

And accidents began to happen.

Maggie didn't believe it at first and then she headed off in pursuit. "Oy, Stop! Stop that man!"

She caught up in time to hear a cameraman tell him, "And this one is delete," and hit a button.

"What did you delete?" Maggie grabbed his arm.

"Tonight's rubbish. Who wants several hours of a boring building?"

"But that showed what it was doing."

"What?" The cameraman seemed slightly dazed. Maggie gave up and turned on the other, golden-eyed gentleman instead. "What do you think you're doing?"

"Saving a few careers. Keeping a few secrets."

"Careers?"

"Do you think some fairly uninspiring pictures of a building will make you top dog?"

"But..." Maggie paused; she was no fool. "All right, I'll grant you that. But once I speak to the people inside, I'll have one hell of a story."

"You'll have a story of a few people who inadvertently got locked in a library. That's all."

"You can't know that."

He grinned at her. "Trust me, I can. Now, excuse me, I have some other journalists to go and... discourage."

"By all means." She watched him go. "Well, you won't discourage me, matey," she muttered and headed back for the police barrier with grim determination. "No handsome secret service agent is going to try and James Bond me out of a good story."

She carefully ducked under the plastic tape and, instead of pavement, found herself standing in a lush summer meadow beside a babbling stream. The tape was still there and people walked about on the other side of it but she was somewhere else entirely.

"What the..."

"I've always found two approaches serve me best," the golden eyed man said conversationally as he appeared beside her and offered her a perfect crimson rose. "First, I try the 'there's nothing to see' route and I usually manage to persuade most people that they really haven't seen anything worth mentioning."

"And if that doesn't work?"

"Well if, as in your case, a person perseveres, I try the opposite extreme. Lovely place this, isn't it? To your friends, we are standing having a chat on a small patch of pavement that looks like... well, like it did to you until you stepped past that rope. To us, it is a veritable paradise." He breathed deep, throwing his arms wide. "Print your story of it, by all means. How many do you think will believe you?"

Maggie opened her mouth and shut it again, fuming. No-one would believe it if they could all still see her.

"It does have an added bonus," the man said helpfully. "Can you see a library?"

She couldn't.

The summer meadow stretched as far as the eye could see in front of her. She knew the library would re-appear if she crossed back over the tape boundary but then she'd have to wait in line for an interview like everyone else. On the other hand… It was galling but it looked like he'd won. "I get it," she hissed between gritted teeth. So much for her big break.

Stepping back across the police line, she made one last attempt. "So, is that what all those policemen inside the cordon are seeing?"

He laughed. "No story there either, my dear. They see nothing unusual. They don't need to."

And he vanished.

Maggie had a definite feeling that no-one would believe that either.

*

It wasn't easy going. They had joined a mass of journalists with notebooks and cameras pressing at the police cordon and demanding they be allowed to get at the people trapped in the library.

"This is ridiculous," Jill said. "We'll never get to them."

Diane tripped the man trying to push past from behind her but then stumbled into Jill as a man with a boom mike thrust it past her.

It sounded like a school playground. Jill had a brief understanding of how dangerous a mob could be. "Let's wait, Di. We're going to get hurt here."

The two of them elbowed their way back out of the scrum despondently.

"I hope they're all right." Jill rubbed a hand across her face. She was tired now, wanted nothing more than to sit down with Steve and hold him.

"Oh they are," a man appeared in front of them. "Let me show you the way in."

"And you can do that, can you?" Jill looked at the dark-haired man with the funny eyes. "Who the hell are you?"

"A friend. Call me Hawkeye. Trust me."

The two women exchanged glances and then Diane nodded. "All right, lead on but we're not in the mood for any nonsense."

The stranger led them away from the main doors to an unsupervised stretch of tape and stepped over it.

"That easy? We could have done this."

"Ah, but you would have been seen." He led them back towards the doors and the policemen did indeed seem blind to their presence. One man stepped aside so they could pass but his eyes looked through them.

In hardly any time they reached the doors, the baying crowd clustered five yards away.

"In you go," He opened the door for them and gave them both a slight push.

Jill stumbled inside to be swept up into her husband's arms.

CHAPTER 2

It was breakfast time before Marshall was happy enough with his organisation to hold a meeting. He sent Mark to find all the participants of the night's activities from their scattered locations around the library. His sergeant had turned up shortly after the real world had reasserted itself with several of the mummers in tow.

Marshall went himself to find Jenny and Lucy to warn them of the impending influx of people.

When he arrived, the office was empty – or nearly so.

Its lone occupant was Wayland, the golden-eyed spirit, stretched out in an armchair before the fire.

"Jenny?"

"They went to see if they could find the bodies," the man indicated the garden entrance.

Marshall frowned. "I don't understand. Ben Martin *and* Annie Williams, the Hunter took them both?"

"The Hunter was offered them both."

Marshall nodded sadly and then made up his mind about something which had been nagging at him. Leaving the problem of Jenny, Lucy and a possible two corpses for the present, he sat down opposite Wayland.

"You didn't see that coming, did you?"

"I didn't, Inspector?"

"Oh come on, Mr Smith, I've been doing some investigation…" He stopped; Wayland had collapsed in gales of laughter.

"Mr Smith? How modern. I am gaining all sorts of new names tonight."

Marshall took a deep breath allowing his training to take over. Laughing, avoidance of questions; all textbook distraction tactics of someone who didn't want to answer his questions. Anger would get him nowhere, perseverance might.

"Mr Smith, you lined up Rick to die tonight, didn't you?"

"The library…"

"Is yours, Mr Smith, I believe?"

"You have been busy." Wayland sat back and looked seriously at him out of his magnificent eyes. "I didn't really bargain on *you* tonight, Inspector."

Marshall gaped, enlightened by the emphasis. "Just me?" He talked through it. "No, you probably didn't expect to get police officers or doctors, I'm thinking. But if everything else… the spirit…" Marshall looked back through the evening. "You have been telling us all night about this 'breach' in the mirror which let the Hunter out but if you say… I'm wrong, aren't I? I thought this Laodhan was unexpected, but you had to have the breach to have the Hunter and to take us out of time, so you had to have arranged the spirit taking over someone's body. So how did you do that?"

Wayland raised one eyebrow but didn't answer.

"So, I wonder if Constable Martin was a deliberate choice or whether it was pure chance." Marshall ploughed on in the face of Wayland's silent scrutiny. "No, not chance because it was Lucy's father who deprived Mike of justice for his death. He needed to be here for Jenny to face him."

Marshall paused; he wasn't sure he liked where this was heading. "So, I guess Annie possibly wasn't supposed to be here getting in her daughter's way and probably wasn't supposed to fall for the policeman she called either. Or perhaps she was, perhaps her love for him was supposed to be what wiped the slate clean." He felt briefly superior to the spirit who obviously knew nothing of love. How on earth did he suppose Annie would continue to love the father of the girl who'd killed her husband?

"The thing is, Mr Smith, if I accept that premise – if I accept that you arranged for Ben to be the 'instrument' of Laodhan's release – then I have to believe that you have ways of influencing the police system. And such an assumption gives you way more power than I'm comfortable with. It also raises the question of what you intend to do with us now?"

"To do with you?"

"Outside, Mr Smith, are a large number of journalists who have all suddenly decided that a night's footage of a flickering building isn't news after all." Marshall was quite relieved about that, but it didn't change his core problem. "They made this decision at about the time you were wandering around out there."

"You saw me?" For the first time the man seemed mildly surprised.

"I'm a policeman and I happen to be a bloody good one. We're trained to notice things."

"Yes… yes, I had… 'noticed'." Wayland smiled fully, lighting up his whole face. "You asked what I intend to do to you. The answer is 'nothing'. I can convince a lot of bored photographers that a flickering building is uninteresting because most of them had come to that conclusion themselves. I can't make them forget that they wasted a night staring at it but their own memories will probably do that for them over time. But you, Inspector, have had an altogether different experience. I doubt all the persuasion in the world would make you consider tonight 'uninteresting'."

"Anything but."

"Besides, Inspector, my librarian needed tonight as part of her education and acceptance. It would do her no good if all those who shared the experience with her forgot it."

"All right then, explain this to me," Marshall demanded. "You had a perfectly good librarian as far as I could see. So why bother with these whole shenanigans?"

"David is nearly four hundred years old."

Marshall blinked, "Well, he still looked fit."

"His body is fine, but he has trouble moving on. You cannot imagine, Inspector, how technology and the growth of knowledge has changed in those years."

"Oh, I don't know. I now chase criminals who live in virtual realities and catch them through computer screens whereas my gran grew up with an outside toilet before anyone invented television."

"Perhaps you will understand, then, my need for someone younger."

"Perhaps. It doesn't excuse the fact, Mr Smith, that you set up this whole thing knowing that at least two people would die to make Jenny your librarian. That's conspiracy to murder in my book."

"I set up a situation, Inspector. How people react in such events is their choice."

"I'm not sure that's entirely accurate."

"Then let me return your question, Inspector; what do you intend to do with me?"

Marshall laughed and let go of it; he was going to have to collude here. "There isn't a court in the land would accept any of what I've seen tonight as evidence." He sobered. "I don't know how to explain two dead bodies though so that's why I need a meeting. The truth is so far outside anyone's experience that I simply can't tell it." He smiled at the other man. "I'm sure that you will say you had it all sorted until I came charging in here uninvited but it's too late now."

"Choice again, Inspector. I will not argue with a person's right to control their own destiny. You came and you chose to stay. I will say that part of me is glad you did. Sometimes the knowledge here may be useful to those outside, particularly someone like yourself. David had no real contact with the outside world. Anyone he was close to was long dead and he chose to shut himself away. I expect impartiality but not frigidity and seclusion." Wayland held out his hand. "You will always be welcome here, Inspector, on one condition."

Marshall shook the offered hand. "Name it."

"Call me Wayland. For all my forward thinking, even I cannot cope with 'Mr Smith'."

"Then, Wayland, I could do with your help. We need an explanation for what happened here tonight, and we need to have one that doesn't actually mention what happened here tonight."

*

"That looks like it could be an interesting friendship." Jenny stood beside the mirror, Lucy a step behind, watching the two of them.

"Formidable," agreed Lucy.

Both young women looked as if they had been crying but, to Marshall's eyes, they looked reconciled. He might even venture at using the term 'friends' given a little while to let the events of the past night fade. Except he had one more item to clear up.

"Forgive me, Miss Williams, but I need to deal with the fall-out presented by the night's events, so I have a couple of tasks."

"Fire ahead, Inspector."

"Are there bodies?"

"None that we could find."

"Do you know if they are likely to turn up elsewhere?"

"I have no idea."

"Wayland?" Marshall re-directed the question.

"Sometimes. The Hunter is a law unto himself."

"Like you."

"Very like me."

The two men exchanged a long stare as Marshall digested this and then he nodded. "Secondly, Miss Martin, I have to arrest you for the death by dangerous driving of Mike Williams and-"

"You can't," Jenny said.

"She killed your father. I heard a confession; you heard the confession and…"

"I didn't," Jenny shook her head and then snapped her lips to, staring calmly into his eyes.

Marshall glanced at Wayland, who shrugged, "People make their own choices, Inspector," he said.

"I have plenty of witnesses," Marshall said evenly, "even if you don't want to make a statement."

"No," Steve said from behind him, "I think you don't. We have been chatting. It's time we all moved on and I think losing her own father is probably more punishment for Miss Martin than you could possibly manage." The mummer smiled at Jenny. "Whatever you want, lass. Time to start over, hey?" He turned away, back into the library.

Jenny nodded her head slowly. "Thank you. I'm afraid I can't help you, Inspector. I heard no such confession."

"But…" Lucy began but Marshall ignored her.

"I need to talk to Matt then, see what he has to say." The only other evidence he had.

"I'm sorry," Wayland said, sounding anything but, "I have been trying to reunite people and clear up loose ends – as you 'noticed', Inspector – so I have helped these good gentleman's wives make it here and, inadvertently deprived you of your witness. Matt wanted home and bed, so he has gone. He is one of those who can probably be encouraged to think of tonight as just a bad dream."

"I hope you don't mind if I ask him myself," Marshall knew as he spoke that it was probably going to prove futile. He had just been neatly sidestepped and wasn't going to have anything to show for an evening's policing. He had a solved case and nothing he could do about it.

By all means," Wayland smiled. "You ought to know that it will be a rather nasty, recurring bad dream, and probably worse after alcohol. After all, I do have some belief in justice, Inspector."

"I ought to pay," Lucy said softly.

"I think you have and now you ought to leave the past behind and get on with living. The dead need to be left to rest in peace." Jenny said and took the other woman's hand. "Let's look forward, Lucy."

"Don't leave it all behind," said Wayland.

As if on cue, a guitar began to play, picking out a Dougie MacLean tune.

"Dad used to play this," Jenny said, her voice catching. "That'll be Julian." A fiddle joined in and then a whistle and they heard Steve's voice raised in song.

"It's a thin line that leads us, keeps a man from shame
Dark clouds quickly gather along the way we came..."

"What are they doing?" Marshall couldn't believe what he was hearing after the night they'd had.

"They're relaxing the best way they know how." Jenny gave the first genuine, stress-free smile she'd managed all night. "All the troubles just melt away. Excuse me; it's too long since I did this."

She left the office dragging Lucy with her and soon her voice was added to Steve and Julian's.

"This love will carry
This love will carry me
I know this love will carry me …"

*

"So much for a meeting," Marshall commented sourly; he was fairly sure that the whistle was Mark joining in too.

"Go along, sing a tune or two and relax. It'll wait half an hour," Wayland told him.

"And you?"

"I believe there's a car out on Northgate Street with two bodies that needs finding by the right people. I might borrow your sergeant if I can get him away from the music."

"You said…"

"I said 'sometimes', Inspector."

Marshall opened his mouth but then shut it again; arguing was pointless. That much, at least, he'd learnt tonight. "So you did."

"Trust me. I think it might be possible that the paint of the car they are found in matches the flecks taken from the body of a mummer tragically killed two winters ago."

"You're going to put the blame on Ben for…"

"People can draw their own conclusions. Trust me," he said again.

"Only to do what's right for your library but currently that seems to work to go some way to solving my cases for me. Take Helen by all means, I think Mark may be busy. I'll stay here and explain." Or possibly, join in a folk song; it looked like he'd lost on all grounds.

Winking one golden eye, Wayland leapt to his feet and strode from the office leaving Marshall to follow slowly in his wake.

EPILOGUE

It was Boxing Day before Marshall made it back to the library. A mountain of creative paperwork detailing a boring evening spent locked in a library, a sad car accident killing a police constable and his girlfriend and tidying loose ends of a two-year-old hit and run had kept him busy.

Having spent Christmas day at home he returned to find a note waiting for him on his desk.

'Inspector, I have something to show you if you'd care to visit. Jenny."

He walked. There was still snow; a white Christmas for the first time in twenty years.

There was a discreet poster above the plaque outside the Foundation Library. It advertised a monthly folk session to be held there. Marshall smiled to himself but also noted the day; he'd come down occasionally just to keep an eye, his sergeant would probably be coming anyway.

Jenny, Eleanor and Lucy met him inside. All three greeted him cheerfully. The tension between them had dissipated and they chatted away as Jenny led the way through the library. The red rims around all six eyes spoke to underlying sorrows but they seemed to be helping each other through mutual loss.

"Where are we going?"

"To show you something, Inspector."

The small troupe passed through the office without stopping and out into the garden. Marshall stepped through the mirror with slight trepidation but, apart from a slight shiver along his skin, nothing happened.

There was no snow here. The garden glowed under early morning sunshine. Marshall breathed deep. Clear air filled his lungs. "This place is amazing."

"I know." Jenny slipped her arm through his. "It's a bit of a walk now."

They strolled through the winding maze, across a manicured lawn beside an ancient summerhouse and then plunged into thicker woods beyond.

After a while of battling along an overgrown path between towering trunks they came to a clearing. The largest tree Marshall had ever seen dominated the small space but beside it a green sapling was reaching upwards.

"This is David's tree," Eleanor said softly, stroking the leaves of the sapling.

Marshall nodded, unsure of what to say to such a thing. "This is what you wanted me to see?" He asked Jenny.

"Partly. The other tree is Laodhan's."

Marshall looked. The tree rose above them, powerful and imposing. Gradually, though, he realised that it wasn't in leaf as the other trees were. Branches stretched gaunt and bare. As he lowered his gaze he saw a naked figure hanging spread-eagled upon the trunk of the massive tree. Marshall couldn't see what held the lifeless body to the tree but he could see that the light had gone from the eyes.

He moved forwards and the spirit vanished leaving him staring at an empty trunk.

"Did you see...?" He whirled round to face three almost identically serious faces.

"Appeared last night," Jenny said. "And the tree is dying."

"So... the Hunter got him too?"

"I assume he was too inextricably linked to Dad to escape," Lucy said. "It's probably best; he was... a troubled spirit."

"He wanted to hold on to the past," Jenny said, "and the library moves on."

"And Wayland makes sure it does," Marshall noted. "Be careful, Jenny."

She smiled. "I know my role, Inspector, and I know my eventual fate. I think I prefer it that way to the sudden and unexpected end my dad suffered."

Marshall shrugged. "So, Laodhan's gone, you're the librarian and I can close my case."

"You make it sound like an ending, Inspector."

"Isn't it?"

"No, this is just the beginning."

ABOUT THE AUTHOR

Emma Melville lives and works in Warwickshire. She is a school teacher of students with special needs who writes in her spare time, concentrating mainly on crime and fantasy short stories, often inspired by her involvement with folk dance and song. She has had several short stories published in anthologies and won several literary prizes. Many of her stories involve Inspector Marshall and fantastical crimes in Fenwick. This is the second novel involving him following the success of *Journeyman*.

Printed in Great Britain
by Amazon